The Second Son

DEE HOODCAMP

Ark House Press
arkhousepress.com

© 2025 Dee Hoodcamp

Cataloguing in Publication Data:
Title: The Second Son
ISBN: 978-1-7641362-8-0 (pbk)
Subjects: FIC042100   FICTION / Christian / Contemporary; FIC042040   FICTION / Christian / Romance / General; FIC145000   FICTION / Places / Australia & Oceania.
Design by initiateagency.com

For Megan Elizabeth

PROLOGUE

'Come Essie, we are going on a long journey. We'll have ourselves a wonderful adventure.' With those words, Lottie had packed her younger sister's belongings and without a word to her father left the paternal home.

Together with many other hopeful women, they had boarded a ship in Southhampton, bound for Australia, where they would find a new life and a husband.

When they arrived in Botany Bay, Lottie and Essie were appointed two brothers: Connor and Elliott Stack.

Looking her prospective husband over, Lottie was well pleased. Yes, he would do very well! A blacksmith, muscled and handsome.

Connor Stack.

The name suggested Irish blood. Those in England would have something to say about that.

No matter! England was behind her. In no way they could they direct her future now.

CHAPTER 1

The early morning fog hung low over Sydney Town. John pulled his coat closer about him so the cold could not get under it. This weather was too similar to the cold in Old Mother England for his liking. He did not want to be reminded of that life, not now, when he had found his perfect place, and lived the life that he had wished for since he was a child. As he walked at a steady pace, his footsteps echoed against the houses, as a constant reminder of the loneliness he felt.

He wondered how his dray was progressing and decided to go past the wagoner's workshop to see for himself how long it would be before he could travel back to his farm. For the hundredth time he thought how much he hated cities. The stinking streets, the sooted houses, the dirty street urchins, the beggars and prostitutes. But most of all, the lack of clean, fresh air. It was no wonder he could not find rest here. Though his room at the inn was quite comfortable, a restless night, had caused him to flee outside and walk around the town in search of something. Of what, he did not know, but anything was better than lying in bed cursing himself for being so stupid as to break an axle.

Here and there a light was lit. City folk were beginning their day. Far off the sound of workmen could be heard, hammering and voices of foremen rousing at their apprentices.

He rounded a corner and a delicious smell filled his senses: Fresh bread! He breathed in deeply and realised he was hungry. He walked in the direction of the sign that announced the bakers shop. Through the slowly breaking dawn a clear voice began to sing. In spite of his rumbling stomach John stopped to listen. More memories, this time fond ones, broke into his thoughts: his mother singing this same hymn as a lullaby, sitting at the edge of his bed, smiling down at him with love. Her voice had always soothed him, yet it had not been as beautiful as the soprano who sang in the grey Australian morning; John thought he had never before heard such an angelic sound. A roar from inside the building put an end to the song. John was comforted by the thought that, if he could not satisfy his love for music, at least he could satisfy his appetite for food.

He stepped into the warm baker's shop. Soon running footsteps brought a pretty young girl to the counter. Politely she asked what his favour was. He ordered some buns and a sourdough loaf. He looked at her while she wrapped the bread in brown paper.

'I heard singing just now.' John started. She reacted by profusely apologising for being so noisy in the early morning.

'Was it you who sang?' he asked.

She nodded remorsefully.

'You have a beautiful voice. Why did you stop?' he asked. Now she shyly smiled up at him.

'Thank you, sir. I love singing, but after being up most of the night baking, my uncle does not want to hear it.' He nodded with understanding, paid for his bread and bid her good day.

As he walked in the direction of the wagoner, he bit eagerly into one of the still warm rolls; they were just how he liked them: The crust was crispy and the inside airy and sweet. It brought to mind a large kitchen, a forbidden place for the likes of him. But when he was a mere boy, Cook had had a weakness for him, and sometimes, on baking day, he had been allowed to enter and sample a few titbits.

As the wagoner's workshop came into sight, a thought struck him so forcefully, that it stopped him in his tracks.

Marry the girl!

Straight away, the reasons against this idea formed in his mind: He did not know her from Adam, the farm was far from ready for a wife, it would put an end to his so very comfortable bachelor life and Perk would not like it. What would he do with a woman? No, a mere girl? What would she know about farm life anyway? No, he was not ready for it. He walked on.

Yet, the thought would not leave him alone. It nagged at him while he talked about the repair of his wagon, which was going to take another two days. It badgered him while he went back to the inn and asked the bemused landlady to add the sourdough loaf to his lunch, with a few slabs of lamb's fry and gravy. It kept him from focussing while he checked the list of necessary provisions for the farm. It ghosted his dreams while he tossed and turned it his bed that night.

The next morning, fed up with the unwelcome contemplations, he went back to the baker shop. He had told himself that the least he could do was to have a talk with the uncle and find out more about her. Even if it was only to block the possibility. He was sure the man would find a thousand objections to a mad proposition like that. And he would be resolved from making the decision.

When he entered the shop, a different girl was serving a rotund woman clutching a wicker basket under her ample bosom. Although her round face smiled readily at the joke the large lady made, she was not as pretty as the girl that served him the day before. When it was his turn, he asked quietly if he could have a word with her uncle.

'Tha's no possible sir, me uncle has been dead for many a year. You can speak to me dad. Him's in the back.' She turned around and in a raucous voice yelled for her father. It took all John's willpower not to run out of the shop.

'What's all the ruckus about? What's the matter with you girl? What do you mean by making that noise, Clara?' The baker, clad in flour dusted clothes and clogs came running from the back. Greasy tufts of flour-powdered hair stuck out from under a white kerchief, bound around his head.

'This here gentleman, wants yer, Pa,' she rasped, pointing at John. The baker saw that John might be a good customer with a complaint; a cockroach in a loaf, or a mouldy bun, perhaps. He bowed slightly in an attempt to show that any wrong would be made right.

'Yes, sir, how can I help you?'

'Good morning, Baker, I am John Beauchamp. I would like a word in private please. Is there a place where we can talk freely?'

The baker perceived that the issue might be far graver than he had first thought.

'Sir, if you would allow me to show you into the parlour upstairs?' He opened the door at the back of the shop and went ahead of him, up a set of narrow stairs, all the while assuring him that they would be totally private and out the earshot of others. John was shown into a small, neat parlour, containing two wooden chairs, covered with knitted shawls, a small table and an escritoire piled with books. He invited John to sit, which was curtly declined.

John was nervous. What he was about to do was against his own better judgement. He wondered for the hundredth time what Perk would say about the whole thing. He paced the room, his boots striking the wooden floor in a severe rhythm. The baker looked with growing concern at John, nervously waiting for the axe to fall.

'I am afraid I did not quite catch your name.'

'A thousand apologies, sir, I don't think I told you. I am Elliot Stack, sir. Your servant.' The poor man bowed again.

'Ah, Baker Stack, I have a particular favour to ask of you. Yesterday I met your niece, I presume she is your niece, and I wish to wed her. Is there any way I am able to speak to her father?'

Elliot Stack was dumbfounded. He sank down on one of the chairs and puffed out his cheeks. A wave of relief followed his surprise, and brought on a train of thought: This request might prove advantageous to him, there might be money involved, plus he would have one less mouth to feed. Yet, he should not seem too eager. So he set sad eyes on his guest and in mock grief wrung is hands.

'Alas, sir, her father is deceased. And her mother. Both died of diphtheria these past six years. In the same year I lost my own Essie. My daughter Clara and Maud, you are right she is my niece, and I are the only ones in our family who survived that horrible disease.' He put his head in his hands for theatrical effect and sat silently waiting for John's reaction.

'Maud,' John thought, 'her name is Maud.' He smiled at the rightness of her name.

'You have suffered much,' said John, trying to sound empathic. 'Your daughter must be a comfort to you, she looks to me like a capable girl.' There was a faint nod of the floury handkerchief.

'I am a man of my word Elliot Stack. I would take care of your niece as a decent husband should. She would have the protection of my name and she would live in reasonable comfort. I have a farm, about two days travel from Sydney Town. I have a farmhand helping me with the work on the land. She would be responsible for the farm house, and for the growing of some vegetables. I am a man of faith and a preacher comes to the hall every fortnight to conduct a service. In the light of that, would you, as the man responsible for Maud, trust me to marry her?'

'But I do not know you, sir. Come and pay court to her, so I can make up my mind.'

'I would love to be able to woo Maud in the customary way, but this time of year, my farm will not yield any crop if I do not attend to the work. Time is not a luxury I possess, Master Stack.' For a moment John saw a way out of his odd scheme, yet he did not give up. 'If it worries you, and I can see that it may, you are always welcome to visit my farm and stay as long as you please.'

'You will understand that being a baker, I have the same problem. I cannot close the bakery for any amount of time. I would lose all my customers.'

'I am glad you understand that because of both our livelihoods this unusual proposal is necessary.' said John.

Elliot Stack thought feverishly how he could make this work to his benefit.

'You understand also, that running a baker shop requires more than just one young female, however capable my Clara may be. Maud is a very hard worker....' He stopped, realising that, of the two girls, his Clara was the slothful one, but it would not do to mention that. 'Moreover, Clara would miss her female companion and Maud would fret for her family.'

John nodded, seeming to identify with that feeling.

'There must be a suitable lady in your church or in circle of friends, in need of employment, who you could hire?'

'Sir, our income does not allow for that sort of luxury,' Elliot Stack declared, seemingly insulted.

'I could take care of that. I could pay you enough to hire a female for two years.' John tried. The offer made the baker look up in surprise.

'But sir, that would amount to …' After a little thought Elliot Stack mentioned a goodly amount of money.

'Yes, Master Stack, I have done my calculations. I am not a rich man, but I have some put by. You would not be out of pocket. Would a solution such as this be acceptable to you?'

The prospect of having a number of guineas like that, played pleasantly on the baker's mind. He held his hand out to strike the deal, stating that it was a shame they had to go on without Maud, but that, providing they were married in a proper church service he would have no objection.

While the men in the parlour made the final arrangements, downstairs Clara pulled Maud in the corner under the steps.

'You are getting married tomorrow.'

'No, don't be silly. Don't tease me.'

Clara pointed up towards the top floor. 'Me father and the man are talking about it now. I heard them.' With that the door opened and the two men came out.

'You will take care Maud will have her things packed so we can leave straight after the ceremony?'

'Yessir. Will you bring me the money on the day?'

'Certainly. And will you be attending the wedding, Master Stack?'

'No, after a night of baking, I will be sleeping. I need my rest, you will understand.'

'Maybe her cousin, Clara, could attend?'

'And who would mind the shop, sir?'

'It won't be a long service, and the church is close by. Surely you wouldn't let your niece be without any family on her wedding day?'

The men had disappeared into the shop and the girls did not hear Elliot Stack's answer.

Maud was unable to move and her eyes were wide open with horror. From their hiding place they had not been able to see the men; she only had seen the high boots: brown, dusty, well-travelled leather boots. In a high-pitched whisper Clara filled her in of what she had overheard, until a roar from the baker made them hurry into the shop.

'What are you girls about? Here I am, finding the shop empty. What if a customer had come in? Go on, get to work!'

CHAPTER 2

n bed that night, the girls discussed the possibility of Maud's marriage. Maud still could not believe that she was going to be sent away to become the wife of a complete stranger.

'Maybe you misunderstood, Clara.' Maud said hopefully.

'You heard what the man said, coming down them stairs. He was clearly talkin' about a weddin' and leavin' straight after. I tell you he is a farmer, who needs a house keeper. I heard it with me own ears.'

'But my uncle hasn't mentioned it at all.' Maud clung to any straw she could muster up. 'Surely, he would have prepared me for marriage. Maybe even gotten me a dress to wear. The only dress that's better than my shop clothes is my Sunday shift.' Clara moved abruptly, pulling the blanket with her. She was annoyed that Maud had been chosen by the man and not her. At eighteen, she was almost a year older than Maud; in her opinion, she should have been the one to leave her father's house to be mistress of her own establishment, however ordinary.

Clara assuaged her jealousy with the negative picture she painted for Maud's future: 'Me mam always said marriage was no pleasure for a woman. Hard work during the day and suffer a husband's base urges in the night. Him bein' a farmer, he'll have no sense of a gentleman. Better you than me.'

'Do you think I will be able to take my mother's books and the little desk with me?'

'Why would you want them? You'll have to keep a farmer fed and happy, you'll have no time for readin'. Me father will sell them, I've no doubt. He has said many a time, how much room they take up in our house.'

Maud sighed. Too often it was made clear to her that she was the poor relative, who had to slave for her keep, who was a burden to her uncle and cousin, another mouth who ate their food and who took up room in her cousin's bed.

'What was that you said about base urges?' Maud suddenly remembered Clara's superior knowledge of life.

'Me mam said she did not like the weddin' bed. Seems men want to have their way during the night; don't know anythink else. Go to sleep now. If me dad hears us talk too late, he'll get you the belt.' She pushed Maud to the edge of the bed, hogged the blanket and soon breathed the regular rhythm of sleep.

For a long time, Maud lay awake, getting more apprehensive by the minute. In the end she took herself to task. Thousands of women were married, and survived the ordeal, if it was an ordeal at all. She would be strong and face any challenge that might come her way. It could not be that bad. Vaguely she saw an image of her parents: her mother in the crook of her father's arm, smiling up at him, taking his hand, his fingers curling gently around hers. The image faded too soon. Her heart cried out for it to come back; it was so hard to remember them. Sometimes it was only a scent, or a sound that brought back the feeling of that one-time happiness.

It was always too short-lived.

The next day the girls went about their usual business, scrubbing the bakery shelves, serving customers and delivering the wares to the gentry. Uncle Elliot did not mention the man or a wedding. Maud began to feel more hopeful that it had all been mistake. There was the smallest pang of disappointment. It seemed she was stuck here, being the add-on in the Stack family, doomed to work for nothing and getting nowhere. The prospect of running her own household had, for a moment, looked somewhat attractive.

Therefore, Maud was surprised when, at ten o'clock the following morning, her uncle came into the shop and told her to take off her apron, put on her Sunday shift, gather her hairbrush and a set of clean under clothes, and go to St Matthew's church. He handed her an empty flour bag to carry her things in.

'You'll find a fine gentleman there, by the name of John Beauchamp, who you are to marry.' He was about to turn his back on her, but she grappled for his arm and begged: 'But Uncle I don't even…' he shook her off and put his head to her face, his voice none too friendly as he told her what to do.

'You will do as you are bid, girl. If the vicar asks if you want to marry the man, you will say 'Yes'. If you don't, you will be on the street where all and sundry will take advantage of you.'

'Can I say goodbye to Clara, please? She is in the back.'

'I will tell her you've gone, now scram!' he turned and left the shop bellowing for his daughter to come and serve customers.

With leaden feet, Maud started her walk to the church. Nervous about what she would find, tears rolling down her cheeks, she sat on the low wall in front of the chapel. The vicar came out, asking her if it was true, that she was to marry John Beauchamp.

'Yes, sir, I think my uncle arranged it so.'

'Are you marrying him of your free will, girl?'

'Yessir,' she whispered the lie.

'Then we better make you look the part,' he said. 'Come with me girl, I think Mistress Williamson may have something to embellish your shift.' He took the calico bag from her and one look inside made him shake his head. Maud followed him into the vestry where he called out to his wife. Ten minutes later Maud looked different from the girl the vicar had found on the church wall. Mrs Williamson had made her wash her face, brushed her hair and bound it in a thick plait. At the top of this she pinned a small corsage, fashioned from scrap of lace and some flowers she had picked from the bush in the church yard. Then she stepped back and told Maud that she was pretty enough to get wed in a burlap sack, and that John Beauchamp was a lucky man to have a lovely lass like her.

'What is Master Beauchamp like, Mistress Williamson?'

'Well girl, you will see that soon enough; here the man is now.'

They heard voices and the sound of boots on the wooden church floor.

Mistress Williamson led Maud to the front of the church where the vicar started the wedding litany. Maud kept her eyes downcast not daring to look up at the man who was to be her husband. She noticed that he had cleaned his boots and almost smiled at the paltry way they both had prepared for wedded bliss. When the vows were spoken, John Beauchamp took the hand of his young wife. His voice was strong and melodious. Her "I do" was almost inaudible. When they were done, he gave her an encouraging squeeze and let go of her hand.

After they were declared to be husband and wife, Maud heard John thank the preacher and his wife. She smiled a thank you to Mistress Williamson; then her husband pulled her arm through his and they walked out of the chapel. Outside the bright sun blinded her and she only saw the outline of the man she was married to. It was the only time she looked up at him. He led her to a dray, helped her up and they drove off, toward a life together.

It took John some time to navigate out of the city, Maud was amazed at the amount of people milling about. A few times she was startled by small children running in front of the two horses, in danger of being trampled. Though it seemed that the man had a good hold on his team and she sighed with relief when they finally rode on the Sydney to Parramatta Road, where the traffic was lighter and pedestrians were few.

Not once did she look at her husband during the trip though the city. And, so he could focus on the driving, she did not speak to him either. Now they were on the open road, she felt his eyes on her. She averted her face, studying the passing fields and farmhouses. She thought of a million things to say, questions to ask, but she was frightened to hear the answers and did not trust her voice.

Next to her John began to suspect how the actions of the last days could make Maud utterly miserable. He had been selfish. To pluck a young girl from the place she knew and trusted. To take her to a lonely farm, where she would only have two men for company. To marry her without court-ship. To marry her without her personal consent, uncertain as he was if the baker had considered his niece's wishes. All this weighed heavy on his conscience.

'Lord what have I done? I was sure I did this on your prompting. Could I have been wrong? Did I misunderstand You? Help this young girl, Father, help her to understand that I mean her no harm.' He prayed.

They drove in silence, both of them in deep thought, well past the midday hour.

'I asked the inn keeper's wife to pack us food for our journey.' He indicated a parcel in oil cloth, tucked behind the seat. 'I have some water; you must be thirsty. Have a drink and a slice of bread. There are some pieces of mutton if you like.'

In silence Maud put out some bread and meat for John, before she took a smaller portion for herself. She had a long swig from the canteen then handed it to him. He thanked her with a smile. She closed her eyes, enjoying the food. The lamb was so tasty; it made her think of better days when she remembered her father carving a lamb roast. At the baker's house meat was a luxury; they only had bread with the broth she would make from the butcher's cut-offs and bones.

'Is it good?' asked John. She nodded; her mouth full.

When she had wrapped the food up again, silence returned.

John's concern for her grew. He remembered how she loved to sing so he started to hum a hymn; first softly, then a bit louder, just in case she did not hear it. Next to him Maud admired his deep tenor. A slight smile lit up her face. John noticed and it assuaged his conscience. He started to point out landmarks to her, telling her what he knew of the area. She listened and occasionally nodded in acknowledgement to what he told her. He tried to ask questions: Had she travelled anywhere in the colony before? Was she comfortable? He only asked because he knew this would be a long journey. Would she miss her uncle and her cousin? She answered him in short sentences. In the end he gave up, he would try again when they had set up camp.

Maud felt elated that she was out of the city, out of the bakery, out of a bed that was so grudgingly shared. When she had been given the bread and meat, she felt life had dealt her a bonus, an unexpected indulgence. Yet now, as the day came to an end and the sun was low in the sky, she remembered the things Clara had told her about marriage. Her intention to take wedded state on face value, to weather any storm that might come her way, weakened by the minute. And when John steered the dray off the road and told her they would camp beside the creek up ahead; her nerves got the better of her. She had the urge to run away, but realised she had nowhere to go. All sensible thought left her.

John helped her down the dray and tended to his horses. When they were tethered to a tree at the edge of a clearing with high grass, he turned to find Maud standing forlornly next to the cart. He should go to her and tell her not to be afraid of him, but he realised that would defeat the purpose. He decided to give her some occupation, to involve her in what needed to be done.

'I will build a fire here,' he said clearing a spot to light a fire. 'Maud, would you start getting some fire wood please, just some small kindling will do fine.'

She gathered an armful of twigs and small branches and broke them in same size lengths. John was amazed at how deftly she went to work.

'It looks like you have done that before,' he complimented her. He took off his jacket and got his axe.

He walked away with his axe on is shoulder to cut some larger pieces of wood. There was plenty of dead timber on the ground so he did not have to go far.

Maud observed him. He was a tallish man, black hair that hung over his eyes as he swung his blade. He looked like a capable man, a strong man. With a shock Clara's words came back to her and she turned around and started to busy herself, trying to find the billy. When she had found it, she walked down the creek and scooped up water for their tea. John and Maud returned to the camp site at the same time. As he dumped the logs on the ground, he noticed that she had been to the creek.

'Ah, you have filled the billy, good girl.' He smiled at her, but as she did not dare to look at him, she did not see it. Before long the fire crackled and the tea was drawing. She had fried two slabs of lamb and made a gravy with the flour that he gave her. There were buns left over which she broke in bite-size pieces to be dipped in the gravy. When they sat down with their dinner, he gave thanks for the food and their safe travel. He ate with gusto, telling her a few times that he enjoyed the meal. As soon as he was finished, she took the plates to the creek to wash them. When she returned John poured out the tea. He looked at his wife again and wondered how she felt. He'd better give her an explanation. Talk to her so she would stop looking like a frightened bird, hiding behind the mug of hot tea.

'I am sorry that everything went so hastily today. I hope your uncle gave you the reason why I could not stay and court you properly.'

He seemed to expect an answer so she said: 'Uncle Elliot told me to go to the church this morning.'

'Did he tell you anything else?'

'He said I was to say 'yes', if anyone asked me if I meant to marry John Beauchamp.'

John regarded his wife, horrified at the thought that she had married him without any explanation. Yet, immediately he was convicted of his own guilt in the matter and set out to put things right.

'Will you let me explain why I brought you here?' She nodded her head and he started to tell her about his farm.

'I have a farm; we will get there tomorrow. I am planning to get a few head of cattle, but for now, we are clearing some land to grow a crop of corn. We need to have the sowing done before the wet season, so we are clearing as much as possible. By we, I mean me and Perk, that is James Perkins, he and I came from England together, a few years ago. We grew up together and he is my best friend. Together we built the farm house; it is small, but it has a kitchen and a bedroom and a loft. I hope you will like it.' He smiled hopefully at her. She stared into the fire. 'There is a shed. Perk has a pallet there. He will eat with us, but he will be in the shed during the night.'

Maud's thoughts whorled in her head; fear for what would happen in the night took a hold of her again and tears filled her eyes. John noticed them glimmer in the fire light. Worry and self-reproach made him reach out to her, but like a caged animal she drew away from him. He was dismayed at her reaction.

'Maud, please don't be afraid of me,' he pleaded, 'I am a God-fearing man and the only thing I want is for you to be comfortable with me. I wish things had been different, but here and now I give you my word: I will not do anything that you do not want me to. I will wait to touch you till you want me to. So help me God, I will take care of you and cherish you, like I pledged in church this morning, but *you* must let me know when we can be united as man and wife. Look at me, Maud. I could not stand it if you were afraid of me.' Finally, she lifted her head and grey eyes met blue ones. 'I promise you will be safe with me,' he said with purpose. A tiny smile lit up her face, and she whispered: 'Thank you.' John's first impulse was to break his promise; she was so vulnerable, so sweet. Instead, he smiled back at her and said: 'John, my name is John.'

'Thank you, John,' she repeated obediently. He let out a sigh; this was not going to be easy, but it was going to be good. There was a promise of good in the future; a future that he wanted to rush toward.

'Now, will you tell me a little about yourself?' he asked.

She told him about her parents; her father had been the son of an Irish convict and her mother was born in England. Her grandfather was a gentleman who had five daughters to be married. Her mother, who was the eldest, had heard about the women travelling to the Colony to find a husband, so she had taken one of her sisters to the Colony to be appointed to a man. They married Connor Stack and his brother, Elliot Stack 'My mother was a bit of an adventuress and rather than end up a spinster, she volunteered to be shipped off to New South Wales, with her younger sister, Essie, to come with her. My father had applied for a bride from Mother England, so they assigned my mother to him and Aunt Essie to Uncle Elliot.'

'Were they happy? Your parents?'

'I think so, but I don't remember much about them.' She paused, trying very hard to see a glimpse of the past. 'Because Uncle Elliot was my father's brother, he took me in when my parents died. Aunt Essie died in the same year and so there were only my uncle, Clara and me left.'

'What do you remember of your parents?'

'I can see my mother sitting at her little desk, writing, I think to her family in England. Uncle Elliot let me keep that desk, and my mother's books, but I think he is going to sell them, now I am gone.'

'Was that the little escritoire in the parlour upstairs?' John asked.

She nodded. 'Mother brought it with her, all the way from England.' She had been talking softly and he found he enjoyed listening to her voice.

'We better get some sleep, I would like to leave at sun up,' John showed her a pallet between the boxes on the dray. 'Here you'll be comfortable,' he handed her a rough blanket. 'I don't think you'll need it tonight; I expect it will not get very cold.'

'Where will you be?' The sensation that she worried about him he found touching.

'I'll be in my swag, underneath the cart.'

'Good night, John Beauchamp.' she said quietly.

'Good night, Maud Beauchamp.' there was a smile in his voice; again, he felt there was the promise of good in the future.

CHAPTER 3

Early the next morning John was woken up by the sound of a crackling fire. Between the spokes of the wheel, he saw Maud stirring the tea in the billy. The image gave him a feeling of contentment.

'Good morning, Maud. Have you been awake long?' He stretched and relaxed; there was something invigorating about sleeping in the open air; it gave him a zest that no bed he had ever slept in had provided him with.

'Good morning, John. Tea is ready. I found some cheese. Do you want it with your bread?'

'Yes, thank you. I hope you slept well?'

'Yes, you were right, I was quite comfortable.' She wanted to add that it felt good to have a mattress all to herself and not to be pushed around in the middle of the night, but she thought that he might misconstrue that.

They ate breakfast in amicable silence; the birds filling the air with their morning song. John was surprised how quickly Maud found a way to do her share of the packing up. She seemed to see what needed to be done and was not afraid to exert herself. Soon they were on the road again. This time Maud participated in the conversation, asking questions and remarking on the things they saw on route. The journey seemed shorter, as he enjoyed her company, and she seemed to enjoy his.

As they came closer to the farm, John began to feel concern for the reaction his friend would have to a woman joining their easy men-only arrangement.

'I wonder what Perk will think when I come home with a wife. He will not expect it.'

'Did you not set out to find yourself a housekeeper?' she asked innocently.

'No.' In spite of his unease, he had to smile. 'Did you think I would marry only to get a housekeeper?'

'I thought that's what happened. Clara said that you and uncle Elliot discussed that.'

'No,' he said again. 'I heard you sing and that's what made me go and ask your uncle for your hand in marriage. The song you sang made me think of my mother. And to me that meant you would be the right person to be my wife. Never think I only married you for the work you can do for me.' The last was spoken very deliberately.

Maud was quiet after that. She was pleased that she had been chosen. Not just hired as a charwoman, but chosen as the right person to be John's wife.

'I must be honest with you, Maud. I think God wanted us to be man and wife. Have you ever had the feeling that God is guiding you?' He looked aside to see how she would react to such a remark. She did not look uncomfortable, which gave him courage to go on. 'I did,' he said, 'when I walked away from your uncle's bakery that day I bought the buns; the thought would not let go of me until I had made the arrangements.' He heaved a sigh. 'I fear Perk will not understand that, but there, it is done.' That speech did not pacify Maud's misgivings about being a married woman. Again, she determined to take one day at the time and see how matters worked out.

'I will do my best to do my part, John Beauchamp. After all, I have made a vow in church as well. But all this infinitely perplexes me. Will you be patient with me?' He looked at her in surprise, and wondered at how different she was from her cousin. She was so much more than a shop chit. Her mother must have come from good stock.

'And I am taking her to a lonely farm to work in the garden and keep house for me,' he thought in self-reproach. Aloud he said: 'I am sure you will do magnificently, Maud. You seem to be a very competent lady.' The road made a sharp bend and John's farm came into view.

'Look there she is!' He pointed down the hill, at a slab hut in a circle of trees. 'There is my farm, Maud.' From the tone of his voice, it was evident that he was proud of his property. She felt happy; this was going to be her home. It looked small, but it was going to be hers to keep, hers to tend, hers to make home for both of them.

As they came closer to the hut, John saw Perk coming out of the barn to welcome him.

He waved and got a salutation in return. He saw Perk stop and squint at the dray; no doubt he had noticed there were two persons, where he expected only one.

When the dray finally stopped at the house, John helped his wife alight.

'Well Perk, I am glad to be home.'

'Good day, Master, how was your journey? I did expect you back at least two days earlier.'

'Perk, may I introduce you to my wife, Maud, this is my good friend James Perkins.' Perk looked from Maud to John and back again. His mouth open in bewilderment.

'Wife?' he asked.

'Yes Perk, Maud and I were married yesterday morning.' Maud smiled at him, before she said cheerily: 'It is lovely to meet you James, John has told me you are his best friend.'

'Oh, a thousand apologies Mistress Beauchamp, I am forgetting my manners. Welcome to *Meare Green*. You must be tired from the ride; I will make some tea.'

'No James, firstly, please call me Maud, that is my name. Secondly, John probably could do with your help unloading the dray; show me where everything is and I'll make the tea.'

Again, Perk looked from her to John, who nodded agreement to the plan.

'Yes Mistress, Maud I mean. Come inside, the fire is lit. Would you please call me Perk, like the Master does?'

'I will, thank you, Perk.'

Before following Perk into the house Maud fetched the left-over food and the water canteen from the cart. Once in the kitchen she set to work. The men noticed her efficiency and as Perk later said to his friend: 'Man, she is no loafer. But did you notice, she is no longer than one moment in this place and she tells me what to do.' John laughed proudly; it had struck him too.

'As my wife, she is mistress of this place, Perk. And by the looks of it, we are not going to suffer under her management.'

While they moved the provisions from the dray into the shed Perk asked John: 'Master, what did you do? Did you go a-courting? Is this why you were two days late?'

'No, my friend, I broke an axle, not two miles before I reached Sydney Town. I had to wait for the blacksmith to fix it and the wagoner was not quick in getting the new one on. But that gave me time to arrange for Maud and me to wed.'

'But where did you find her? I don't mean to be impertinent, but I did not know you knew many people in Sydney Town.'

'Perk, you and I have always been able to talk freely to one another. Don't excuse yourself for asking me questions. Truth be known, I have asked them of myself. I heard Maud sing one morning,' John explained. 'She reminded me of my mother. Then when I saw her…aw Perk, you can see for yourself, she is beautiful.' He stopped unloading the cart and leant against the side of it. His peace of mind disturbed by the inner battle between delight in Maud and self-reproach at his selfish actions. With a grimace he continued: 'I told myself that God had put the thought of marrying her in my mind, but now and then I have my doubts.'

Perk stood in front of his boss with his arms crossed, his usual stance whenever John talked about his God. 'Why would God want me to take a lovely girl like that to a solitary place like this?' John went on. 'You know, she wasn't even asked if she wanted to marry me. She had not met me before she spoke her vows. Would God want that for such a one?' Perk shrugged. Like John, he was in two minds: now Maud was here, life would be easier as he would be relieved of a lot of chores. On the other hand, he knew their easy bachelor's existence would be at an end. He would have to share his friend with a woman, which would mean many hours spent without his company, alone in the shed.

'What of her parents? How come they parted with her so easily?'

'Both are dead. She lived with her uncle and her cousin. It seemed there was no love between Maud and her uncle. He accepted the price I offered without much objection.'

'You bought her?' Perk was visibly dismayed.

'I offered the uncle money so he could hire someone to do the work Maud used to do,' said John, realising that the excuse was feeble.

'How much did you offer him?' When John told Perk the amount, Perk whistled.

'I bet that bowled him over.' he said. 'Few people would deny themselves such a sum of money.'

'I think we will be the winners in this case,' John shrugged. His friend eyed him suspiciously.

'I think you are quite under the spell of that little lady,' he suggested.

'I don't know enough of her yet.' John answered curtly. 'Come let's finish this confounded job.'

While the billy boiled Maud took stock of the inside of the farmhouse. John had not exaggerated when he had said it was small. The kitchen had enough room for the woodstove, a side board, and a rough wooden table with a bench on one side and a large chair on the other. There were shelves on the walls and two large bags of potatoes and onions stood on the floor. She walked into the other room. The only furniture was a large bed, made of saplings strapped together, and a make-shift bedside table, fashioned from a plank nailed to a stump, with a candle and a bible on it. On the wall were a couple of hooks on which John's clothes hung and a pair of leather boots peeped from under the bed. Maud felt the bed, the kapok mattress promised a comfortable night's sleep and the bedding looked well taken care of. Yet the bed gave her an unnerving sensation; there was no other place where John could sleep. With a sigh she went back to the kitchen and made a hearty stew from the food they had taken from Sydney Town and whatever she found on the shelves. Then she called the men in.

Even though the evening cool had set in they were all sweaty and hot from the work. On the side board she had put a bucket of water and the piece of lye soap she had taken from the baker's place.

'I have put out water for you to have a wash; you need to show me where I can find a towel for you to dry yourselves.' She said it in a friendly tone, yet the men knew that they had been ordered not to come to the table unwashed. They looked at each other and John grinned: 'It looks like our uncouth habits must come to an end, Perk. Oh, but it smells good.'

'I think you will feel more at ease when you have washed the dirt of the day off your face and hands,' Maud reasoned. After John had said grace, the men fell on their food like they had not eaten in days. Perk had two helpings and avowed that he could eat this sort of food each and every day of the rest of his life. Maud laughed, content that she had succeeded in pleasing them.

After she had cleaned up the kitchen, John told her to make a list of things she needed for the house and garden. He gave her a slate and a stylus. When she did not write anything down, he realised that she might not be able to read or write. He gently took the slate back out of her hands.

'I am sending Perk back to Sydney Town to get things to make the house look better for you. Do you have any wishes? I will put them on here for you.'

'Things are so expensive, John; you need not spend your money on pretty things just for my sake.' He laughed, relieved that she was frugal and regarded the progress on the farm more important than her own comfort.

'I want Perk to buy you some material so you can make yourself a dress for church. And you may need more linen, I think. She beamed at him; the extravagance of new clothes was unknown to her and she was unable to hide her pleasure.

'Maybe we could have some curtains as well?' She tried carefully.

'Good idea,'

'Do you have writing paper, John? I would like to write a letter to Clara. She will not be able to read it herself, but if she goes to the vicar's wife, I am sure she will be willing to help her.' Relieved he nodded in affirmation. After that Maud added chickens to her wishes, so they could have eggs, some garden implements and seeds. John scribbled her wishes on the slate and before long it was full. Maud looked at the slate in dismay.

'John are we able to afford all that? Please don't spend any money on my account. Just the chickens will do. It will be good to have the eggs.' He laughed at her.

'You are to trust me,' he said putting his hand on her shoulder. 'I never spend more than is wise. Do not think that I will make you to live in poverty. A church dress and a few things to make our house a home, are no frivolities.' Maud felt an emotion she had not experienced before; uncertain if it was because of his words or because of his touch, she looked away, and murmured a soft thank you. Perk saw her embarrassment and was moved to try and make her feel more at ease. In a nonchalant way asked her what her favourite colour was and if she preferred material with a floral or checked pattern.

CHAPTER 4

The next day Maud got up before the men. In the first rays of the sun, she quietly went about her business, making the fire, boiling the tea, and cooking porridge. She added lard, she had found in an earthen jar, to give it more substance. Contented, she saw that the woodpile for the fireplace was well stocked.

She wondered what had happened to John. He had not come into the bedroom, yet his clothes had vanished from the hooks. She hoped he had not slept in the barn, where Perk had his pallet. She realised that that would be shameful for him and her alike.

She had been the first to bid the men goodnight, professing she was tired from travelling and the many new impressions she had experienced. Once in the bedroom she had decided to wait to see what would happen, but John did not appear and she had fallen asleep almost as soon as her head sank into the pillow. The bed was so much more comfortable than the mattress she had shared with her unruly cousin for years on end.

There was a creak and when she looked up, Maud saw John coming down a ladder.

'Good morning wife. I trust you slept well after the long voyage yesterday?'

'Yes, thank you, John. Where did you sleep?'

'In the attic.' He walked over to her, and stood close behind her; for a moment she thought he would put his arms around her. She almost took a step back, but with effort she stayed put, stirring the porridge. 'I have a comfortable pallet there.' He gently assured her. 'Don't worry. I slept well.'

She turned around and looked into his face. 'I am glad,' she said, thankfully.

His voice turned more matter-of-fact when he said: 'Shall I call Perk for breakfast,'.

'Yes please, I will dish up the porridge.'

During breakfast, the men spoke of the work Perk had done while John was in Sydney Town and the plans for the next stage. Maud's only contribution was her question if the men wanted more tea. After the meal John picked up the bible from the highest shelve in the kitchen. Maud realised that he had been in the bedroom after she had fallen asleep, to take his clothes and the Good Book.

He read a Psalm, thanked God for His Word and put the bible back. Throughout the reading Perk had been unable to sit still. Restlessly, all he seemed to want is get up and start his day. After breakfast Perk was sent on his way, back to Sydney Town, to get the extra provisions.

'Maud, I will be clearing the far field; I will not come in for the midday meal. Will you please pack me some food and some water?' John asked 'I will get my tools, while you do that.'

She wrapped up bread and cheese in a clean cloth and filled his canteen with fresh water.

'Do you mind if I have a look around? I can hear the gurgle of water. Is there a creek close by? And is it permanent water?' Maud asked, again surprising John with her astute questions.

'By all means, you need to know this place well. Find a spot you think is good for a vegetable patch. Tomorrow, I will start digging it over.'

'Thank you, John. I hope the rain stays away today; it feels like a storm is brewing.'

John looked up at the cloudless, blue sky. He smiled wryly, unable to see what made her say so. Then he took his lunch and walked off, giving Maud a quick wave goodbye.

After the house had been straightened, Maud stood at the bottom of the ladder leading to the attic. She wavered. Would it be an intrusion in his life if she would go upstairs and have a look where John slept. Maybe she should straighten his bed. She deliberated for a while. After all she was his wife, though only in name. Uncertain if it was the right thing to do, she decided to ask him first. While Perk was away, they would take the opportunity to arrange things between them in comfort. It would not be easy to broach the subject, but she felt John wanted her to be honest with him.

She went outside to explore the surroundings of the farm. She found the barn open and was struck by the tidy way tools were set away. The only messy corner was the place where Perk had his quarters. She shrugged, that spot was none of her business.

Walking further out, she found that the house was skirted closely by the bush. A narrow path led to a grassy knoll that sloped down to a creek. A smile crept over Maud's face. John had had the wisdom to build the farm house close to the creek; this would make life so much easier. She could do her washing there. They could bathe in it. She could water her garden with it.

Thinking of that made her look around for a good place to grow her vegetables. At the bottom, close to the creek was about an acre of flat ground. Looking at the greenery that grew there Maud thought it would be a perfect place. With a frown she remembered something her father had taught her, way in the past. Patiently he had explained all things to do with gardening, telling her never to grow edible plants too close to the edge of a creek.

'When the rains come, Maudie, this place will flood and all your work will be for nought.' She remembered sitting on his lap while they decided where she could plant her beans. His strong arm around her tiny frame and her hair tickling his chin. Why did she remember him now? Showing her to push the seeds in the ground with her little fingers, not too deep, but deep enough to cover them with soil. At Uncle Elliott's place she had kept those memories hidden, as they made her immensely sad.

Yet now, when she needed the lessons learned from her father, here he was telling her what to do. She felt her eyes tear up. Annoyed, she wiped them with the back of her hand, telling herself to get on with the job at hand.

On the other side of the knoll, she found a sparsely wooded section, where only a few saplings stood. It had an open path to the creek and though it was a little further from the farmhouse, the soil did not seem as stony as the flat section.

She went back to the house and found the tools she needed in the barn. When she returned, a couple of kangaroos were quietly grazing on her chosen patch.

'It seems we'll need a fence around our patch, to keep you lot out,' she told them. Yet she was relieved to see them hop away.

After roughly surveying the area, Maud started to break away a straight line in the topsoil, the length of her desired vegetable garden. Taking a stick, she drew a line perpendicular to the dug over ground and chipped away the soil along the line. She worked intently making the outline of three vegetable beds. It took her quite a while and she was so fixed on her job that she did not see the sky cloud over. When she was finished, she looked over her work and realised she was quite dusty and hot.

'I was right, it is going to rain,' she said to herself as she noticed the dark clouds rolling in. She looked longingly at the babbling creek. 'I will have a quick rinse off, then I'll make it home before the storm breaks.' She peeled off her clothes and sat in the cool water, letting the current wash all the grime and perspiration away.

John also noticed the change in the weather. In amazement he remembered Maud's words.

'She was right. I wonder how she knew.' He gathered his tools in his wheelbarrow and made for home. Tomorrow the ground would be softer; it always was easier to work the soil, after a good bit of rain. He had planned to do more than he had achieved; he missed Perk's help. It was so much better to do the clearing with two of them. And with the horses gone to pull the dray, he was limited in what he could achieve. The stumps and young trees had to wait till his friend came back.

Coming to the house he found it empty. He called out for Maud but there was no answer.

He put the tools away and noticed a mattock and a spade were missing. He frowned. Worrying thoughts entered his mind.

He looked around and called out for Maud, widening the circle of his search. Coming close to the creek he heard singing. He recognised Maud's voice. A relieved smile crept over his face.

He walked over the knoll and stopped, stunned by the spectacle before him: Maud sat in the middle of the creek, swirling the water with her arms, singing the sweetest song. His breath stuck in his throat. The sight of his wife, her back turned toward him, was a most serene vision he had ever beheld. His heart beating double time, he slowly stepped back, not wanting her to know he had seen her. On his way back he noticed the outline of the garden Maud had chosen.

'God, you gave me a wonderful wife,' he prayed. 'Teach me to love her the way I should, and help her love me back.' Back at the farm he sat down in the kitchen, waiting till Maud would come back. He only got up once from his chair when he thought the darkness promised a potent storm, worried that she would not make it home in time. But as he stood in the door, he heard her song coming closer and knew she was on her way.

'Oh, you are already home?' Maud asked, surprised to find him sitting at the kitchen table.

'I thought it would be prudent not to be in the open when the storm hits,' he said. 'Your hair is wet.'

'Yes, I set out the vegetable garden, and I was hot and dirty. I found the creek.' she sat opposite him and her voice took an exciting tone. 'John, did you know the creek is so close by? We can use it for washing and watering the garden. I was so delighted when I found it.'

He laughed at her enthusiasm. 'The very reason I chose this piece of land. Did you find a good level area?'

'Yes, but it was too close to the creek. It will flood when the rains come.'

He nodded agreement, amazed by her knowledge. Again, he thought she was much more than a serving girl from the city. He never expected to find she had practical skills that would contribute to the work on their farm. Now he was certain that God had guided him to her.

'Do you think we'll have enough time for you show me where you have been working?' he asked.

She jumped up from where she had just sat down and went ahead of him. 'It is not far; I think we can make it.' She talked about her plans, as she tripped down the trail, how she was of the opinion they would probably have to widen the path to make access to the garden easier and how soon they could benefit from the vegetables. He admired her work and asked if she thought it would be large enough.

'We can have a herb garden at the house.' Maud suggested. 'The only thing I am worried about it where to get some manure. I can remember Dada digging manure in the ground so it would not dry out too quickly. And for better growth of course.'

'Do you think Jess and Jill will supply enough manure for our garden; I know of two farms that have cows and horses. Maybe we can ask if we can gather some off their fields.' John thought a while. 'Or we could buy a cow. Do you think you could milk a cow?'

'I can learn. Oh, wouldn't that be wondrous, to have a cow of our own.' She clapped her hands. 'Can we afford that John?'

'I'll do my best. Next time I go to Sydney Town, I will have a talk to the bank manager.'

'No, don't go into debt; not for a cow.'

'Think of the milk! You could make cheese and butter.'

A large raindrop fell on Maud's nose and she let out a yelp. John grabbed her hand and yelled: 'Here's the storm, run!'

Hand in hand they ran homeward. As they fell into the house they laughed, trying to catch their breath.

'Wet again!' Maud said. 'Look at you: you look like a drowned cat.'

'Thank you for the compliment!' John chuckled. He looked at her: joking, laughing and happy. With a shock he realised, that he was falling in love with his wife. So soon, so deeply!

'We better dry ourselves.' Maud fetched some drying clothes. She sniffed the petrichor purposefully. 'I love that fresh rain smell. I am glad I thought to let down the shutters.'

John stood in the door staring out at the deluge outside. What had happened just now was playing on his mind. Together they had run to the farmhouse. They had laughed together. They had discussed a common goal. They had behaved like any married couple. He revelled in his new-found sensation, knowing deep down that it was sanctioned by his Heavenly Father. To top it off there was the rain. Rain meant that the soil would be softer. It meant an abundance of water in the creek. It meant they could grow a crop.

'You did very well, setting out the vegetable garden, Maud.' He turned towards his wife.

'Well need to fence it off, there were kangaroos grazing this morning. Do you think it is large enough?' She had her own doubts now.

"I can always enlarge it if it proves to be too small. Time will tell. I am glad I asked Perk to buy a variety of seeds.'

The rain held on for two days. In the afternoon of the second day, Maud asked John if Perk would have difficulty coming home. 'The roads will have turned to mire and they will be hard to navigate.'

'Perk was used to the English weather; I don't think he'll worry about the roads here.'

'Surely in England the roads are better?'

'Not necessarily. It would depend where you are. The main roads might be very good, but not so the country lanes. I trust he knows the Sydney Road well enough not to take risks. I would not be uneasy about him.'

'But I am, John. This is no weather for travel.' He looked at her anxious frown and felt the pangs of jealousy. Perk? What if she liked Perk better?

'Well, I am not worried,' he said grimly, 'Is there any tea to be had?' Maud busied herself with the mugs, realising the happy mood had been broken, yet not knowing the reason.

After his tea John went into the barn to sharpen the saws and put them away. When he returned, he found the kitchen warm and filled with the aroma of dinner. It restored his good humour.

During the meal John and Maud talked about the happenings in Sydney. They wondered how the colony would get on now the convict transports had stopped.

'I think we will get a better sort of people into the colony now,' suggested Maud.

'I don't know. Some of the convicts are hard workers, Maud. We will wait and see. How did your father come to be here?'

'His father was transported from Ireland. I have no idea what his crime was. Both Grandfather and Grandmother Stack were from Limerick in the north of Ireland. Dada was very proud of his Irish ancestry.' John smiled at that, knowing that the Irish were not always popular. 'My father inherited a beautiful Irish singing voice,' Maud went on. 'He knew the sweetest songs and Mama used to harmonise.'

'Were they happy, Maud?'

'Yes. I can remember there was a lot of laughter in our house. Not like Uncle Elliott's place, he always seems to be angry.'

'Was your father a baker as well?'

'No, he was a blacksmith in Parramatta. He was as strong as an ox. I think Uncle Elliott was jealous of my father. He had the better of the two sisters. Aunt Essie was not beautiful like my mother; she could not sing and she was painfully shy. Just as well he chose her, because I don't think Uncle Elliott would have been able to bully my mother, like he did Aunt Essie.'

'You seem to know a lot about growing food. Did your father teach you that?'

'He did. We had a small garden plot and he always took me with him when he worked it. He explained why he did the things he did.'

'That is why you have the makings of a great gardener.'

'I hope so, John. It would be nice to make a stew with other ingredients than just onions and potatoes. What about your family? Were they farmers too?'

'In a manner of speaking. We always had food from our own property in the South-West of England. My mother had a fine rose garden. She loved roses.'

'Do you miss your family, John?' Maud asked, seeing a softness coming into his eyes.

'I miss my mother, she was a wise woman, the sweetest mother one can imagine.'

'Yet here you are, on the other side of the world.'

'Yes,' he grinned, 'and without the wish to return.'

'Do you have brothers or sisters?'

'I have one older brother, Charlie; a younger brother called William and three sisters: Marianne, Frederica and Annabelle.'

'How wonderful! I have always wanted siblings, now I have them through you.'

'We are all too far away to enjoy our relations, Maud.' John said. 'I am sorry to say, I am the only person from my family who wanted to move to the Colony.'

'And you do not miss them?' Maud was puzzled.

'No. Charlie and I did not get along, and the others were still so young when I left. I hardly knew them.'

'Can your mother write? Does she write to you?'

'I have had news from home via a friend in Sydney Town. My mother has sent letters to me there.'

'Poor woman, she must miss you.'

And so, they told each other about their families and their lives before their marriage.

When Perk came home, he had a cart full of exquisite surprises for Maud.

While he dismissed her exultations, John looked on with amusement, as his wife's happiness with his worldly goods grew.

'Oh, look at this material, it looks like cambric, but it is so soft. John is it alright if I make a church dress of this? The thicker, floral material can be made into curtains. Heavens, there is enough to make a table cloth as well. What luxury! How lovely this all will look!' Perk handed her the pouches with seeds. Explaining which was which. She took it all in and then put them away on the top shelf, next to the bible.

Without Maud noticing, he handed a small package to John saying: 'I hope this is to your liking, Master. The goldsmith said you can exchange it if you find it unsuitable.' Without looking at it or the contents, John put the package in his pocket. He nodded thanks to Perk. He had made Maud happy. At that moment, that was all he was concerned with,

CHAPTER 5

Maud loved her new life. After her domestic duties she sat in the sun and sewed her curtains and her Sunday dress. Somehow, Perk either had an understanding of what was needed for a lady's dress, or he had had some good advice from the milliner, when he shopped for Maud. With the soft blue material came laces and ribbons, cotton and needles, and a small pair of sewing scissors. Maud used the decorations sparingly, so she would have some of them left for future creations. Besides, it did not do for a farmer's wife to have too ornate a church dress.

When the dress was finished, she could not wait to show John her handiwork. She twirled before him telling him she never had something pretty like this. He laughed happily as she thanked him again for the luxury of new clothes. He responded in telling her he was proud to have a wife who was clever enough to make such a comely dress of a straight piece of cloth. In the coming months, the gift of the material was followed with many other things that John, or Perk, purchased for her on their trips to town. From the successful wool trade around Melbourne, there had been skeins of wool. These were knitted into jackets for the men and woven into a large shawl for Maud. It seemed that there was no end to the new skills she learned with the aid of the ladies she met at church. For the kitchen there were plates and cups with pretty flower patterns.

Perk often remarked how things had changed for the better since Maud managed the household. 'Master, I think you made an excellent choice. Maud is all that a man would want in a wife. Did you see how well the garden is progressing? And to come home to a solid meal each day is a true comfort for any hard-working man.'

In turn, Maud had wondered why Perk always addressed John as 'Master'. When she asked him, he answered that was because he was his master and always had been. After that, Maud did not consider it so strange; after all there were many convicts who were attached to the free settlers and who called their supervisor 'master'. Maud thought it typical of John that he considered Perk his friend. When she remembered John had said that they had grown up together, she deduced that John and Perk had been friends in the old country. She suspected that Perk had done something bad enough to be sent to the Colonies. John had followed him as a free settler and asked for Perk to work for him to earn his ticket-of-leave. That way he had shielded his friend from a harsher boss.

Perk never joined them when they went to the Windsor Hall, where, if the weather permitted it, a preacher visited once a fortnight. John and Maud would travel for over an hour in the cart, Maud in her blue dress with her shawl draped around her. John, fine-looking in his white shirt with a waistcoat and cravat, his boots polished to a shine. John would help her out of the cart and pull her arm through his, like he had done on their wedding day. On those Sundays Maud felt proud to walk beside him. He was such a strong, handsome man. Sometimes, in a show of tenderness he would put his hand on hers, which always made her smile. They looked like any other happily married people and people around them thought they made a lovely couple.

One Sunday Maud heard Milly Craig, one of the ladies, remark to her husband; 'Look Patrick, how well-suited Mr and Mistress Beauchamp are; mark my words there will be a little one before the year is out.'

The words made Maud blush; she hoped John had not heard them. But it struck her that he was very quiet on the way home.

From that day onward John dawdled in the morning, leaving Perk to gather the tools from the barn. He would stay in the kitchen and compliment Maud how well she looked, or put his hand on her shoulder and tell her how neatly she managed the house or what wonderful progress she made in the garden. He would smile at her and she would cast down her eyes lest she would see the question in his eyes. Though she cherished these moments, she also feared them. She knew he expected her to reciprocate his advances, yet she found she was unable to do this. In her heart she admired John; his strength, his care and his attitude of respect towards her. She felt safe with him. She found the greatest attraction were his eyes. His soft grey eyes that followed her as she prepared and served the food. His eyes that held an expression of tenderness for her.

She felt it. She knew it.

Sometimes she wished his arms would draw her close to him, and not let her go. Sometimes she wished she had the courage to say: 'Don't go up to the attic tonight, John'. Yet, at the last minute, her boldness would leave her and all she could do was bid the men a friendly goodnight and retreat to the lonely bedroom.

And so, the rhythm of their life did not change much for eight long months.

The menagerie grew steadily. Besides Jess and Jill, their horses, and the six chickens, there was Mols the Friesian cow. After which Baz, the dog joined the household. They met and made friends with their neighbours: Liza and Jim Calder, on the North side. On the South side there was Helmut, who they tried to comfort when his wife Constance died in childbirth. They became part of their neighbourhood.

Yet the prophecy of Millicent Craig remained unfulfilled.

On a cloudy day in May, Maud was weeding in the garden, and setting out some seedlings. As she worked, she had the feeling that she was being watched. Yet every time she looked around her there was nothing to be seen, and no other sound than the gurgle of the creek, the varied chirps of the birds, and the rustle of the leaves in the wind. The feeling that she was not alone was so persistent, that she sat down on a stump and scanned the surrounding bush.

Suddenly there was movement on the other side of the creek. A dark face, with piercing eyes, soundlessly appeared. Blue and brown eyes observed each other from afar, then Maud called out: 'Hello there. Don't be afraid, I am your neighbour, I think.'

The face looked back at her in astonishment, and mumbled something in a language that Maud did not understand.

Maud got up and walked toward the edge of the creek, making sure her face wore a pleasant smile. The figure on the other side of the creek did the same and now Maud could see that it was a native woman. Amazed that she was naked, but for a kangaroo skin around her shoulders, she made an inviting gesture. In a rumbling sentence the woman seemed to ask her a question.

'I cannot understand you,' Maud spoke over the water, 'but I hope you are friendly.' Again, she beckoned the woman to come to her, knowing that there were many large rocks that made for an easy crossing. The woman shook her head, but kept on watching Maud.

Maud thought she would go over to the other side, to show the woman that she wanted friendship. As Maud was making the first move the woman seemed confident enough to walk to the edge of the water and negotiated the rocks. When she was on Maud's side, she stood still, a little undecided.

'I am Maud,' Maud indicated herself by putting her hand on her chest. She took a step towards the woman.

Again, the woman answered in a language that was unfamiliar to Maud, so she repeated her name, now pointing at herself with her index finger.

The woman seemed to grasp what was meant now and tried to repeat the name pointing at Maud. Maud reacted with a smile and a vigorous nod. Then she pointed at the woman with a question in her eyes.

Hesitating the woman slowly put her hand to her chest and said: 'Lowanna.'

Now it was Maud's turn to repeat the name and Lowanna reacted with a wide smile and an outstretched hand. Maud tapped the ground indicating they should sit together, and sat down; Lowanna followed her example. She slowly started to explain that she often felt lonely and how she would appreciate a female companion. Lowanna listened, seemingly interested. When Maud stopped, waiting for an answer, Lowanna spoke at length in her language. Though neither woman could speak the language of the other, there was a certain understanding between them. For ten minutes they took turns in telling the other little titbits about their lives. Then Lowanna stood up and spoke what Maud knew to be a goodbye. Maud asked her to come and talk with her again. Then they parted, feeling they had made a friend. Before Lowanna disappeared into the bush, she turned around and held up her hand. Maud smiled and waved back at her.

At dinner that night, Maud told the men what had happened.

'I made a new friend today!' she declared jubilantly.

Both men were suspicious of who she had met.

'You did not let one of those sales men, who roam the country in, did you?' John said. 'They are not to be trusted, Maud, you need to be very careful.'

'No, my friend is a lady. Her name is Lowanna, and she is a native girl. We sat and talked for a while; she lives on the other side of the creek.'

'A blackie,' said Perk with contempt. 'You can't trust them. Next thing you know they empty your garden.'

'Not so,' Maud was not intimidated, 'We just talked, she did not want anything. We just talked.'

'A black woman who speaks English?' John sounded unconvinced.

'No, she spoke in her own language and I in mine.'

Perk uttered an expression of contempt.

'You can say what you like, but I consider her to be my friend.' Maud defended the other woman.

'There are a lot of things you still need to learn,' John suggested. 'Just be very careful.'

The reaction of the men put a damper on the delight that Maud had felt. But she was not easily beaten.

'John, do you mind if I make a shift for Lowanna? She only wore a cape of animal fur. I don't know if she would like a dress, but I do have some of the floral material left. I was going to make cushions of it. I think I'd rather see Lowanna dressed. She might come one day when you or Perk are home.'

John looked at his wife and decided to indulge her. 'I think you should do as you think fit, Maud. But I do want you to be careful,' he repeated. 'They have different ways from us, she may not like to be dressed.'

'But you don't mind if I offer it to her? She is my size so it will be easy to make her something that fits.'

To Maud's disappointment Lowanna did not show herself after the first meeting and for some time the shift hung, unused, on the hook in the bedroom.

In August Perk went to Sydney Town for provisions. John remembered that Maud had inherited her mother's little desk. Besides the usual list of shops to visit John charged Perk with the following task:

'Perk, when you are in town go to the baker again and ask for the escritoire,' he instructed his friend, 'and any of Maud's books that he may still have. Don't offer him any money, he had enough of that, but make it clear that these things are not his to keep.'

'Master, you never go to town yourself anymore. You realise that there may be letters from home waiting for you at the post office.'

'Yes, but my wish is to stay home, with Maud. So if you don't mind. I know you may find some entertainment to your liking in town,' Perk laughed at that, well understanding what his friend meant.

When he came home after more than a week, he brought the desk and the books for Maud. She was elated when she saw what Perk had brought back from town. She covered her mouth to stop her from screaming out, and her eyes teared up.

'Come now, Maud. This was to make you happy.' John said when he saw her tears.

She stood close to him and grabbed his arm. 'Oh John I *am* happy, you have made me very happy.'

'But this is not all, Maud.' Perk delved in the pocket of his jacket. 'I have a letter from your cousin. As you suggested, she went to the minister's wife who wrote it for her.' He handed her the letter, a little crumpled but still it was a missive from her relative. She read it aloud.

Dear Maud, the letter read. *Mistress Williamson is writing this for me, for as you know I have not learned my alphabet. I hope you are well and like your new life. Is John Beauchamp good to you? My father has married again and now he has a wife, I am in the way. The lady's name is Cornelia and she does not like me. I have to make room for her brood of children. She has three and there seems to be no room for me anywhere. Sometimes I wish John Beauchamp had chosen me to keep house for him. I am sure that your life is better than mine. Mistress Williamson has asked around if anyone wants a maid, so I can move out of my father's house. Your cousin Clara*

'Oh dear, I think I know the woman my uncle has married. Poor Clara. Her life must be very unpleasant now.'

'Remember that she made your life difficult, Maud.'

'That is in the past. I pity anyone who lives under the same roof as Cornelia Beacon.'

'You mean Cornelia Stack, now.'

Maud shrugged.

'I wish I could do something to help her, John.' Maud conjured up visions of her former life when a single bed was shared by her and her cousin. Now she slept all alone in a bed big enough for two people and suddenly she found she could share that bed with her cousin again. She had to try, for Clara's sake.

'John, can Clara come and live with us, please?' John looked long and hard at his wife, hoping she realised what that could mean. He saw her large heart for others and wished he would be included in that love. Before he could answer, Perk spoke up.

'I would not mind if there was another woman living with us. I was quite charmed with your cousin Clara; she seemed to me a girl with her heart in the right place.'

'Well Perk when you put it like that… I need to tell you, that it would mean another journey to town for you. Or maybe we should all go.' He looked at Maud searching how she would feel about that.

'I am happy to stay here, John,' said Maud, who had secretly savoured the times when Perk had been away and she had John all to herself.

'I will sow the small paddock, meanwhile you can fetch Clara.' John decided. 'Will that make you happy, Maud?'

'Thank you, John, you are a good man.'

'I don't want to be a good man,' John thought, pulling a face. 'I want to be *your* man.'

'Where will she sleep?' Perk asked

'We will decide that when she is here.' was John's short answer.

CHAPTER 6

The following Saturday Perk made the journey to Sydney Town again. He seemed excited with the pleasant mission he was given: the saving of a damsel in distress. He had a letter from Maud to her uncle in his pocket. In it she thanked him in the most cordial way for the return of her mother's escritoire and suggested that Clara could stay with her on the farm for an indefinite length of time.

Perk entered the bakery in the best of moods. Before giving the letter to Elliott Stack, Perk had held it up to Clara, who was serving at the counter and said: 'Here is an invitation from Maud to come and stay with her.' Clara had visions of freedom from her step-mother and step-siblings. Yet on reading the missive, the baker started to wail: 'My only child! You want to take my only child away from me? What kind of father do you think I am?'

Perk saw through his piece of theatre and jingled the shillings in his pocket. Instantly, the wailing stopped. Perk smiled and made to walk away, saying: 'I am not a father myself, but I can understand your predicament. I will tell Maud that her cousin will not come to stay. She will be disappointed, but so be it.'

When Clara heard her father's edict, it was her turn to moan. When her father vetoed the visit, she made such a racket that it was heard by the baker's new wife, who came down the stairs to see what the fuss was all about.

'What is happening here? Can a lady not sit in peace, without being disturbed by a vulgar din? Stop your grouse at once, girl, or you will feel the end of your father's belt.'

The eldest of Cornelia's brood, a pimply boy of about fourteen, now spoke up: 'This man wants to take Clara with him. Ma, tell your husband to let him take her, and good riddance.'

'Is this true, Stack? '

'Cornelia, she is my only flesh and blood, I want to keep her with me; think of the work she does. Who will do it in her place?'

'Nonsense,' said Cornelia, 'she is a lazy chit. I am sick of her impudence; tell her she can go. And stop your belly-aching, man! One less mouth to feed, one less ugly face to look upon.' She turned around, went up to the parlour and deliberately closed the door. For her the issue was decided.

'Tell the man you don't want to go, Clara,' the baker begged, pointing at Perk.

'No Pa, I *do* want to go. Cornelia hates me and I am better off with Maud.'

'What about me?' the baker asked pitifully.

'You never speak up for me, Pa. You married that shrew. You made your bed, so you can lie in it.'

'You are not getting anything to take with you.'

'I can't very well take anything that I do not have, can I? You have given all Ma's things to her.' Clara said with a sob, indicating the parlour upstairs.

'Good, away with you then.' Elliott turned away from his daughter and went back into the bakery. Clara stood, a bit lost, not knowing what to do. Perk took pity on her.

'Come, we will get you some necessities and then you may stay in the inn for tonight. Tomorrow we will travel to the farm. I am sure you will be more welcome there.'

Meanwhile at the farm, it had been a church Sunday. Taking immense pleasure in walking into the hall on John's arm, Maud had seen the women's eyes on her dress, checking if she was with child yet. She had looked up at John, seeking reassurance and he had smiled encouragement at her. During the trip home and all through the afternoon, she had thought of ways to tell him she loved him, and that she wanted nothing more than to be held by him.

Yet, even after a day like that, her courage failed her at bedtime, so she bid her husband a polite goodnight.

In bed she tossed and turned, unable to sleep, not knowing how to approach him. She thought back at what the preacher had said: 'God has a solution for all your problems, just read the Good Book and the Holy Spirit will guide you. Be open to His message.'

Then he had read the story about Ruth. The Moabite widow, who had lost her husband, who had refused to leave her lonely mother-in-law and who had gathered the left-overs so she could feed the two of them. Then she had laid at the feet of Boaz, her future husband.

And suddenly, Maud saw the way to her own husband. He lay asleep in the attic, just like Boaz had. Now she would lay down at his feet, just like Ruth had done.

She tip-toed out of bed, and carefully climbed up the ladder. Apart from the regular breathing of a sleeping John, all was quiet. Gently she laid down at the end of his pallet and waited.

'Maud?'

'Yes John.'

With one movement he threw the covers back and she was carried close to his side. She savoured the security of his strength, and the warmth of his body. She eased herself against him with a happy sigh.

'You have come to me, my sweet Maud. I have loved you for such a long time. And now the wait is over, I am perfectly happy. At times, I thought it was a hopeless case, but now you have come to me. All is well.'

'I have been wanting to come to you for some time too. But I did not know how to go about it. Today when the preacher talked about Ruth and Boaz, I think God thought it was time we loved one another.'

John laughed with delight; he kissed her, tenderly at first, then his kisses became more passionate.

In the night Maud had asked if they would not be more comfortable in the big bed down the steps. But John had said that for one time he wanted to enjoy her being with him in the place he had, for so long, called his own. 'You have no idea how often I have imagined how it would be if you came to me.' he had said, caressing her. He promised that the following night they would sleep in the little bedroom. The pallet was not as pleasant as the bed, but she had slept like a baby after they had talked, laughed and loved. She smiled as she remembered his tenderness.

In the dark John had taken Maud's hand and solemnly put a ring on her middle finger. He had told her that had had had the ring waiting for such a time as this, and that he had prayed each night that she might come to love him.

Waking up next to her husband was another wonderful experience. She was the first to stir, and she could vaguely distinguish him in the dim morning light. She observed how relaxed he was, how handsome, and when a slight smile crept over his face, she had let out a tiny giggle and his arms went around her, pressing her close to him.

The following day it was difficult for Maud to stay focussed on the house keeping. Before John had gone to the far field, they had joked together. He had taken her in his arms and kissed her for the hundredth time and told her that he looked forward to the night, when they could be together again. All kinds of silly things were said. Then he had finally set off to work.

Repeatedly, she had to chide herself to finish her tasks that day; dreaming away the time, with memories of the night before, seemed to come more naturally.

In the afternoon she decided she would see to the garden. Outside the work seemed to be easier than inside chores. She sang her favourite songs as she weeded. After an hour she stood up, stretched and surveyed her work. Yes, it looked a lot better; she was happy with the result. Just as she bent down again to pick up her hoe, she saw a shimmer between the plants. In consternation she saw the long curving body of a snake. She yelped in fear, but seemed unable to move. Standing rigidly, her eyes on the serpent weaving through the plants. Instinctively, she knew she was in mortal danger, yet she was debilitated with fear. As she saw the menace come closer, there was a voice coming from the creek: a torrent of rumbling words spoken in the language of Lowanna. The tone of her voice was insistent and deliberate. It sounded like her friend told her what to do. Like never before, Maud wanted to understand her; to know what she ordered her to do. From the corner of her eye, she saw Lowanna come her way in great leaps and jumps. It struck Maud how fast she could move, without making any noise. In a moment Lowanna was in the garden and had the snake by the tail. She flicked it hard and Maud heard a slight crack. Then it hung motionless from Lowanna's hand.

Finally, Maud dared breathe again.

'Lowanna, you saved my life. What providence that you saw the snake.' Then when she realised how far Lowanna had been away from her, she added: 'But how you could see? It is a miracle; your eyes must be like those of an eagle.'

Lowanna did not heed her; she answered in her own way: 'Nggununy gan.' while she made like she was eating.

'Oh, you are hungry? You want some food?' Maud took Lowanna's hand, but the woman pulled it back at first touch.

'Come with me, I have stew and this morning I baked fresh bread.' Maud laughed and Lowanna laughed with her. Maud tried to hold her hand again with the same result. Maud gave up and only signalled Lowanna to follow her. Reluctantly Lowanna followed Maud, yet stayed at a distance, looking behind her as if to make sure the road back was kept open. She looked in awe at the farm house when it came into sight. When Maud went inside, Lowanna gave a shout of fear and warning, she seemed relieved when Maud reappeared with the dress over her arm.

She held it out to her friend, who took a step back. With many gestures and giggles Lowanna finally agreed to put the dress on. More giggles and calls of glee and admiration ensued. Together they were just two girls understanding each other without knowing each other's language. Maud kept on telling her friend she looked very pretty; they laughed when Lowanna tried to repeat the word.

While they were trying the shift on, Lowanna had let go of the snake. But now she picked it up again and pointed at an open spot in front of the farm, where the cart was usually parked.

'Guwiyang badallya gan?' It was a question that Maud did not understand. Lowanna pointed at the snake and then, again made a gesture like eating.

Maud caught on, and made a face that expressed disgust. 'I am not eating a snake.' She said showing disdain. Lowanna understood that this meant a refusal, and was amazed that Maud did not want to share the delicacy with her. She shrugged, turned around and walked back to the creek.

'You look very nice in your dress,' Maud called after her; Lowanna did not respond.

At the dinner table that night, Maud told John all about her adventures that day.

'And John, she knew exactly what to do; with one sweep she killed the beast and I was safe. I can honestly say that I owe my life to Lowanna. She is a veritable guardian angel' John put out his hand and she laid her in his.

'How can that be? She is a native woman, a heathen, Maud.' He told her again to be careful, yet this time he meant of the reptiles and not the people on the other side of the creek.

'John, can you go to her family and thank them? I think it is only fair, and a matter of good manners.'

'I would love to, my sweet, but I am not sure if I would be welcome. I think our ways are different from theirs. You said she came to you without a stitch of clothing?'

'Yes, but I gave her the shift I made for her. And we had so much fun trying it on. She is not used to be dressed like me.' Maud thought for a while. 'Do you think her family will like her with clothes on?'

'I don't know.' He smiled at his enthusiastic wife. 'Maud, you have a heart of gold.'

Maud noticed John was not his usual carefree self.

'Is something bothering you, John? You seem worried.'

'Yes, but it has nothing to do with us. It is Helmut. Since Constance died, he has not been himself and he has taken to the drink. I did not know how bad it was until I talked to Jim Calder today. He came over to tell me, while I worked at the far field. He told me Helmut has let the farm go. He had to sell it to someone from Melbourne. He had to let it go for a song.'

'Oh, the poor man. After all the misery he has had, the loss of his farm must be the end of the world to him. It makes me shudder thinking of all the work he put into that place. Is there anything we can do?'

'It is too late. I wish now I had taken more notice of my neighbours. When all the fields are cleared, we will be able to visit them more often, I think. It is just such a big job to get things going.'

'What do you mean by it being too late?'

'He has moved in with Liza and Jim Calder. They have a little extra room now Noah has gone to Melbourne. He needed someone to take him under their wings, now the new owners have moved in. Like Helmut they are from German descent.'

'Do you know their names of our new neighbours?'

'He is called Philip Werner. His wife is called…' John thought for a long time but could not remember.

'But I am glad there is another woman closer by now. Sometimes I like talking about female things; I cannot do that with you, can I?'

'You can try me,' John grinned.

'No John, it would not be the same. Poor Helmut though.'

'Yes, his farm was the oldest in the district and the largest. The farm house is so well set up. You are right, all the hard work he put into that, all that beautiful furniture he made; he is a real artisan. Now it has all gone to someone who paid less for it than it is worth. I hope the people who bought Helmut's farm are worthy of it.' Maud heard the doubt in his voice.

Two days later Maud had a visitor. A man, with a scrawny face and haughty attitude walked up the drive way and without being invited in sat on the chair in the kitchen.

'I am Philip Werner,' he said with a heavy accent. 'And I am vondering where your mother is?' While he spoke to her, he looked her up and down, which made her uncomfortable and angry.

'I am Mistress Beauchamp and I am wondering why you have left your good manners at home.'

'Ach ein feisty one. I like that very mush.'

'I do not like the way you speak to me, and I would ask you to come back when my husband returns from his work. You can do your business with him.'

'Nein, I will talk with you.' He looked around. 'You have a very small house. I have a mush bigger house. You will come and work for me, jah.'

'I don't care for your impudence. I would like you to come back when my husband is home.' Maud repeated. 'You need to go.'

Philip did not take her advice. Instead, he said: 'You will make me a cup of tea.'

That did it for Maud. She called Baz and sooled him on the German man. As he was taught the dog grabbed hold of the man's trousers and pulled him.

'If you don't move,' Maud warned the man, 'he will draw blood.'

'If he hurts me, I will shoot him,' he threatened.

'Not on my land you won't.' Maud answered coolly.

Philip Werner saw that he was not getting anywhere with Maud so he hobbled home muttering all kinds of threats to Maud and John.

It upset Maud to have a neighbour like Philip Werner. Her hopes of having a kind friends nearby were all but dashed. She hoped that at least Werner's wife would be more pleasant.

CHAPTER 7

Shortly after Werner had gone, she saw Baz, who had returned to his favourite spot in the door opening, lift his head. Knowing it was a sign that he heard someone come down the road, she went outside to see what her faithful dog was about.

To her relief she saw the dray come down the rise. Next to Perk was another person: Clara had been allowed to come and stay with them.

In anticipation she put on the billy and washed out some of the pretty china cups that John had bought for her on one of his trips to town. Then she sat on the bench outside to welcome her cousin.

The girls hugged each other and then Maud led Clara into the house.

'Ow, it's very small.' she said. 'Where is your husband?'

'He is at work in the far field. Did you have a good journey, Clara?'

'Yes, Perk is funny; he is good with the horses.'

'She is afraid of them.' Perk explained. 'I told her that you would teach her to milk Mols; I don't think she is looking forward to that.' He smirked cheekily before he went off to unload the cart.

'You got a cosy kitchen, Maud,' Clara said. Maud was sad to hear the undertone of jealousy in her cousin's voice.

'It was a bit bare when I arrived here, but John has bought me material for the curtains and cushions.' She tried to change the subject. 'You should see my church dress, Clara! John has spoilt me ever since I moved here.'

Maud noticed Clara's eyes filled with tears. 'What is the matter, Clara? Do you miss your father?'

Clara shook her head, she whispered: 'Me father gave all Ma's things to Cornelia. She wants everythink, and she gets it. I am glad I am here, Maud, but I can see how little I have and how lucky you are. It is a bit difficult.'

Maud was impressed with Clara's candid confession. She put her arm around her cousin and assured her that it would only be a matter of time for things to look up.

'Soon you will find yourself a strappy farmer, Clara, and you will have your own house and family.'

Maud showed her the attic, where she would sleep. She had brightened the place up a bit with a coloured quilt, made with the off-cuts of her dress and the curtains, a candle holder and a jar with gumtree blossoms in the corner. Perk had brought a kapok mattress and together the girls made the bed. Though it was tiny, Clara had her own room.

Clara told Maud about the things that Perk had bought for her: some toiletries, a night gown and yellow material to make a church dress.

'Because he said that Master John would want me to have all that.'

'Good! See, before you know it you will have more than you ever had in your father's house.'

'One thing puzzles me, Maud. Why does Perk call John Master?'

'I understand they were friends in England. Perk must have done something unlawful - don't ask me what - and was transported to the Colony. John decided to come here as a free settler and he asked to have Perk assigned to him as a convict-worker. I am sure that by now he has done his time and must be a free man, because he is able to move around without John being there. Now they have stopped the convict transports, I never talk about it; it must be so painful for someone as nice as Perk.'

They sat together on the bench in front of the farm house. There were two mugs with tea and three slices of fresh bread with dripping. Maud would pour Perk's tea when he was finished unloading the dray.

'I have so much to tell you, Clara. I made a friend; her name is Lowanna. I was almost bitten by a snake. Lowanna killed it for me. Later I will show you the creek and my vegetable garden.'

The girls caught up with events of the last year until John came home.

Clara's first meal was an eye opener for her: Never had grace been said in the baker's home, never had the Bible been opened, and never had happy conversation been a part of the meal. Besides this, she was treated with respect. Clara decided that, even in a small house like this, life was going to be good.

Later that night when everyone had gone to bed, Maud confided in John.

'I had a visitor today, John.'

'Did your friend from across the creek come and visit you?'

'No, it was the German man who bought Helmut's farm. He was quite rude. I did not feel safe with him around, and I sooled Baz on him.' In the dark John laughed at the way his wife had handled the situation. But then he turned serious and asked her to tell him more about the visit.

'He told me to come and work for him and ordered me to make him a cup of tea.'

'Did you?'

'No!' Maud was almost offended that John thought she would be ordered around by such an uncouth person. 'I told him to come back when you got home.'

'Good girl!' he pulled her closer to him as if to protect her against the neighbour. 'I have a worrisome feeling about him, Maud. I would love to say I'll have nothing to do with him, but he lives on the next property, and that makes it almost impossible.'

'It is good that I am not alone anymore when you and Perk work out in the field. Clara will be a great help for me. I cannot always count on Lowanna to be there to rescue me, can I?'

When John discussed their new neighbour with Perk, the next day, his worries seemed to be justified.

'Master, I would not trust them as far as I can see them. Jim Calder invited Helmut to stay at their place. Helmut said that as soon as the Werners arrived, they threw him out of the house he built with his own hands. He had to beg to get the picture of Constance, you know the one that Liza drew of her.' Perk sounded angry. 'He was not allowed to take any of his furniture either. They said that it was included in the sale.'

John shook his head. 'Helmut worked so hard to make those chairs. Such craftsmanship! I have always wondered if he could make our furniture when we get a bigger house.'

'Yes, he is a clever man. You know he told Jim that they called him all kind of names in German, not realising he could understand the language. How low is that, kick a man while he is down. I would have nothing to do with them, Master.'

John told Perk about Maud's visitor.

'So she sooled the dog on him,' Perk said with admiration. 'I say it again, Master, you got yourself a good one!'

'Yes, but the problem remains, Perk: The Werners are our neighbours. We need to at least be polite to them.'

'After they have treated Maud so disrespectfully?'

'Well, I will not sink to their level. You said Helmut stays with Jim and Liza?'

'Yes. It will be good for Jim; he has that long paddock to fence; an extra pair of hands will come in handy.'

'I wonder if the Werners are church people.' John though aloud. 'That would give us an opening to put them right.'

That is where Perk stopped talking. He disliked the mere mention of anything to do with God or the church.

Maud and Clara worked together as they had done before. They took care of the house, the bread baking, and the vegie patch. Then they started to cut out Clara's dress. Clara admired the sewing paraphernalia that Perk had bought for Maud, especially the dainty scissors. She run her thumb over the pretty pattern on the handle.

Maud saw how much her cousin had missed, living with a stingy father and a smallminded step-mother. She said: 'When you get your own place, Clara, I will give you those scissors, it is not much, but I don't like to ask John for pin money; he already buys me anything I ask for,'

After some time, they decided to visit Liza Calder, so Clara would get to know some of the people in the neighbourhood.

When they walked through the bush, on the barely used path to the Calder farm, Clara became apprehensive.

'What will you do when the wild people see us? Will they kill us?'

'If they are all as nice as Lowanna, I would love to meet them.' Maud smiled to herself. 'The worst will be that they will not wear any clothes. But they are people like us, with just a few different habits.'

'I am frightened, Maud.'

'Don't be. I am with you, aren't I? Look there is the Calder farm, you can see it from this hill.

Liza was happy to see the girls. She had not expected visitors. but because they had Helmut living with them now, she had made extra bread and even a sweet bun.

'How lovely to see you, Maud. This must be your cousin you hoped would come to live with you.'

Clara smiled, feeling welcomed. She was gratified to see that Liza's home was much bigger that Maud's and that she had better pieces of furniture. It was gratifying to see that her cousin was not as high and mighty in this community as she had thought. There were richer people than her, even though she made out she got anything she wanted. Somehow the thought stilled Clara's envy.

Liza was a wonderful hostess and they heard more particulars about poor Helmut.

'He has a corner in the barn and the first thing he did was hang the picture of Constance next to his pallet. I don't know what will happen to him. He is a broken man. I don't know what to do to cheer him up.'

'I think you are doing all you can by taking him in.' Maud said putting her hand on Liza's shoulder. 'He needs to grieve for what he lost, Liza. Give him time and give him an occupation. There will come a time he will be his old self again.'

After that the ladies discussed their dressmaking and the progress of their gardens.

Liza had a wonderful flower garden in front of the farmhouse. Her vegetable garden was much larger than Maud's. When Clara commented on this, Liza said with a smile: 'Those two men have been living by themselves for too long. Maud has not been here long enough to get things more attractive. Wait till she has been here as many seasons as we have. I can see that the house will be twice as large and the garden will grow as well.'

Liza told them about her son, Noah, who was an apprentice carpenter in Melbourne.

'He is doing so well and he wrote that he has met a girl,' Liza's face shone with pride. 'She is a teacher and has been in the Colony a little over a year. Her folks come from the same county where I was brought up, which means that she must be perfect.'

'Will they take over the farm when Jim gets on?' asked Maud.

'I hope so. Yet, I think that will be a decision that he has to make himself. It will be quite some time so I am not thinking about that yet. How are your men going?'

'The little field is coming up well. With the rain we have had lately, I think we will have a good crop. They are still clearing the far field. We might have to fence it well; it borders onto that horrible man's land.'

'Hush Maud,' Liza cried out. 'We have to live in peace with our neighbours. If we start being hateful to them, even in private, it will be hard to be nice to them when we meet them in person.'

'I have met him in person and I sooled Baz on him.' Maud said almost belligerently.

'What!' Liza cried out aghast. 'Why did you do such a thing?'

'You would have too, Liza, if he had been as rude to you as he was to me. Ordering me around in my own house! Telling me to come and work for him. Who does he think he is?'

'Oh Maud, be careful. He may well be an unpleasant sort of man, but to sool Baz on him is down-right unwelcoming.'

'Liza, he came into my house without an invitation. He ordered me to make him a cup of tea and told me to be his servant. Would you not be horrified by such behaviour?'

'Did he do all that? You did not misunderstand him?'

'No, he ordered me around, like I was an underling. And I had to ask him twice to come back when John was home. Don't you think it is unseemly to visit a lady who is alone, and not wait for her husband to be home?'

'Yes,' Liza was quiet for a moment. 'That doesn't sound right. I hope he will not come here. But,' she brightened up, 'you are lucky Clara is with you now, at least there are two of you.'

'Let's talk about more pleasant things,' Clara said a little bemused. 'I am worried about that man, but I know Maud is very strong in doing the right thing.'

'You are right.' Liza offered them another cup of tea and not another word was spoken about nasty neighbours.

CHAPTER 8

Clara came to love the life on the farm. Both girls chatted and sang while their hands did all the necessary work. Clara asked Maud if she could teach her to speak like she did, and show her how to read and write. From then on Maud would correct Clara when she did not pronounce her words properly and they would laugh at Maud putting on a silly accent to break the monotony of her lessons. Using the slate that John had shown her the first night she had been at *Maere Green*, Clara practised her letters. Maud remarked to John, that Clara had always been told that she was stupid, unable to learn, but Maud found her a quick learner and during the lessons, the girls grew close.

It saddened Maud that Lowanna did not show herself after Clara had joined their household. She would have loved to introduce her friend to Clara, even though her cousin shuddered at the thought of having to talk to one of the "wild people". To her disappointment, Liza had also warned her off, talking to people who were not of her kind. Maud often wondered why it was that many folks were so disinclined to make friends with the local inhabitants, especially when she was expected to be polite and neighbourly to the likes of Philip Werner.

Perk and Clara got along very well also. They joked at dinner time and teased each other about their bad habits. When they were on their own,

Perk tried to ridicule the part that God played in the daily life of John and Maud. Yet that was something Clara did not tolerate.

'What would you know about the Bible and God, Perk. You see how good John and Maud are to us, and yet you cannot see where they have learned this?'

'I can't see *you* understanding all those stories he reads every night.'

'No, but I go to church and the minister explains them.'

'My Mam was full of religion too. And look where that got her.' Perk's bitterness showed itself loud and clear. 'She rotted from the inside out. Starvation is not a nice thing to behold, Clara. I was lucky as John's father took pity on me; else I would have turned out just like that.'

'How old were you when your mam died?' she asked thinking how she had lost her own mother and how difficult it was to remember her.

'I was ten years old and doing the job of a grown man to keep her alive.'

'Can you remember your mam?'

'Yes, but mostly when she lay dying. Sometimes I see her before she got sick, singing those damned hymns. When she still had a voice, then she looked happy, praising her God.' He laughed sneeringly. 'What good did that do her, when she so cruelly perished?'

'I am sorry she suffered Perk, but you have food each day, friends who value you, surely you must see that is a good thing; something to be grateful for.'

'Not to God. I am not grateful to him!'

'I lost me ma when I was ten too. My problem is that I cannot remember the face of her. She was sick for a long time and me da hated her for it. I don't think he loved her at all. Not like John loves Maud. When I get married, I'll be wanting a man who loves me like John does her.'

'Did he marry for love the second time around, your father?'

'Cornelia? Oh I doubt it. She is a lazy so and so, wanting all the protection a man can give her, but not wanting to do no work.' Clara became pensive. 'I wonder who'll be doing my work now? It won't be Cornelia.'

With the weather getting warmer, the men often started work before the girls were up. On days like that the girls would prepare an early lunch meal and carry it to them in the far field. With only the horses to help them unearth the roots of the trees it was heavy work and they were always glad to see the ladies bring sustenance. They could rest their weary bones for a while and the female company was an added bonus.

On one of those days, Maud, who was carrying the water canteen and the beakers, suddenly cried out; 'Clara stop. I can't…' and to Clara's dismay she sank to the ground.

'Maud! Maud. What happened?' She looked around to see what could have cause her cousin to swoon. 'Did you get bit by a snake? O my God, what to do? What to do?'

It did not take long for Maud come to. 'Oh, what a silly thing to do!' she complained, angry with herself spilling the water. 'I don't know what came over me. All went black all of a sudden.'

'You sit here and I'll get new water.' Clara offered. 'Here, you better drink the little that is left in the canteen.'

'Thank you, Clara, that is very sweet of you.' Clara smiled to herself; she had never had a compliment for service rendered, and it made her feel valued. She walked back to the creek and after fifteen minutes was back with a canteen-full of water.

As they walked on, Maud thought it best not to worry the men with her mishap.

'It was only a silly thing to do. It is no wonder, it is so hot I probably need to drink more water. Let's not say anything to the men about my swoon.' Clara nodded, but at night, when she went to the barn to call Perk for dinner, she mentioned it to him: 'We were late with the midday meal because Maud had a stumble and lost all the water.' Proudly she told Perk she had gone to the creek to get more water, all by herself, even though she was frightened that she would meet wild people or a snake on her way. Perk told her it was a brave thing to do, which was all she wanted to hear.

At the dinner table he broached the subject. Clara silently chided herself that she had not told him not to say anything to John.

'How are you, Maud? No broken bones after your tumble?' he asked lightly, as to make fun that she had tripped on a tree root. Maud looked at him, then at Clara, a question in her eyes. Clara looked down at her plate, suddenly very interested in her food.

'It was nothing Perk, I am quite in one piece.' To her relief John did not want to know any particulars. Yet, at night when they were lying in bed, he asked her about it.

'Did you stumble over a rock or root, Maud?'

'No, John, it was the funniest thing: everything just went black, I just swooned. It is the first time this ever it happened to me.'

'I don't think that it is funny at all, Maud. Are you sick in any way?' He pulled her close to him. 'Do you want to talk to Liza about it? She is quite clever she may have a draught you can take to make you feel stronger. I think it is no wonder, you work so very hard.'

'There is nothing wrong with me, John,' Maud was irritated that he would think her weak. 'I just need to drink more water, I think.' Yet, when John was fast asleep and Maud still tossed and turned, she had to admit she would like to talk to Liza, lately she had not felt like eating her porridge in the morning and that was unusual.

The next day she told Clara to tend to the evening meal by herself as she wanted to see Liza on a private matter. Clara did not object. When she was by herself, she would imagine she was the mistress of her own farm; she would dream of that day she would have her own home and her own man.

Maud took care to take the walk to the Calder farm at an easy pace. She had taken a small canteen of water and often took a sip.

Liza was pleasantly surprised to have a visitor. Visitors were scarce, most of her days were spent waiting for the men to return from their fencing. It was a lonely life.

'Come out of the sun, my dear. How good it is to see you. Where is your cousin? Did she not accompany you?'

'No, Liza I come alone today. I need some advice from you.'

'Let me give you a drink; after your trek through the bush, you need refreshment first. Then you can tell me what is on your heart.' She poured a glass of lemonade.

Once they sat cosily in the kitchen, Liza asked what her problem was.

'I am not sure, it is anything at all, but John felt I should talk to you. I fainted on my way to the far field yesterday.'

Liza tut-tutted: 'And now you come all by yourself, over the rise, and all, don't you think that it is a bit reckless? What if you swooned again with nobody there to pick you up? I take it Clara was with you when it happened?'

'Yes, she went and fetched fresh water; I spilled all the canteen I was carrying. I did not think it would happen again. I have never fallen in a swoon before.'

'No, I can understand that. Tell me, do you eat well, my dear?'

'Yes - not so much in the mornings. I feel a little queasy, so I eat later, after we have done the house cleaning.' Liza nodded knowingly.

'What about your menses?'

'They have not come since Clara moved in with us.'

'There you have it, my dear. It is my conviction that you might be with child. I had an inkling last time you visited, as your figure has taken on the shape of an expecting mother.'

'Oh,' Maud was quiet for a moment, savouring the idea that she and John might have a child. 'That would be wonderful. I hope John will be pleased.'

Liza had to laugh. 'I think he will be delighted; you can take my word for it.'

They discussed the time the baby might be born and how they would go about it.

'I will come to take care of you when you're ready to give birth.' Liza offered. 'I have helped quite a few other women in the neighbourhood. I was at the birth of Constance's little Sarah. It was a pity that mother and child were so poorly from the very beginning. You are a healthy young lady; you will do fine.'

'I will ask John if I can come to Sydney Town next time he goes. I want to buy wool and cotton for the baby clothes.'

'I suspect John will make a cradle for you. He is such a clever man,' Maud smiled proudly. Yes, her man was clever, and she hoped she would present him with a son to help him make the farm flourish.

Liza gave Maud some general advice and walked along the path with her till she was halfway home.

Clara was waiting for her in anticipation to be told what the visit was about, but to her disappointment, Maud did not let on what she and Liza had discussed. When she came inside and saw the extra work Clara had made of the meal, Maud complimented her on the stew and the way she had set the table.

'Clara this looks almost festive! What a lovely idea to put the greenery on the table. One day you will make a man very happy. I hope the men will appreciate your efforts.'

They did. When he saw the table John asked what they were celebrating. Maud gave all credit to Clara, who beamed with pleasure, forgiving Maud that she had not been taken in her confidence that afternoon.

Later that night when they were alone in the little bedroom, Maud told her man that she was pregnant.

'Liza said she had expected it, because she had seen a change in my body shape. Isn't that amazing John?'

'It is. And you are amazing too. I cannot tell you how wonderful this is, my love. I pray that you keep well and strong. You need to be careful and not walk too much. Don't go digging in the garden and carrying heavy things. Let Clara do that. She is a strong girl.'

'John I cannot leave all the heavy work to Clara. That would not be fair. I promise you, I will rest, but I need to put my hand to my own housework. Liza said that I am a healthy woman, so I will go on as I did before.'

When he withdrew from her to go to sleep, she would not have it. She followed him and wrapped her arms around him. 'John, I am the same as I was yesterday, don't turn away from me.' He turned towards her and took her in his arms.

'If you are sure it will not hurt the child?' he asked, uncertain, yet wanting to make love to her.

'Liza told me to go on as we have always done.' She smiled as he nuzzled her neck.

John and Maud made a special trip to Sydney Town, leaving Clara to look after Perk. Maud was able to buy all the things she needed for their little one. At least a hundred times she warned John not to spend money that was needed to buy the necessities for the farm, on her child, but he urged her on to get all the things while they were in town.

When she showed them to her cousin the pangs of jealousy stirred in Clara's heart again. She thought of her age and as she would be twenty on her next birthday, she was in danger of becoming an old maid. Even the time she had spent alone with Perk, in which he had hinted that he would not mind to have a wife of his own, as soon as he could have a farmhouse to offer her, did nothing to assuage her envy. Perk had kept a respectful distance from her, yet giving her clear indication that in time that would change and she would be his chosen one. She thought it was praiseworthy that he wanted to stand on his own two feet before starting a family, on the other hand she regretted that she had to wait until he had a chance to pay off his debt to John.

Maybe, sometime in the future, she would mention it to John; she was sure he would not want to stand in the way of his friend's progress.

Yet, that needed courage and Clara had very little of that.

CHAPTER 9

As Maud's pregnancy progressed, she did leave some of the heavier chores to Clara. She often sat sewing in the sun at the front of the house. The pile of tiny clothes grew. John was amazed to see the things Maud produced, but, she said, that she could only do this with the help of Liza and Clara.

The ladies in the church looked on smiling, as Maud's girth grew and her face glowed.

'How long to go now, Maud?' Millicent would ask, when the men would be out of earshot.

'I feel like I am ready to burst,' Maud would quip. Liza would give the right answer: 'Another three months to go, and she'll produce a beautiful baby.' Other ladies also offered their services: 'Maud, I am knitting you a blanket for the cradle.' or 'Maud, I have a rattle that our Georgie had when he was just born, would you like it for your little one?'

All through it, Clara was Maud's greatest help. Every night John carved the head of the cradle he had made for his child.

Yet, not everything was a path of roses. John's greatest worry was the new neighbour. Not content with taking all Helmut's belongings, he often came to *Maere Green* to hassle John or Maud.

'I will take that girl,' indicating Clara, 'she can work for my wife. Gerda needs a maid,' he said on one of his unwelcome visits

As so often, he had come when John was at work, which made Maud's hackles stand on end, as soon he had entered the kitchen, uninvited.

'Mr Werner, you must not come into my house without being asked. My husband is not home and it is not seemly that you barge into my house.'

'I will take that girl.' Werner reiterated.

'No!' Maud felt the discomfort of pregnancy, combined with the summer heat, taking every bit of patience from her. 'You go home. Clara stays with me.'

He needed more encouragement to leave, but in the end he did so, very disgruntled.

He did come back on a Sunday while John and Maud were at church.

Perk had no patience with him either and refused to talk to him after he had told the German that the farm belonged to John and if he wanted to discuss anything with him, he needed to wait until he returned. Werner sat down on the bench in front of the farmhouse, and refused to move.

John sighed when he saw Werner sitting there. 'Maud, go inside, I will talk to him away from the house.' He smiled at her. 'Don't worry I will tell him to go home.'

As the ladies went inside, they acknowledged Werner with a slight nod. No more.

When Werner looked Maud up and down in the most offensive way, John tried hard to contain his urge to floor the man.

'Werner,' he curtly greeted him. 'Why are you here?'

'I will buy the fields from you. I have money.'

'No,' John answered, 'they are not for sale. I have them both under seed now and I have not done all the work so you can walk away with my crop.'

'But I have money.' He mentioned an amount that was insulting to John, who felt it not necessary to be courteous anymore.

'I find your offer offensive, Werner. Take your money and go home.'

'You are a stupid man, to refuse my money.'

Baz, who had been at the back of the house now came to stand next to his master. One look at the dog and Werner got angry. 'You send that dog to bite me again, I burn your crop.'

Perk, who had been in the barn, now came outside and joined John and Baz.

'I can get your gun, John.'

'Not necessary, Mr Werner is going home to have his Sunday dinner.' He said this with such authority that Werner, went, mumbling furious threats in German.

'What do you make of that, Master?'

'The man is an uncouth fool.'

'A dangerous one?'

'Could be. Could well be, Perk.' He looked at the figure getting smaller and then disappeared into the undergrowth. 'But let's leave the ladies out of this. I will not have Maud worrying about him.'

Going inside he reassured both Maud and Clara: 'I sent him away with a flea in his ear. Don't worry about him, He won't be back.' Sounding more confident than he was.

'Dear God, don't let him come back,' he prayed softly.

A few days later, when Maud was particularly tired, Clara came running into the house.

'Maud, Oh Maud, I hear gun shots. Do you think the men are in danger?'

Maud moved as quick as she could. They ran outside, where Maud stopped Clara.

'It sounds so close by. We might be in danger if we get in the firing line.' She put her hand on her belly, as to protect her child. 'We should stay inside.'

'Who could be shooting?' wondered Clara as they walked back into the house. 'I hope it is not that horrible Werner man.'

Maud was very worried. Why had she not asked John to teach her to use his gun. She looked at the weapon as it stood in the corner, hidden between the wall and the cupboard. How was she going to defend their house and their baby?

They let the shutters down, but the sound of the shots came closer and did not stop until they heard voices.

'John. I can hear John.' Maud wanted to run outside, but Clara stopped her.

'He will come here; don't go where they can shoot at you, Maud. Think of your baby.'

Maud could see the sense in that, but she tried to peep through the shutters to see if John was coming closer.

The door was thrown open and Perk yelled out to no one in particular: 'They are safe. The girls are both inside.' as if to placate himself.

'Where is John, Perk.' As he stepped inside, Maud could not stop herself from holding on to Perk, wanting him to answer her. While he grabbed the gun from the corner, he set the girls' minds at rest. 'John is fine. It is that fool Werner; he is shooting at the blackies.'

'Oh no, Lowanna!' Maud's mind raced to find a way to help her friend. 'I wish I knew her better; I wish I knew where she lives, so I could warn her.

Why didn't I try to lean her language so we could understand each other. Please God, let her be safe!'

Before Perk could stop her, she ran outside towards the creek.

'Lowanna, Lowanna!' she called out. 'Lowanna, hide. Lowanna, don't show yourself. Hide.' She kept on calling to her friend to be safe. She crossed the creek, slipped and almost fell into the water. With one wet foot, she ran on, warning her friend.

At the house, John had arrived from the far field, only a few minutes after Perk. When he heard that Maud had run into the bush, he ran after her. As he passed him, Perk threw him his gun. Clara, left by herself, followed at a distance. She was too frightened to stay in the house by herself. The shooting, though it became less frequent, it kept on cracking through the bush in intervals. John cursed as he crossed the creek, then he stood still to listen when Maud had gone.

He heard her cry out in agony. That is when he started praying: *'Lord, don't let her be hurt, keep her safe, Father, I cannot possibly lose her. Please Lord, have mercy on us.'*

He ran in the direction of her cry and found her at last, kneeling on the ground, sobbing her heart out.

'Lowanna, *Lord don't let her die.* Oh, my friend, why did this have to happen?'

John knelt next to her. He saw the woman who had saved his wife from the snake. The woman who had helped her in her lonely days. He felt her pulse and at his touch she opened her eyes wide and started to speak in her language. He understood she was begging something of him. He could only surmise that she was asking for help.

'Maud let me carry Lowanna to our house. Then you can take care of her.' He tried to lift the woman in his arms, she moaned pitifully. Maud picked up something that had laid next to her. She recognised it was the dress she had made for Lowanna. It was soaked in blood.

'Let me put this over her, John. Lowanna we will take care of you,' she put the hand, that was hanging down, on her body thus securing the dress over the naked body.

As John carried the lady, he felt the life slip away from her. At the creek he stopped and put Lowanna carefully down on a patch of green grass.

'Maud, I think she has gone. Let's wash her here, and then we can decide what to do.'

Maud was broken; she sobbed softly now, tenderly wiping wet strands of hair off Lowanna's face. Relieved that at least Lowanna would feel no more pain, she worried about her friend's soul. She was unable to talk. She just looked on, while John went about his business. John took the dress from her and rinsed it out in the creek. Then he came back and gently washed the blood from her arms and torso. As they were busy Clara, who had not dared to cross the water for fear of falling in, called out to ask if she was going to be fine.

'No Clara, she has passed away.' John answered. Clara covered her mouth with her hand in a gesture of horror. All of a sudden Maud jumped up and crossed the creek, as fast as her swollen body would let her. She disappeared over the knoll. And John, thinking she had gone home, let her be. He asked Clara to see that she was alright. Then he went on till Lowanna was looking quite peacefully and clean. He gathered her hair and shaped it under her head, like a little pillow, then he covered her body with the wet dress. He stepped back to look at the peaceful face of his wife's friend, whispered a word of thanks, slowly got up and walked home also.

He was half way crossing the water when he saw Maud returning carrying a spade. She began to dig the earth on the flat like one possessed. John ran to her now. He put his hand over hers, to make her stop.

'Maud, my love, what are you doing, Stop!'

'I have to bury Lowanna on our land. She must have a proper grave.'

Now John took the spade out of her hands.

'Maud, I do not know what the proper rites are when the people, who live here, die. You need to think of what she would have wanted.'

'I want to give her a good Christian burial, John.'

'That is *our* way of doing things. If there are people of her family left, they might be looking for her to bury her in their own way.'

Maud sank against him, empty of tears. He comforted her holding her tightly whispering soothing words.

'Come let us go home. I left her on her side of the creek, she looked peaceful, Maud. You know, I wish now I knew her too.'

He led her to the farm where Clara hid in the kitchen and Perk paced outside, seething with anger.

'What happened, Perk. What was the shooting all about?'

'It was that fool Werner, Master. Helmut just came by to tell us. Werner noticed there were blackies on the other side of the creek so he and one of his cronies went on a shooting spree.'

John was white with anger. 'What a bastard! We need to have a serious talk with that man. This is the end of what I can endure. You know Maud's friend was shot? In her back! She was running away from him and he shot her in the back! The coward!'

Then his attention was drawn to Maud who suddenly turned pale. He was just in time to catch her before she fell down.

'It is all too much for her, Perk. I will put her to bed. Clara, will you make tea please?'

Nobody slept well that night. Even though Maud was exhausted, she kept on thinking of the lonely figure on the other side of the creek. John had said that her own people did not find her, they would bury her on their land in the morning.

'Will the wild animals not take her away, John?'

'I don't think there are animals here that eat anything other than plants, Maud.'

But she was not to be pacified until he prayed over her and for Lowanna's soul.

After that she fell in a restless sleep.

CHAPTER 10

The next day Perk and John went to see if Lowanna's body was still where they left it. John took care to wash the ants off her before he allowed Maud to see her again. Between them the men carried her to the other side of the creek where John dug the grave while Perk carved her name in a rough wooden cross.

Maud and Clara put a ring of rocks around the mount and Maud sprinkled flower seeds on the soil.

'I want her place to look nice, John and I can always get other ones from the flower heads in the front yard.'

John said a prayer and left Maud to sit by the grave for a while.

'I am going to speak to Werner. I need to empty my spleen to him, if it is the last thing I do.' John declared when Maud had come back to the house.

'I'm coming with you; I don't trust him.' Perk went to grab the gun, but John told him to put it back in the corner. 'I am not visiting anyone with a gun in my hands, my friend.'

'John, you need to be careful. In my opinion, Werner will shoot anyone who stands in his way.'

'I will not stand in his way. I will just tell him a few things he needs to know about being a good neighbour.' A thought struck him and added with a cheeky grin: 'And then I will invite him to come to church next Sunday.'

Maud was not mollified. But John stopped her from protesting by kissing her. 'I will be back before you know it. Do not worry, my sweet.'

They remembered the Werner place from the time when Helmut and Constance lived in the large farm house. Yet, now it looked different. Gone were the inviting flowers by the gate. Instead, there was a chain, locking the entrance to the front yard.

Perk wondered if they should go further as it was obvious that the Werners did not like visitors.

'Perk, this man barges into my house and sits in my kitchen without so much as a by your leave. I will knock at the door, but I will not be kept away by a mere chain.' In one jump, John was over the fence. Perk followed suit.

They walked up to the house noticing that the garden looked quite derelict.

'Constance would turn over in her grave, if she saw this. I can't imagine how someone can do so much damage in so short a time.' Perk was disgusted.

'You withhold water from plants and very quickly, the heat will do the rest.' John walked up the three steps onto the veranda and knocked at the door. While he waited for an answer, he looked around and said: 'One day I will build a veranda like this on to my house. It is good to sit outside, but as it is now, Maud is always in the sun.'

The door was opened by a rotund lady of indeterminate age. Her hair was blond and her cheeks were rosy, she was dressed like a frump and wore a scowl.

'Good afternoon, I am your neighbour, John Beauchamp, this is my friend James Perkins. Is Philip home, please?'

'Nein,' she waved her hands around to suggest she did not know where her husband was.

'I would like to speak with Philip, please,' reiterated John.

'Out. He is out.' She considered her part done and tried to close the door.

'We have come from the next property, could we wait for him please?'

'Ja, you wait there.' She waved her hand again, this time in the direction of a bench on the veranda.

'Thank you,' John was determined not to be as ill-mannered as Gerda Werner.

They had waited for about ten minutes when they heard Philip's voice from inside the house.

'Hell, he *is* home, Master.' Perk was sickened by the attitude of the Werners. 'Typical!'

'Hush Perk. I will try again.' He got up and knocked on the door once more.

This time the door was answered by Philip.

'Yes, what do you want?' he barked.

'Philip, we come to talk to you about the shooting, yesterday.'

'No need to talk. I see the blackies, I shoot them. They want to steal my sheep, goodbye.' Like his wife he was about to shut the door in John's face, but this time he was not given the chance. John put his foot in the door.

'Listen Werner, you have proven yourself to be a boorish oaf. I, and most of the people in this neighbourhood, are fed up with your antics. We do not shoot other people. We do not barge into other people's houses, and we do not order people around. What we do is invite visitors to come and have a drink if they have walked a long way like we have.'

'No, you don't; your wife never gives me a drink.' Werner defended himself.

'I would not come into your house if you were away and your wife was home by herself. It is a matter of courtesy.' John pointed at the bench where he and Perk had been waiting. 'We sat outside till you were home. That is what you should do too. I know for certain that Maud has told you, every time you came to my house, that you should talk to me.'

'I have no time to wait for you. Besides, you have a pretty wife, who is pleasant to have in your bed, and who can have your babies. I am not that lucky.'

It was clear that Gerda had been listening to what was going on outside the house. A stream of angry German came from inside.

'Look, now you have upset my wife,' Philip jeered. 'You have no manners yourself, John Beauchamp!'

'The point is,' started John, who saw that there was very little reason in Philip Werner, 'that shooting the native people is murder. They always stay on their side of the creek. They have their own way of living, as we have ours.'

'Oh, now you are changing your tune. They can have their bad habits, but you cannot live with mine,' Werner scoffed. 'You are a case, Beauchamp, a sad case!'

'If you start shooting people who have done nothing wrong, where is it going to end? The people in our neighbourhood have lived in peace with them, hopefully you can do so too. What have they ever done to you?'

'Ha, there you have it! I saw them on the other side of the creek; they looked at my land. They were making plans to take my sheep.'

'So you went on *their* land and started shooting them?'

'Yes. I did not get them all. Some of the cowards ran away.' At that, John's patience left him.

'Werner, I am going to teach my wife to handle a gun. You set one foot on my land and any person in my household will have the order to shoot you.' With that John turned on his heel and walked off.

'Have you thought of selling me your land?' Werner called after him

'Over my dead body,' John returned, without looking back, or slowing down his angry stride.

'That can be arranged,' Werner mumbled with an evil grin, and went inside, where he was met by a torrent of hateful censure from his wife.

As they walked away Perk and John could hear Gerda bellowing at her husband.

'It looks like Philip doesn't have a peaceful homelife, poor fellow.' Perk remarked dryly. 'I think he has every reason to be jealous of you, Master.'

'Maybe,' John said sadly. 'But with all that, I let him get to me, so that I lost my temper. I totally forgot to invite him to come to the church service. I feel like I failed.'

The result of that afternoon was that the folk around the region became divided about the Aboriginal people, who lived on the other side of the creek. John certainly had his followers, but so did Werner. He discovered that even the families in the congregation were split in two camps. John was discouraged to find that some of his best friends were on Werner's side and condoned his actions. Jim and Liza Calder were two of those and this was a hard blow for him.

'I don't understand you, Jim,' John had argued, 'the Almighty made us, and them, in His image. How can you think they are less in His eyes? How will you answer when you stand before our Lord and you are asked why you thought you were better than they?'

'Have you seen how they live? Running about without a stitch of clothing. Looking at us with their dark, satanic eyes. Don't you ever say that we are the same as us.' The friends had parted angry and disappointed with one another.

Liza had acted the same as her husband when Maud tried to convince her that the people of the colony were no better or worse that the British settlers.

'Well Maud, I do not see any of them ploughing a field or planting a crop. They must live by stealing what others work for. How else can they stay alive?'

'They don't need to steal. I know that they eat things that we don't. Lowanna planned to eat the snake she killed, to save me.'

'What sane person would eat a snake?' Liza shivered with repugnance. 'There! does that not prove to you that they are evil. The same snake that made Eve sin in the Garden of Eden.'

'Come now, Liza, do you really think that an earthly snake is the same as Satan in the Garden?' Maud shook her head. 'Surely you are not that simple.'

'If you think I am simple, I wonder that you want me to help you with the birth of your child.'

And so, the harmonious life of the community of the settlers became blighted.

When Maud told John about the conversation with their neighbour, he shook his head. 'Don't worry, you have still some time to go before the baby is born. I am certain Liza will be your friend again when all this blows over.'

Again, he sounded more confident than he really was.

A week later events took a turn that nobody expected.

Maud and Clara had prepared dinner and were waiting for the men to return from the far field. In the afternoon they had brought fresh water and some savoury cakes to the men. As the days were getting longer, John and Perk worked on the fencing till the sun went down.

The girls waited long after night had fallen, getting hungry themselves. Yet the men did not return home.

'Where can they be? I should go and see if they got hurt. Maybe a tree fell on one of them.' Maud paced the kitchen, thinking of the worst scenarios.

'No Maud, you cannot possibly think of going out in the dark.' Clara worried. 'You might trip and fall. Or an animal might get you. Think of Baby. The men probably want to finish a part of their work. It is a full moon, so there will be enough light to work by.'

'They must be exhausted by now.'

'I wish they were not in such a hurry finishing that fence. It is all because of that man Werner, they think the fence will keep him out.'

Clara's explanation sounded reasonable and in the end the girls had a little to eat and went to bed. Maud fully expected to find John next to her when she woke up in the morning.

CHAPTER 11

Early in the morning, Maud woke up and saw that John's half of the bed was left untouched. She threw off the cover and, in her nightgown, ran to rouse Clara.

'Wake up, Clara! John has not come home. Oh dear, where can he be?' Clara came down the ladder with a tousled head of hair. She rubbed her eyes and frowned.

'Let's look outside, maybe they both slept in the barn, so they would not wake us up.'

They ran outside, where the sun just peeped over the rise. The barn door was closed. When they opened it, they were met by an eerie silence.

'Baz? Where is Baz?' asked Clara. 'Why is Baz not around?'

'You milk Mols, Clara, I am going to see if they are still at the far field.'

'Think Maud. Don't go alone.' Clara reasoned. 'Let's do the work together, and then we will both go and see about them. I wager that they just camped out; John will laugh at you when he hears you made so much fuss about it.' She mimicked John: 'Silly girl, do you think two grown men need looking after? Go home and take care to bring us some breakfast, we are starving.' In spite of her worries, Maud had to laugh. She prayed that Clara was right. Yet, she could not shake the disquieting feeling that made her sick to her stomach. Maud did not feel she could eat breakfast while the men did not have their meals, so with a canteen with water and a cloth containing bread with cheese, the girls went on their way.

The far field was deserted. The wind in the trees was the only sound. The tools the men had taken from the barn, only the day before, lay discarded on the ground. A tree, half sawn swayed precariously in the breeze.

'That tree is going to fall, Maud; come away!' Clara pulled Maud to the side.

Maud could only stare at the terrible emptiness of the field. She dared not think what could have happened to her husband and his friend. In her mind she heard the shots that were fired at the people from the other side of the creek, and she was petrified.

For once Clara did not have an explanation. Or rather, she was not going to voice the fear that filled her thoughts.

'We need to take the tools home,' said Maud at last. 'We cannot leave them here.' They filled the wheelbarrow with whatever they could find, not touching the saw that was still stuck in the half-sawn tree trunk.

Silently they took turns to push the barrow down the narrow path. They were hot and bothered when they came to the farm house, but before they went inside to drink, they put the tools away in the shed. Then they sat at the kitchen table with a cup of water and some bread and dripping. They were too anxious to talk about what could have happened.

'Maud?' Clara finally tried, but Maud did not want to hear what could have happened to her husband. She sat in silence, tears dripping on her apron.

'No! Don't say it, Clara.' she clipped.

'What will happen to us? The little field needs to be harvested soon; I heard John tell Perk only yesterday.'

Maud just nodded. She did not want to put her fears into words.

It was not until the afternoon that Maud came to life. She did not have any more tears left. She had unleashed her worries to her heavenly Father, and she knew instinctively that if she did not do something, her troubles would only multiply in her head.

'I am going to Liza. They must know what happened.'

'What do you think happened then, Maud?'

'I am sure it was Werner. He wanted the land and he wanted you to be his wife's maid. I think they quarrelled and he shot them,' she ended with a sob.

'Perk as well?' asked Clara.

'Perk would have come back to us, if nothing had happened to him.'

Clara sniffled all the way to Lizas place. On arrival her face was blotched and her nose was running. Liza, who was surprised to see them come to visit so late in the day, and wondered what had brought them to her farm.

'Oh my dear, you look like you have been crying for an awfully long time. What can have upset you this much?'

'The men, John and Perk! I think they have met with a terrible calamity.'

'Oh no! I will come with you; I'll see what I can do. I have bandages and some laudanum for the pain.'

'No, Liza they have gone!' Maud screamed her agony out. Once she had been told the full extent of their plight, Liza was aghast and her commiserations were genuine.

'They ran off?' she asked, not believing what she heard.

'No, they were working in the far field and they must have been disturbed. Their tools were still lying about as if they were plucked away from the spot. I fear that someone killed them and took them away.' Maud started crying; now, as she put the horrific situation in words, she lost the self-control that she had held on to so stoically.

Clara went on to tell Liza about the half sawn tree. 'We had to stay away from there; even a slight breeze would have caused that tree to fall,…' she stopped, letting Liza fill in the possible outcome.

'They were finishing the fence around the field. I think they were only three days from having it all done. And the little field needs to be harvested soon.' Clara explained their predicament further.

Liza had turned white. It was a well-known fact that Werner wanted to expand his property, and while *Maere Green* had been a buffer between Philip's land and theirs, now the land would become available, he could become their close neighbour, and that would be too close for comfort. Bad neighbours were a curse.

'Maud, how terrible to have this happen to you. I will make tea. You will stay for dinner and Jim or Helmut will bring you home. But wait for them, they will want to know the details of these awful events.'

When Jim and Helmut came in from their work, they were as horrified as Liza had been.

'Unbelievable,' said Jim. 'Are you sure it is Werner?'

'He has been wanting to buy our land,' said Maud. She mentioned the amount that Werner had offered for the property and the crop. Both men were disgusted.

'He is a crook! But we knew that already, by the way he treated Helmut,' said Jim. 'He is a greedy villain. His wife is very unpleasant as well. I have only met her once, but the language that came out of her mouth was atrocious!'

'I don't know what will happen now,' Maud said. 'I feel that whatever we do, Werner will be there to get things his way.'

'Why would you think that? You are two capable women. I can help with the harvesting, after my own fields are done. Helmut and I will be happy to lend a helping hand. For half your profits I will take the corn to town and sell it. At least you'll have something to live on. Then you might want to go back to the bakery. I am sure Clara's father would have your back.' Both girls looked aghast at him. The spectre of Elliott Stack and his wife Cornelia loomed large.

'Half the earnings from that one field? That is a lot, Jim. I think a quarter sounds more reasonable.' Maud was appalled that her friend would take advantage of her.

'Take it or leave it,' Jim said. 'I am not going to work and travel for less. I am not a young man anymore and I have to put by enough money for when I am not able to farm anymore. My son seems to like city life better and will not promise to come back to help out. I am not going to work extra, unless you can make it worth my while.'

'But you have Helmut working with you.'

'Yes, but that is not going to last much longer. He has different ideas from mine and I will not have someone telling me what to do. Besides he wants to go back to his own country.'

That was a surprise for Maud. But she was not beaten yet.

'Helmut do you want to work for me?' she asked the German, who had sat quietly listening to the conversation.

'No, he will not!' Jim shouted, not giving Helmut a chance to speak for himself. 'He owes me, we picked him up when he was in dire straits, so he owes me.'

Helmut looked away, ashamed that he could not help the women.

'I think we will have to find another way out of this.' Maud got up. 'I thank you for the drink you gave us, Liza.'

'But you should stay for dinner, it is dark soon; one of the men should bring you home after dinner.'

'No, thank you. We will not eat your food. I do not think I could afford it.' Maud's voice was chilling.

'Not so hoity-toity, missy, you have no choice in the matter,' said Jim. 'I am sure you will come back to me. I am the only help you can get.' Maud shook her head, unable to believe the turn-about her friends had made.

'Come Clara, we are going home,' she said wearily.

'You will be back!' Jim called after her, 'You'll be back and my price will be higher than a measly fifty percent.'

Liza followed the girls out. 'I am sorry, but my husband is a proud man. I know he drives a hard bargain, but at least you can trust him.'

Maud stopped and looked Liza in the eye. 'Your husband is a crook, Liza. He knows I am in trouble and he uses that for his own benefit. I thought you were my friends. What kind of friend does that? Now I see why you helped Helmut. You helped yourself to a free worker. I am disappointed in you.'

Offended, Liza stomped back into the house, and Maud was relieved; there were too many things, nasty things, that she was tempted to say.

Clara trudged after Maud, who, in her anger, had found new energy.

'What will you do now, Maud.'

'I am going to have my dinner and then I am going to have a good night's sleep. Tomorrow I will make plans.'

'Do you think we'll ever see John and Perk again?' There was a hint of hope in Clara's voice.

'No Clara, I think someone has done them in. But let's not think about that now. We need to make the most of our future as we can.' Unconsciously her hand went over her round belly.

They woke up in the morning unaware that there had a severe storm in the early morning hours. When they saw the garden full of debris caused by the wind, they wondered if they should check if the half sawn tree had blown over.

'I hope it fell towards the side and not into the field. It would be a pity if it destroyed the seedlings that have already come up,' said Clara.

'We'll first have some breakfast; we'll do the chores and then we'll have a look.' Maud decided.

During the night she had laid awake for a long time considering what could have happened. She had thought of every possible scenario. One moment she was convinced that Werner had killed them and buried them on his own land, the next she thought they had walked off the job, too tired and too overwhelmed by the magnitude of the work and the long wait for a return. She remembered how exhausted they had come home each night. The last thought had sounded more plausible to Maud as Baz had disappeared also. He would have followed the men, or they would have taken him with them. Then she recalled John's love for her, his tenderness and his joy at the thought of becoming a father. He would not have left her. No, he would never leave her to fend for herself, even though he had often said how ably she coped with the problems that were thrown her way. But then, maybe his funds were severely depleted. Oh, she wished she had not spent valuable pounds on material for curtains and other luxuries. Contrasting thoughts twisted her mind in all kinds of knots. In the end she did not know what to think and when she came out of the bedroom, she looked wan and worried.

'I am appalled that they took the dog with them. Baz could have been the only safeguard against the likes of Werner,' she complained to her cousin.

'You don't know that they went out of their free will.' Clara's voice betrayed her astonishment at the change of heart Maud seemed to have.

'Let's just get on with it, shall we.' was the crabby answer she got from Maud

CHAPTER 12

On their way to the far field, they passed the little field.

'Look how beautiful those ears of corn are, Clara, I think they should be harvested soon, else they will be past it.'

Clara nodded.

'This is why I think the men met with adversity, Maud. They would never leave the crop so soon before they could make good money out of it.'

Maud had to admit that Clara had a very valid point. Her judgement must be clouded by her lack of sleep and churning over the worrisome events of the last few days. To think that John would leave her, to think that John would leave a crop that was near ready, it was all too ludicrous. Yet, to think that some terrible fate had befallen them was even harder to contemplate.

They trudged on to the far field where they saw to their relief that the tree had fallen. And it had dropped to the side, so that the field was intact.

'Oh look, how lucky that we did not lose any of the seedlings. Maud, this will be the another good crop,' exclaimed Clara. Maud sighed, at least something had worked out.

But coming to the stump they saw that the tree had been fully sawn and the saw, John's saw, had disappeared.

'Someone has helped themselves to the saw. And finished the job that John and Perk could not.' Maud slumped. For one moment she imagined that their only option was to go back to the bakery and be the servant of Cornelia Stack.

No! every fibre within her revolted. She was going to do the best she could, she was not giving up, even though she realised that she had lost John and the urge to wail was great.

'You can do your crying in bed tonight,' she told herself, 'Now is the time you need to make the most of what is left.'

She turned to Clara. 'Will you help me, Clara? I want to start harvesting the corn and pack the wagon. I will ask Helmut to teach me to drive the cart and I will take it to town myself. I know they will not give me as much as they would John, being a woman and all, but I have to try. I cannot give up what John started. The last thing I want to do is give Werner the satisfaction that I am an easy prey.'

Clara nodded. 'I will do anything you say, Maud, I will work like I have never done before.'

'Thank you. I knew I could count on you.'

'But Maud, you will not be able to work for very long. The baby will be born in little more than two months. We need to do as much as we can.'

'We will start tomorrow. Today we will work on the vegetable patch so we have enough food to keep us going.' Maud looked around. 'This looks like a promising crop also. If we get the rains, we will be able to cope.' As she surveyed the field, she became more hopeful that they would be able to make it, just the two of them. Two capable women.

'Look Maud,' Clara pointed up at the ridge where the Sydney Road ran. Isn't that Werner?'

'It looks like he is coming back from Sydney Town.' Maud followed her neighbour's progress for a while, then said, more or less to herself: 'I wonder what he has been up to?' She shrugged and started walking home.

The rest of the day they worked at the vegetable patch and gathered enough food for a few days. Maud decided to ration out the flour, cheese and dried meat they had in store, so they could live as long as possible on the provisions they still had.

The next day they went back to the little field with a wheelbarrow and some tools. They planned to work half of the first day, and carry barrow-loads of corn to the cart that was still parked in the same spot where Perk had left it after his last trip to town. In the afternoon they would visit Liza again to see if Helmut would teach them to drive the cart.

'I am glad that the dray is still here,' Clara had said. 'And again... it is proof that they did not go of their own free will.' As if that still needed to be proven.

While the morning was fresh, they found the work was not too hard on them, but soon the sun did its worst on the women and long before noon they were parched and exhausted with the heat.

'Tomorrow we need to bring more water, Clara. One canteen is not enough.' Maud licked her lips in an attempt to conquer her thirst; to no avail. 'I think we need to go home now. Before one of us passes out.'

As they passed the cart, they realised that half a day's work had not rendered much result: the cart was far from full. Maud sighed at the sight.

'Oh, my John, it is so much harder than I thought,' she mumbled. 'Where are you? I would love to go back a week and stop you from going to work on that fateful day.'

'That is nonsense, Maud, and it does not help much; it only makes you sad,' reasoned Clara. 'We need to have a rest before we walk all the way to the Calder farm. Besides, you have to accept that both men are dead. Werner would not do things by half.'

Maud knew that her cousin was right. But she dared to hope against all odds. She had to hope, even if only for the sake of her unborn child. She had to plan for the future because of John's child. She put the hand on her round belly. The baby, having had to endure a lot of bending over, now was moving about. Maud softly talked to her child, reassuring it, and with that, herself.

After a little food and a rest the girls felt strong enough to tackle the walk to the Calder farm. For the second time Liza was taken aback to see them again, especially as their last visit had ended in discord.

'Please tell me you are the bearers of good news,' she called out as she saw them approach.

'Alas, we have to disappoint you. The men have met with a calamity, I am sure.'

They talked about the missing Baz. Liza suggested he might have run away.

'I would be very surprised if he did; dogs are faithful, and Baz was very protective of any of us,' said Maud, 'but maybe he did get spooked by gun shots.' The very thought brought tears to her eyes. Liza was moved to put her arms around her.

'Come, let's have some tea. You two look tired. What have you been doing?'

When they told her the reason for their visit Liza looked worried.

'Jim is not going to like that.'

'Liza, do you think that Jim owns Helmut? Surely that would be a very unchristian attitude. I do not want him to go to town for me, I just want to learn how to handle the horses and the cart.'

'I will talk to Jim if he does not approve of Helmut helping you.' Liza acceded.

'Thank you. I don't want to be unkind to your husband, Liza, but I think his love for money outdoes his love for his neighbour. I understand that you took Helmut in, but you give him a pallet in your barn and treat him like a servant. It does not seem right to me.'

Liza slumped. 'I do not agree with the way he treats Helmut, but Jim is so disappointed that Noah does not want to follow in his footsteps, that he has lost all reason, it seems. Noah likes the city too much, and finds working on the farm a waste of time. I think he will change his mind once he gets a little older, but for now, Jim feels deserted. He is obsessed by the idea that he needs enough money to keep him in his old age.'

'I understand,' Now it was Maud's turn to comfort Liza. 'But can't he see that he will lose Helmut altogether if he goes on like that?'

Liza was true to her word and when they woke up the next morning, Helmut was waiting for them outside the farm house.

'Maud, are you sure you want to go to town on your own?' he asked.

'I have no choice Helmut. But I would appreciate it if you could show me how to handle the team and the cart. I have never driven them before.'

'I wish I could go with you.' Helmut said wistfully. 'But the least I can do is teach you to drive. They are a very good team, so you are lucky in that. John must have a lot of knowledge of horseflesh to choose them.' He went ahead of her to the barn where the horses were stabled.

It did not take Maud long to grasp the art of driving the cart. The horses were calm and obedient; besides, she had been watching John whenever he had driven them to church.

'You are doing fine, Maud.' Helmut said before he left to go back to work with Jim Calder. 'I have never seen a woman with such dexterity in handling the reins. I am sure you will do fine in Sydney traffic.'

The remark was meant to set Maud's mind at ease, but it had the opposite effect. She realised driving on the tracks was nothing compared to navigating the cart through narrow streets full of people and children. It caused her to have second thoughts about the plan to sell her crop herself. Yet she could not leave the job to her neighbour; the amount of money that Jim would demand of her, worried her no end.

For the next two days Maud and Clara worked to fill the cart. In the early afternoon of the third day, while they were contemplating going home, Werner, came to the field.

'Good afternoon, ladies,' he greeted them in a most courteous manner.' I must sincerely commiserate with you. I heard your men have disappeared.' He spread his hands out in the general direction of the field. 'And at a time like this, when there is money to be made. This is a great misfortune.'

'Good day, Mr Werner,' Maud said coolly, surprised that Werner seemed to have manners after all. 'You have heard right. But as you see we have no time to stand and chat, you must excuse us. We have a cart to fill. It is as you said: there is money to be made.' She turned around to continue putting the tools in the wheelbarrow.

Werner did not move.

'How are you getting your corn to the market?'

'We are filling the cart and as it is almost full, I will drive it to Parramatta to sell within the next two days. Good day, Mr Werner.' Maud wanted to make it clear that where she was concerned the conversation was at an end.

'I could help you, you know,' he offered.

'Yes, I realise that, but I am not prepared to lose most of my money to anyone else. I had the same offer from Jim Calder, who was taking half of my profits away with it. I thank you for the offer.' Again, she turned away from her neighbour.

'I will pay you, before I take it away.' He promised an amount that was very attractive to Maud. Even Clara who had listened to all that was said, gasped at the amount. Maud became suspicious.

'And why would you do this?'

'To help a neighbour in need,' he said simply.

'But you are not usually the helpful kind of person,' Maud suggested, thinking of the way he had treated Helmut.

'Do you want to make a contract? I know I have a bad name, but that does not mean I am a bad business person.'

'Mr Werner you have always treated me like I was inferior to you. You have tried to order me around; you have been rude to my husband. Why would I trust you?'

'I am not the bad person you make me out to be. I know you need help, I offer it to you. Payment first. One of my men will drive the cart to Parramatta, and you get an empty cart back.'

The thought that she would not have to drive all the way to market, over a bad road, while she was almost seven months pregnant, looked awfully attractive to Maud. Yet in the back of her mind there was a strong feeling that she could not trust Philip Werner.

Clara spoke up: 'Mr Werner, can we think about it?'

'Of course, you can. You said your cart is almost filled? I will come back the day after tomorrow; we can talk again then.' He turned and, without a greeting, walked away.

The girls did not discuss the offer on the way home, but at night when they were having their evening meal, they considered all the benefits and hazards of the plan.

'Once you have the money, it does not matter if he gets more or less for the crop. And you can stay home.' Clara reasoned. She had not looked forward to be left alone on the farm for possibly more than a week. 'And it would also save you the cost of staying overnight in an inn.'

'That is true. I know the road is hard to travel, especially with me being pregnant. But Clara, I think he is too much of a weasel. I am afraid he will trick us. He has never treated us with much propriety before. That, I find worrying.'

'There is always the chance that he will cheat you, though I do not see how,' Clara admitted. 'He is not a person who would help if it did not benefit himself. Maybe he knows he can get more for the corn than he paid us. Though the amount he offered was generous.'

In the end they resolved to sleep on it.

CHAPTER 13

The next morning, while they were doing the chores, they had a visitor. Clara saw him come down the rise, on his horse.

'Good morning, Clara,' he greeted her as she stood at the door to welcome him.

'Good morning, Preacher. Maud is milking Mols; she'll be finished soon. I will boil the billy for some tea.'

'That would be nice, Clara. Have John and his friend gone to Sydney Town?'

Clara shook her head.

'You've not been told what has happened?'

'No. I came to visit because I missed you at church. It sounds like something nasty has befallen you?' Clara started to explain the situation they were in. The preacher did not quite understand her haphazard account.

Maud came into the kitchen with a bucket full of milk.

'Hello Preacher, what brings you this way?'

'I missed you at church, Maud. I know what sticklers for Sunday services you and John are, so I thought I'll have a look how you are going. I thought maybe the baby might have been born early. But now I hear this strange story from Clara, that John and his friend have disappeaed? What is that all about?'

Maud filled him in, not leaving out the smallest detail. She finished her tale with: 'It is really good that you have come, Preacher. Maybe you can give us some advice. We have not decided if it is safe to accept Werner's offer.'

'It sounds like a perfect solution for your problem, Maud. Do you plan to go back to Sydney Town, to your uncle? Clara will probably love going home,' He turned to Clara. 'I expect you must miss you father.'

Clara just smiled at him. She did not want to say anything bad about her home and family to the pastor.

'I love living with Maud. I need to be here when the baby is born; she will need all the help she can get.'

'Very commendable, my dear, but when the money is gone… what will you do then? You will not be able to keep the farm going between the two of you, especially after your child is born and needs your care.'

'We have thought of that. I had hoped that Helmut would like to help us, when he has finished the harvest with Jim Calder.'

'I don't think that Jim will be amenable to that. He needs a helping hand too; he is getting older. And you are two females. I think it is quite unsuitable.'

Maud did not agree, but did not want to discuss it further. She turned again to the problem at hand.

'Preacher the first thing we need to do is sell our crop. Do you think it is safe to trust Werner with our corn? You know the misgivings I have about him.'

'I do not know the man but the offer sounds sincere. He said he would give you the money up front? In that case you can hardly go wrong, especially since you were surprised at the amount he offered, am I right?' Considering the problem solved, he asked more questions about John and Perk's disappearance.

'It is very unusual. I had not expected John to be so fickle to run away from his responsibilities.'

'Oh no!' Maud cried out, ready to defend her husband. 'I am sure that they met with foul play.'

Preacher looked surprised. 'What makes you say that, Maud? I know that it is hard to accept that the men might have been overwhelmed by the work, and may have just left.' Maud noticed he did not say: He left you, as that would be more painful for her. 'Consider though: once, they have rested, they will be able to think more clearly. They will miss the people they love, and John will realise that he has a family to take care of.' he pointed at her belly, 'And, when they come back, will you welcome them back with good grace?'

Maud looked at the preacher and wondered how a man she had thought of as a sensible person, could believe such nonsense, even though she, herself, had considered the same a possibility.

'They would not have left the tools, and the saw halfway through the tree,' she argued. 'John would have come and talked to me,' she added stubbornly.

Preacher regarded her with pity. Here was a woman, almost due to have her first child, and unable to give up on the man she loved. Or rather, she had given him up already.

'Do you really think that he has gone... forever.' He could not say 'died', that was too final.

'I think he has been killed. In cold blood. There are some people here who do not count a life as being sacred. Werner,' she pointed in the direction of the Werner homestead, 'has shot several people; those who live on the other side of the creek. Just because he suspected them of planning to steal his sheep.' All through Maud's speech, Clara nodded her head in agreement with her.

'Yes, I know the kind,' Preacher said pensively. 'But John...? He would not make enemies easily.'

'Werner wanted to buy our farm, he came to John and offered him pittance.'

'And now you ask me if you can trust this man?'

'He is giving us money up front ...' started Maud. 'And I have very little bargaining power. I would not know what to do if the baby was born while I was on the road.' Maud's voice trailed away.

'Just so,' said the preacher, all of a sudden decided. 'Then you must take his offer. And wait till the baby comes. After that you will be able to make the difficult decisions that are before you.' He sipped the tea that Clara had put before him. 'I will have a talk to Jim Calder and Helmut, I am sure you can expect a bit of help from that quarter.'

Maud was not so sure, but as the decision was made. She felt relieved.

Soon after, Preacher took his leave from them to ride over the hill, to the Calder farm.

In the afternoon, just when Clara and Maud wheeled the last barrow to the cart, Philip Werner came by.

'Have you made a decision, Mistress Beauchamp?' He did not enter the house but stayed a few meters from the front door.

'Yes Mr Werner, I did. Are you still prepared to pay me the money you promised to me yesterday?'

'I am. What kind of business man would I be if I changed my offer in one day?'

'In that case, let's shake hands on it.' Maud held out her hand to him. He took it and held it longer than necessary. Observing the soft skin, he said: 'And a very pretty hand it is.'

She withdrew her hand, unnerved by the remark.

He smiled and took a number of billets out of a pouch hanging by his side.

'Please, count the money, Mistress Maud. Even if you know you can trust me.' Philip smiled in a way that unnerved Maud.

'It looks fine, thank you, Philip. I appreciate your help. Will your man pick up the cart tomorrow?'

'No, I will drive it home with me now; Kurt will leave at sun-up and we would not want to wake you.'

She hesitated for a moment, before she asked: 'Is it possible for your man to bring us back some victuals?'

'Of course. What is it you need?'

'Just flour, and oil. Some tea, as well.' She gave him back one of the billets and added: 'However much you can get for this amount of money.'

Taking it, he smiled again. 'You will have the goods when he returns with your cart.'

For a moment it looked like he wanted to grab her hand again, but he took his leave of them in the politest manner possible.

Maud went inside with a sigh. She had money, still, there was that feeling of unease again. All she could think of was how wonderful it would be if John would be there. If only she knew what had happened to the men. If they were dead, there would be an end to it. But it was the lack of certainty that made it so frustrating. Maud was tempted to hang onto the opinion of Preacher, that the men had only temporarily gone. That every moment now they would be back, telling Maud they were sorry for having gone their own way. Of course, she would forgive them, she would be too happy and relieved to have them back. Yet deep down, she knew John would never put her through an ordeal like this, just on a whim. He loved her. He was looking forward having a child. He was too proud of his farm. He was a man of integrity.

Deep down she knew he had been killed.

Little did Maud know that the men were very much alive. They were bound and, locked away in the basement of an inn. They were fed fairly well. They had enough ale to drink. But they were not free to go home.

It had come about very unexpectedly.

While they were at work on the far field, two fellows had approached them. They were carrying a rifle each and, after a friendly greeting they had asked where there was good hunting to be had. John and Perk discussed the wildlife and the chance of getting a good feed. It had all been very amicable. They came from Mother England and there had been a joke about the size of the Royal Family, a discussion about the difference in climate and the need for rain. One of the men had talked about a strange tree he had found on the way and he asked if they could identify it for him.

'That is his domain,' John had indicated his friend. 'You show him any tree and he'll tell you what its name is.' John had sent Perk with the man, who, a little later, had returned by himself, explaining that Perk had to relief himself and he was not going to stand by and watch. They had had a good laugh about that.

But suddenly the laughter had stopped, when the two men grabbed John and covered his mouth so he could not yell out. John was a strong man, but against the two burly villains he was powerless. They had tied him up and made him walk up the hill to a waiting carriage. He had tried to run off, but that had cost him painfully. He realised that these men meant business. They were out to get him and, he had to accept that they well and truly got him. He thought he would cooperate, and take his chance when their guard was down. Then he would try and escape. He wondered what had become of Perk. Obviously, the curious interest in a tree had been a ruse to get Perk away. He had seen the man put his gun against a tree so his friend had not been shot. But they also carried hunting knives. He prayed that Perk had not been hurt, so he could take care of Maud and Clara. And the child. What a terrible time for this to happen. All of this went through his mind while he stumbled, bound and pushed, through the bush to a carriage waiting for them on top of the rise.

Once inside it, he noticed that the carriage door had bars on the windows and a lock on the outside. That would severely diminish his chances of escaping. In the roughest of manner, he had been shoved into the carriage, where his feet were bound together. Then he heard the key turn in the lock. One of the men sat in the coach with him. He looked at him with a strange mixture of pity and awe. He did not speak a word of explanation. It took a few moments until the horses were ready to forge ahead. Then the carriage plunged forward, in the direction of Sydney Town.

John wondered who was behind all this. Werner came to mind. He remembered his words: 'I want to buy your farm,' and the pittance he had offered. Sadly, John thought of all the toil and hard times it had taken to wrest the fields from the bush. Perk and himself. The days of sweat and grit. No money could pay for all that. The farm was his. His and Perk to share. As mates, as partners. The plans they had talked about: the next winter they would build a farm house for Perk, at the south end of the little field, so they would be near the creek as well. Perk would ask Clara to marry him and they would live and work together, the four of them. These were good plans; plans that convinced John he had to get out of this scrape as soon as possible.

His fear for Perk's wellbeing grew. What if he had been stabbed? What if he could not take care of the girls? He pictured Maud waiting for him with the evening meal. He imagined Maud and Clara coming to look for them. He remembered the half sawn tree. He closed his eyes as he thought of the danger his wife could be in if it fell while they were there. Again, he prayed for their safety. And for his release from these two crooks.

Charlie! Maybe it was Charlie who had organised this. He would not put it past Charlie to spoil his life. Ever since he could remember his older brother had had it in for him. Resenting the fact that he was called the better son. Resenting the way his mother asked John for advice, and not of him, her eldest son. Resenting how he had to hear the proud bragging of his father to his friends. His achievements, were always compared with the silly scrapes of his older brother. Maybe Charlie had heard about his farm and his beautiful wife. Maybe England was not far away enough, as he had thought. Maybe the distance between his parental house and the far land had not been wide enough to keep the jealousy of his brother at bay.

CHAPTER 14

The carriage had not gone for long when it suddenly came to a halt. John heard voices outside and recognised Perk's to be one of them. Faithful Perk! He had found a way to get help. John could not speak with the cloth that was quickly stuffed in his mouth but he groaned as loud as he could, earning him the vitriol of the man next to him: a firm kick in the shin and a rough hand over his mouth. But as Perk was outside, John was sure that this ordeal would soon see its end.

He was wrong.

A few minutes later, the door was opened and Perk was forcibly pushed inside. The men bound Perk's feet together and his hands behind his back, then they told him to be good and sit tight. Then they were locked in again. His head had a deep cut in it and he was bleeding profusely. John grunted to ask how he was. He nodded, and asked their guard to take the cloth out of John's mouth so at least they could talk.

'You have us well locked in, man. You can afford to give us at least some comfort.' John was impressed with the authority with which Perk spoke.

The guard looked from one to the other, and said: 'Which one of you is Beauchamp then?' John nodded at Perk.

'A thousand apologies, sir,' the man was clearly flustered. 'If I had know'd it was you, I wouldn't have clonked you in the head so hard. But we has our orders. And a good packet of money to go with it.'

'Who is paying you to take us away from our farm?' Perk asked.

'Man in Sydney Town. Wanted to have you alive and well. Now we has got you, we gets our pay. Us don't care for this one much,' he indicated John with a nudge of his head. 'Us only gets paid for the Beauchamp fellow.' He obliged John by taking the cloth from his mouth. Relieved, John tried to get the acrid taste out of his mouth.

The voyage to Sydney town was not a pleasant one. With their hands and feet bound, the limited movement soon caused the men no end of irritation. The many ruts in the road did them no good either. There were no stops and they drove through the night. The guard was without mercy. He gave them a little water from the same canteen he himself drank out of and bread with cheese, fed to them with a dirty hand. But no attempt was made to relieve their aches. Never had Perk been so glad to see the dirty streets of Sydney Town, where they stopped in front of an alehouse that looked as worn as, no doubt, its reputation was. As darkness had fallen not long before, the men were careful not to unload their human cargo too publicly. They waited till the street was empty and after taking the ropes off the ankles of their captives, they walked them to the back of the inn and ushered them into a dark basement. There, they were told to sit down and hold their peace, if they cared to stay alive.

John and Perk were too tired to speak and, as they each had a rough pallet on the ground, they decided they first should have a rest before thinking of what this all meant. Their poor muscles needed to stretch out after the long journey without movement. They were convinced that, sooner or later, they would get a chance to escape. But to be able to think clearly and make sound plans, they first needed sleep.

They spent a restless night. As the basement had no windows, they had no idea what time of day it was when they woke. The inn had fallen very quiet and as no sounds were heard they concluded it was still night or very early in the morning.

'Their interest lies with me, Perk. You should get yourself back to the farm. I don't know how Maud and Clara are faring, but they will not know what has happened to us, they must be worried out of their wits.'

'No Master. Those oafs think I am John Beauchamp. Let them think that. I am of no value to them. You act like me and they will probably set you free. You heard them; they only get paid for you. Besides you have more clout than I, and you can be more effective as a free man: you can go to your lawyer, or to your bank and get me freed. Who would listen to the likes of me?'

John saw the logic in that. If the crooks wanted money, they would not get it for Perk. If they thought Perk was John Beachamp, there would not be any reason to keep him and he could set the soldiers on the miscreants as soon as they let him go. John realised he looked as unkempt and dirty as Perk, yet, the people in the bank could vouchsafe that he was indeed John Beauchamp and that would speed up the chase. Once that was done, they could go home.

Home. He thought of Maud, and the child. She would be so worried. He hoped the neighbours would help her. He was sure Liza would be a great support to his wife. That thought calmed his concerns somewhat. At least she had friends to see her through.

Perk played his role well. Making the most of the moments the guards spent with them, he told them to let his servant go as he would only be an extra burden to them. John, acting like a good valet, begged to get some clean water and lint, so he could wash and bandage his master's wounded head.

'Don't just stand there gaping at me, fellow; bring my man what he asked for.' Perk was visibly enjoying his part. 'I am no good to you if the wound gets infected and I die in this Godforsaken hole.'

'Master do not exert yourself too much,' John added to the drama. 'You have lost too much blood already.'

At the threat of losing their money-cow, they brought anything that their prisoners asked for. When the felons whispered outside the basement door, John and Perk clearly heard them discuss the tides and a ship. The look they exchanged was one of worry. Later that night one man was heard to say that to feed one man was bearable, but why they were feeding the servant also, one who would not be of any benefit to them, was madness to him. On hearing that the men smiled. And decided to use that to their advantage.

The next time they were brought a hunk of bread and a bowl of soup, John took one of them to the far corner. 'Listen, I don't know why you have taken my master, but..'

'Orders, just orders from the boss.'

'So you are like me, just taking care of the money-bags of them rich ones, who don't really care what happens to you, as long as you do as you're told? You run all the risks while they pocket the larger share of the loot.'

'Yes, us jus does as we was told.'

'And your boss-man takes the big money, don't I know it. Allus the same,' he made it sound bitterly resentful. 'There must be a pretty penny riding on this if you are able to feed two men for the price of one.' Then, as he was about to turn away the weaselly man pulled him back by his sleeve.

'Throw your lot in with us, we can use a man with muscles like you.' He looked admiringly at John's wide shoulders. John feigned interest.

'Yea? And what would I be doing?'

The poor soul thought he had recruited a fellow underling. In a friendly way he put his arm around John, who had trouble to not to turn his head away for the smell of the man's clothes.

'Well, us does all kinda jobs. Never a dull moment, that's what I'm telling you. Let me have a natter with Will. Him's the man that's the boss.'

John pulled a serious face and just nodded. He did not trust himself to answer. He considered how easy it would be to overthrow the man and thus escape, but he had no idea what he would find at the top of the stairs. They had to be careful, in case there was another guard who could sound the alarm. He went back to his pallet an sat down, dejectedly, playing the victim of the higher echelons of the population.

Meanwhile Perk acted like he was preoccupied with the wound on his head, and had not heard what had been going on.

'I say, Perk, have a look at my head. The blasted thing is hurting like hell. I hope it will not leave a scar. I don't think I could live with a scar on my head.' The man looked at Perk with contempt. His prisoner might be an important person, but when it came to mettle, there was a lot of room for improvement. He exchanged an expression of scorn with John, who shook his head and shrugged, indicating he did not get the quality either.

When the scrawny man had gone up the stairs again, they laughed.

'Please tell me I don't behave in that obnoxious manner,' said John.

'No master, but if I must convince the sod, I might as well have some fun doing it.'

'Yes, you certainly are in good form. Do you think they will take the bait?' He pointed to the upper floor.

'I hope so, although, I wonder what they will do with me what they find out they have the wrong man.'

'I will not take long to get you out of here, that I promise you.'

It did not take long for the man to come back with the announcement that Will did not need the servant, and he certainly did not want him as a member of his gang.

'Will don't care to share his readies with another person. Nor does he likes to pay for your feed. And the innkeeper ain't a patient man. He tole me to let you go. But don't you get ideas of going to blab on us. I'm keeping my peepers on you. His Lordship can wait here till that capting is ready.' With that he took John by the neck of his shirt and led him out, slamming the door shut on Perk, who was left, somewhat dejected, sitting on his pallet.

As John walked out into the taproom, he started a chat with the man.

'So you're taking hisself back to Mother England, are you?'

'Yep, just waiting for the good ship *Sea Eagle* to be loaded and then he'll be out of our hands onto the deep brine. And we gets the loot.'

'Lucky you! Say, I would not refuse an ale. Of course, his lordship carries all the ready…' he thumbed in the direction of the dungeon they had just left.

'I likes you! Come and tell me why you stayed with the Quality so long. I saw you kow-tow to his lordship like I'm never seen before. This here country is full of good opportunity for the likes of us.' he said in a conspiring tone.

John had an ale with the man and listened to the plans that had been made for himself. These plans convinced him that his brother Charlie had been at the bottom of it all. He wondered how a hatred had gone so deep, that he was not left to live his life in peace, thousands of miles from the Beauchamp home. It seemed that those in England wanted John back and no money had been spared to search for him and hire strongmen to get him on the good ship *Sea Eagle*. Once on the ship the captain would be responsible to get him safely to the Motherland. Why they wanted him back that badly was an enigma to John.

'Oho, his lordship will not like that,' John laughed, thinking how he could get word to Maud not to worry, and that as soon as he could, he would be back on the farm. 'Does anyone know that hisself is married and his wife is expecting?' he tried.

'None of my concern,' the man said nonchalantly. 'I does what I'se told. Will don't care either. He only wants the loot that was promised.'

'Well, I'll be on my way then. Thank you for the drink, you are a good man. A word of warning, my friend: that man down there might give you some trouble. I wish you good luck.' He clapped the man on the back and walked out of the inn into the sunny street. His new friend stood at the door, thinking to himself that it was a great pity Will would not let him join their posse.

Just as John thought how easy his escape had been, he heard his name called out: 'John! John Beauchamp!! I say man, well met, well met! Did not know you were in town.' Noticing John's dishevelled attire, the dandyish partner in his solicitor's office, added: 'Heavens, where have you been and what have you done to yourself? You look like you are in dire need of a new valet, my boy.'

It was said loud enough for the man at the door to hear, and though he had proven not to be one of the smartest in the bunch, he now reacted with lightning-like speed. He turned to the patrons of the inn and called on a couple of heavies to help him catch 'the bleeding blighter who cheated me out of me winnings!' which was enough to set a few burly men out on the street to oblige.

John tried in his best slang to deny he was called John and stressed that he did not want to be called a name that his father had had. So believable was he, that the man of law meekly retreated, convinced he had made a mistake and pronouncing in dulcet tones to himself that it was strange that my lord had a doppelganger among the lower ranks of the populace.

This gave the felons time to reach John. They lay in wait till the solicitor had turned the corner, then he was forcefully returned to the inn and under constant recrimination of his gaoler, he was restored to his pallet next to Perk.

CHAPTER 15

As she saw Werner drive out with the dray filled with the crop, Maud expected to feel a sense of relief. Her problem was solved. She had money; more provisions were coming as soon as Kurt came back from Parramatta, and, most importantly, the crop had been saved. John could be proud of her.

Yet, there was a gnawing feeling in the pit of her stomach that would not go away. True, John might not come back, but she was sure that this was not the cause of her apprehension. These were times in which two girls, left by themselves, were vulnerable. She was decided: as soon as Jim Calder's crop was in, she would ask Helmut to live permanently with them. And she resolved to learn to handle that gun in the corner of the kitchen.

The following days were quiet. In the mornings they worked in the garden and they watered the crop of seedlings in the far field. As the field was some distance from the creek, it was not an easy task, but with the help of the wheelbarrow they worked together till it was all done. In the afternoons they took it easy, sewing and talking about the men: crying about losing them, laughing when they remembered their antics.

At the end of the week, as they walked home from the far field, a terrible smell struck them.

'The wind must have turned, I wonder what that smell can be, it is almost unbearable,' Maud said as she walked off the beaten path a little.

'Oh no! Clara, come and see what I found!' she called out. There were the remains of Baz, his throat cut and covered in ants. He was not a pretty sight.

'We have to bury him, the stench is too ghastly.' said Clara, trying very hard to hold on to reason, and not to gag, when every feeling inside her revolted. 'I will go and get a shovel.'

When she came back, she found Maud in tears.

'This proves that the men will not come back to us.' she said with a sob. 'Oh Clara, what are we going to do?' Finding the faithful dog had cancelled all Maud's confidence. It was clear that they were completely on their own.

The rest of the day Maud was inconsolable. As long as she had thought there was a glimmer of hope, she had been able to keep her emotions under control. But now it was certain the men had been murdered, she seemed to have lost the will to go on. Clara, who was mourning the chance to ever be Perk's wife, had great difficulty to keep her from giving up and being sent back to the bakery to live out her life in drudgery. In the end, Maud just lay on the bed and sobbed quietly. When Clara noticed she had finally cried herself to sleep, she ran to the Calder farm to ask Liza to help her. Liza brought laudanum, should she wake up. Maud desperately needed to have a good night's rest.

The following day Maud just sat staring into nothing. Liza was worried; she had always thought Maud a strong person who would be able to bear up to any difficulty that life dealt her. Yet without hope she seemed to have completely abandoned the will to live.

'Maud is grieving,' Clara said to Liza the next day, when she came to see how the girls were faring. 'We need to give her time; she will liven up when she is done with her sorrow, not a minute before.' Liza looked at Clara, amazed that a girl she had thought quite puerile, would show such strength and understanding when it was needed.

'You are right, Clara; I am glad she has you. I saw Kurt coming back from town this morning, did he bring the cart back?'

'He has not come yet. He may be tired after the journey. We can wait till tomorrow morning; our provisions are low, but we have enough food for another few days.'

After that Liza had gone back home, leaving Clara to watch over Maud.

It took two days for Maud to get up and face their uncertain future. In a rare show of affection, she hugged Clara and said: 'Thank you, for letting me be for a while. Now I need to make some decisions. John would not want me to give up so easily. Today we will go to Helmut and ask when he can come and live with us.'

Clara's face shone with pleasure; being complimented was something unknown to her. She told Maud that Kurt had been sighted coming back from town, a few days before.

'Liza saw him drive back when she came to see us. I wonder that Werner did not come to bring back the cart and the food you asked him to buy for us.'

'We'll see about that too, but there is work to be done now. I am sorry that I wasted precious days that could have been used better. But there is nothing that I can do to change that now. Come, we will see to the watering first.'

It seemed that the field had not suffered much from their absence, and when, later that day, they came to the Calder farm, Helmut was quite amenable to help them out.

'Ho-ho Helmut, you cannot leave me that easily,' Jim did protest, but this time Helmut stood his ground.

'Jim, I have helped you, as you have helped me. Now these ladies need me more than you do. Your crop is in and I am sure you are able to bring it to the mill yourself.'

As if that was not enough, Liza gave her opinion also: 'Jim, Helmut worked hard for you. Now, be a good neighbour and let him go where he is needed most. Maud is having her baby soon and they have tried so valiantly to keep the farm going. They deserve a helping hand.'

Jim knew his wife was right. He had been very surprised that the women had contrived to harvest their crop. Even though he had belittled their achievement, because it only was the little field, deep down he knew it had been a rare feat.

Maud smiled gratefully at her friend. They were saved. Helmut would pack his small bundle of belongings and move into Perk's former quarters.

The next afternoon Maud walked up to the Werner homestead to see about the cart and provisions. She had left Clara to take care of dinner and Helmut to settle into the barn. As the track was leading uphill, she was quite out of breath when she came to the house. No doubt Werner's wife would offer her a drink of water. She noticed how Constance's garden had been neglected and hoped Helmut would never have a chance to see the devastation of his wife's hard work.

Gerda Werner opened the door to her without a greeting. The woman's beady eyes bored into Maud's belly, making her quite ill at ease.

'Good afternoon, Mistress Werner. I am Maud Beauchamp; I have come to take my cart back.' She tried to smile at the lady of the house to show she came as a good neighbour.

'Ask Philip,' Gerda growled, waving her hand in the direction of the shed. Then she slammed the door shut in Maud's face.

Maud stood for a moment, uncertain what to do. Wondering what had happened to Gerda Werner to make her such an ill-disposed person, she went down the three steps and walked to the barn. A flow of angry German emanated from the open door. Maud hesitated before going in. The tirade stopped as soon as she was spotted. A young man, who Maud assumed was Kurt, slid past her, out of the barn, out of reach of his master.

'Ah Mistress Maud, a good afternoon to you.' Werner cooed. 'No doubt you come for your cart and the food Kurt bought for you.' Maud was amazed at how smoothly the change from rough German to polite English was achieved.

'Yes, I heard Kurt had come home a few days ago, so I came to see how he went on.'

'Come with me; the clod put your cart in our little shed,' he grinned wickedly at her. He led Maud to a smallish tool shed, away from the house. 'Here it is.' He opened the door and went in ahead of her. In the dark she could see very little. Suddenly the hairs in her neck stood up: something was very wrong! Then she felt his hands on her and he forcibly pushed her in. She stumbled and fell to the floor. Though, against the harsh sunlight outside she only saw the outline of him standing in the door, she noticed the hunting knife in his hand.

'You stay here, be a good girl and be quiet. If you don't,' his voice grew sinister now, 'if you only make one little noise, I will cut that baby right out of you.' With that he flashed the knife, menacingly. 'And don't think I won't!' He turned, locked the door and left her alone.

Werner's threat ringing in her ears, she was so overcome, that she sat on the floor, not knowing what to do. When her eyes became accustomed to the dark, she saw there was a rough pallet on the floor with a jug of water and a chipped cup next to it. The shed held nothing else. Slowly Maud came to the realisation that he had planned this. He had just waited for her to come for her belongings, so he could lock her up. It was unnerving. She now was sure that he had gone through all that trouble to get their farm. She was certain that he had killed John and Perk in cold blood and that it was her turn now. She wondered why he would keep her in the shed, and for how long. Maybe he wanted to wait till Clara came to see if something had happened to her, and then kill her too. It was clear to Maud that, at whatever cost, he wanted *Maere Green*. He could say to the other neighbours that he had given Maud money for the farm, and that it was obvious that the girls had returned to Sydney Town, to Clara's father. Be it far from the truth, it would sound plausible. Werner did not know that Helmut had moved in with them. That was a good thing. Maud hoped fervently that Helmut would come with Clara. Clara would not dare come by herself, like she had. Oh, why had she been so foolish to come here by herself? Why had she not asked Helmut to accompany her? Why had she been so stubborn?

'Oh Lord, let Clara not come looking for me by herself; let her stay safely on Maere Green. Or even Helmut. I would not put it past Werner to shoot Helmut. Please let them stay safe.' Maud prayed. At some time in the future, he would have to get rid of her, one way or the other. She was heavy with child; she could not have the child here, in the dark. Not by herself. Liza would have to come to help her. She chided herself, thinking that way. No, don't think like that; by that time, she should be well and truly out of this hovel. She prayed that Liza would be worried about her and come with Jim. And Clara, and Helmut. In the end she did not know how or what to pray for; she was tired, hot and desperate.

When it was night Werner came to the tool shed and brought her food. It was simple, but tasty, and because she was very hungry, she ate with gusto. He did not speak to her, and she said nothing to him. She hoped that in the dark he was not able to notice she had cried. She wanted to show him she was made of sterner stuff than the average girl, and that she was not afraid of him either.

Werner waited till she was finished and took the bowl, the spoon and the cup away with him. There was nothing in the shed that she could use to dig herself out with. He had thought of every possibility for her to be securely locked up.

After she heard the key turn in the lock, she curled up on her mattrass. She might as well go to sleep. Tomorrow she would be able to think more clearly.

In the meantime, Helmut and Clara sat at the kitchen table, too worried to enjoy their dinner, waiting for Maud to come home. Helmut was sorry he had let Maud convince him she would be able to do this errand on her own. At least a thousand times he had said: 'I wish I would have gone with Maud. You cannot trust Werner; he is a crook!'.

Clara had a distinct feeling of déjà vu. She remembered the night that John and Perk had not come home after a day's work. She was terribly anxious, not wanting to entertain the thought that Maud, and her baby had met with the same fate as John and Perk. They had been so happy, working hard, joking with each other and making a success of the farm. Where had that wonderful time, full of promise for the future, gone? She could not voice her fears, she was too overwhelmed. She did not want to think about tomorrow for fear that the next day would bring more tragedy.

CHAPTER 16

Under the cover of night, four forceful felons brought John and Perk to the *Sea Eagle*. The clipper lay, fully loaded, in wait for the high tide. While the captain did not welcome them personally, he kept an eye on proceedings from the poop-deck. Neither of the men noticed him.

'Come on, sirs, no dawdling now. You'll soon be travelling the high seas.' With a push and a shove their gaolers led them to their quarters, where they were unceremoniously thrust onto their bunks. A duffel bag was dumped in the middle of their cabin with the announcement: 'Here's the necessities for a pleasant journey.' The door was shut and locked.

After John's escape fiasco, they had waited another two days before they were taken to the harbour. Their hands bound, and with a tight grip on their breeches, they had spotted a man going before them and two behind, just in case either of them wanted to make a run for it. Obviously, it was imperative that someone was desperate to be rid of them and needed them to be on their way to the Motherland today. In the basement their gaolers had served them their food and drinks in pairs, one staying at the door at all times, to prevent any more breakouts. Perk had remarked that it was clear that their worth was severely being overestimated. But the guard had been tight-lipped. Banter was something of the past, lest their talk would convince them to become too friendly and they would be hoodwinked again. There was a quietly mumbled comment that 'an honest person could not trust the quality to speak with accuracy.' And that it was 'better to keep right away from the natter, as it would only lead to more trouble for Will'.

On the ship, the men observed their surroundings. The cabin was small, but it was clear that they would travel in relative comfort.

'Perk, I guess we're on our way to mother England.' John said in resigned tones. He squinted at the porthole that was clearly locked in case they had thought it a way to escape. He folded his hands saying: 'Oh, my Maud!'

'Now Master, don't start your praying again. You know I cannot abide talk of the Almighty. Look at us: caught and transported. Like common convicts!'

'I think we are a lot better off than convicts, Perk. Look about you. We have a bunk, a pillow and a blanket. I'll wager the food will be quite palatable also.' He paced the two steps to the door and, against knowing better, he tried the handle. 'Locked,' he stated quite unnecessarily.

'Do you think they will leave us locked up the entire journey?'

'No, I hope they have mercy on us, and let us out on deck once we are at sea.'

He stepped to the porthole again and looked out. Through the thick glass he saw the vague shine of the harbour lights; no movement was seen and no sound was heard besides the clanging of the ships bell every now and then.

'I am going to bed, Perk,' John stretched out on his bunk. 'My body is aching for some exercise, and as there is none to be had, I am going to sleep.' He lay down on his bunk, and turned his back to Perk. All he wanted to do was to talk to his Heavenly Father. Pour out his heart over the worry for Maud and the child. Beg that the neighbours would help her, and that somehow, there soon there would be an end to the awful separation.

In his mind's eye he saw Liza and Jim's face, smiling and joking. He prayed for them. He saw the sullen face of Gerda Werner, and he prayed for her and Philip. *'Lord have mercy on all of us.'* He prayed for Perk, his good friend, who resisted the love of God, for fear he would be hurt again. And he prayed for the person who had landed him in this mess, that he might be able to forgive them. Then he fell asleep.

He did not notice how Perk moved about restlessly on his bunk. Having no God to turn to, he felt lonely and defeated.

At dawn, as the sun tried to peep over the horizon, the *Sea Eagle* glided out of the harbour. Both men in the small cabin below deck had made the voyage before. Neither had suffered sea sickness then. But now, when they had left the still waters of the harbour, they felt their bellies rise against the groundswell of the waves. Being locked up, with a lack of fresh air, did nothing for their empty stomachs.

'If they do not come either with either food or to let us up onto the deck, I think I may have to use that bucket in the corner.' Perk said, trying to swallow his gut into submission.

'Yeah, if I don't beat you to it. Just remember that every one of the crew is busy getting this ship to go in the right direction, so I don't think we are on their "important-things-to-do" list.' said John, holding his head.

They did not have to wait long: a well-dressed lady, opened the door and brought a jug with ale, two glasses, and two rolls with thick slices of meat, to them.

'The captain asked me to bring you this, and he wants you to come up to say farewell to the Colony.' Her speech was friendly, but John could see that she was far from easy.

'I thank you very much, Ma'am.' John said with a smile and a slight bow. 'My name is John Beauchamp; this is my friend James Perkins. We had despaired that anyone would remember us.'

She smiled back at him, not surprised that he would treat her with deference. 'My husband is well aware that you find yourself in a delicate situation. He said he would try to make your journey as pleasant as possible. I will leave the jug and glasses. You may come up on deck at your leisure.'

Never minding the food and the drink; John and Perk had an urge to push past her to breathe the fresh air and see the last of the mainland. Good manners forbade them to run.

As soon as they reached the deck, they put their faces into the breeze and greedily sucked in the fresh sea air. It did not take long for them to feel more comfortable. John went to stand at the railing and looked longingly at the disappearing landmass. Like so many times during the last two weeks he sighed: 'Oh Maud, I wish you were here with me. I wish I knew what is happening at the farm.'

Perk squinted at him thinking of their spoiled plans and about the girl he had left behind. Regret swept over him; he had left her without telling her he wanted her for his wife. Yet, his feelings did not run as deep as John's, and he mostly mourned the loss of the freedom he had enjoyed in the Colony. He knew that was lost to him now: England would not be that charitable to him.

The captain approached them. 'Sir John, my name is Jeremy Hirst. I am the captain of this vessel. Let me first assure you that I regret the measures necessary to get you aboard my ship. Your mother is adamant that you return to your paternal home in England.'

'My mother?' John was puzzled. 'Did my mother orchestrate all this?'

'Yes. To a certain extent. She was convinced you would not come of your own free will. Come into my cabin, if you please, and I will explain the situation to you.' He turned, expecting John to follow him. John motioned Perk to join them. At the door the captain said to Perk: 'This is a private matter. Please, wait for my lord at the door.'

But John would not have it. 'James will come in with me,' he spoke with authority, 'he is one of us.' Perk was astounded. Gone was the easy-going man of the land; the lord of the manor had resurfaced with a certainty that was not to be mistaken or ignored. Perk wondered what this might mean for their friendship. In England John was a scion of one of the great earldoms of Britain. His mother's family was closely connected to the cousins of Queen Victoria and his family owned large estates in the south. Then and there, Perk had witnessed John resuming his old position as the second son of an old family, confident to be obeyed and accustomed to act with authority. Perk had regressed to his old identity: the son of the earl's gamekeeper.

'But Sir, I don't think…' The captain was not given the chance to finish his protest.

'Captain Hirst, I realise that on this ship you are in command. Yet, what you are going to tell me will have a lot of bearing on Perk's life. He will need to hear your explanation.' John had started in a friendly tone, as to pacify the captain; yet his last few words left no doubt that that Perk was going to stay with them.

The three men settled on the ornate benches in the captain's room.

'Firstly, I have the unhappy task to inform you of your elder brother's demise.' The captain spoke sombrely. He waited to let the news sink in.

'Charlie? Dead? How did he die?' John was more curious than sad.

'I understand he had a riding accident.'

John nodded. 'That sounds like Charlie. Always tempting fate.'

'This is why your mother needs you at the estate. Your father did not take well to the loss of his first-born. He has contracted a wasting disease and the doctors do not give much hope of a cure, or many months to live.' The captain looked down, to show the gravity of the situation.

'There is Wills, he could take over the reins. He was only a whipper-snapper when I left for the Colony, but he must be over twenty by now, and an able man to take on the running of the estate.

The captain sighed. 'I think your mother has explained it all in this letter.' He stood up and walked over to his bureau. Out of the drawer he took a sealed envelope.

John recognised the elaborate writing hand of his mother. He held the missive in his hand and felt the weight of its contents lay heavily on the rest of his life.

'I will give you a few moments to read it in peace.' The captain left the cabin. This time Perk went with him, leaving John to meet the nemesis of his future by himself.

On deck Perk sat on a coil of rope. John would be My Lord John Beauchamp, Earl of Cheltenham, while he would still be good old Perk, son of an underling, no title, no name of substance. The mainland was now almost enveloped in a cloud of spray. Almost invisible, totally out of reach. And so was the dream of his own family with Clara and his own farm. Perk felt cheated. It was alright for John, who had a home to return to, a family who would receive him into the fold with open arms, a mother, charming and stylish as the queen herself. And who had an income that would leave Perk far behind.

Perk had no siblings, no mother, a father who, through the shroud of alcohol, would not recognise him; that is, if he was still alive. He had no home to which he could retire, John might give him a job on the estate, and if no one was about, they would reminisce about their time in the Colony. But he would not have the same friendship with him. That would be impossible. He got up and leant on the railing. The face of Clara came to mind. 'Perk, you are such a strong man,' she had once said. 'I bet you there is nothing you cannot do.'

'Sorry Clara,' he mumbled, 'I could not get the master free from those crooks who caught us.'

If only they had not been so trusting.

If only.

Inside the cabin John looked at his mother's handwriting. 'Mama, what are you doing to me?' Now he regretted not writing to his mother, about his lovely wife, about their unborn child and about his happy life on the farm. But he had been so busy, so preoccupied with the farm and Maud. Had she known, maybe the countess would have thought twice before having him kidnapped and brought home. How he would tell her about the baby, and his worry about his two most beloved people, he did not know.

He opened the letter. It was dated four months earlier

> *Dearest John*, it said, *I have sent this letter to your lawyer, to be given to you when you are safely on your way back home. My boy, we desperately need you here. Papa is so unwell. He took ill after Charlie perished. Dear Charlie! You remember how wild he was? Always wanting to win, and laying bets that he could be more daring than anyone of his acquaintance. And he always was more daring. And now it has cost him his life.*

John stopped reading. Even though they had always come to him for advice, his parents always had adored his older brother. He was so different from John, who was concerned about others, constant in character, and helpful.

Charlie had everyone's admiration because he was a daredevil, a risk taker and the eternal optimist. Knowing he was not as reliable as his younger brother he had tried other avenues to gain attention. His antics had been known throughout the county.

John read on:

This is the reason I need you to come home and take on the responsibilities that are now yours. Papa will not last very much longer and I am loath to let William inherit the title. He has made some very unsuitable friends and is more occupied with his apparel and with gaming than with his family. He will let the estate down, till there is nothing left for any of us and he will bring scandal on your sisters.

Since you have gone, Marianne has married. A most advantageous alliance, my dear. She is now the duchess of Somerset. Sweet Cornelis is a great husband to her. Frederica is engaged to be married to the third son of Mr Swanson, not the connection I had hoped for, but this is a love match and dear Freddie is prodigiously happy. Annabelle is coming out this October and we hope to bring her to court just before Christmas. So, you see, you are needed here. I pray that you will make it home before Papa breathes his last, as William has made some very unpleasant remarks and thinks he will inherit the title.

I have spoken to The Earl of Rutherforde, who has a suitable daughter, sensible like you. We have decided she would make a pleasing Lady Cheltenham. When you come home, I will invite dear Cressida to stay with us. My darling son, I hope you will travel safely and I will soon be able to embrace you. Your loving Mama.

'Sorry Mama, I am a married man.' He grinned wickedly, as he pictured Maud in his mother's boudoir.

CHAPTER 17

The four weeks after Maud vanished, was an terrible time for Clara. By the third day she was almost convinced that Maud had been killed just like John and Perk. She had remembered the good times and cried, worried and worked hard, trying to cope with the tragedies. Helmut had gone about the farm business, letting her sob when she needed to and valiantly attempting to comfort her with words of hope against hope.

The day that followed Maud's disappearance, Werner had come to return the cart and deliver the provisions that Kurt had bought for them. He was surprised that the mistress of the house was not home and had shaken his head about the chance she had taken to walk the bush by herself, especially in her condition and with the natives around. But he had not given any possible explanations, or offered to look for her. Helmut had not been at the farm house when he came and when he heard that the neighbour had said he had not seen Maud, he was not convinced that Werner was speaking the truth.

'But why would he lie?' Clara had asked. 'He brought back the cart and did you see the amount of food he bought? It will keep us fed for a long time.'

Helmut had shaken his head. 'I know Werner in a way that you may not. He is not a person to change overnight. He has proven that he is a bad one.'

Clara was too tired to get angry with him. Helmut was such a great worker and so understanding of her sorrow. He had listened when she told him about her former life, how Maud had taken her up and saved her from the miserable days in the bakery. How her cousin had taught her to read and write and to speak properly. How she had trusted her, and treated her as an equal. How, after having been put down by an unloving father, and later, by a jealous step-mother, she had learned to become an independent person, not afraid to voice her opinion. She had remembered how wonderful it had been to work together with Maud, and see the results of a good day's labour. How her life had changed since she started to live with Maud, John and Perk. And how she had hoped to, one day, become Perk's wife.

Helmut understood how great her loss was. As he tried to comfort her, the two got closer in their shared experience of bereavement.

One day after dinner, Helmut said he wanted to speak earnestly with her. He sat her down and started shyly: 'Clara, you are a very capable woman,' Here it looked like he was lost for words. She looked at him expectantly. Nothing followed.

'Thank you, Helmut, that is a lovely compliment!' she said finally. 'I think it is wise to keep the farm going, after all the work that John and Perk did. You are such a hard worker. And I admire you for the respect you have shown to me,' not to single herself out she added: 'and to Liza and Jim as well.'

'Yes,' At her positive reaction, he seemed to have found a new courage to go on. 'I do respect you, Clara. That is why I feel it is not seemly that we should live in this house together. Before people in the district are going to spread gossip about us, I think we should do something about it.'

'But you sleep in the barn!' Clara was bewildered. 'What kind of gossip could they spread about us?'

'Oh, how innocent you are!' Helmut said gently. 'They will say it is not proper for two unwed people to share a house. Even if I sleep in the barn. Clara, I have lost the love of my life. Constance was my all. I think you loved Perk, ja?'

'I did,' Clara admitted, 'but we never spoke of it. I think in time we would have…..' She could not go on, so Helmut took over where she left off: 'You would have married once he had a farm of his own. I have heard the men talk about it. I know those were the dreams of Perk.'

Tears welled up in Clara's eyes. She nodded silently. 'I think so too,' she whispered.

'So you see,' Helmut ploughed on 'both of us have lost people we loved. As it is, it would be good for us to marry, and live and work together on this farm.'

'No,' Clara was not about to give up. 'What if he comes back?'

Now Helmut looked at her with pity. 'I wish it could be so, but all things taken into account, I think that that would be a miracle,' there was tenderness in his voice. 'I can see Werner wanting to take over this farm and he will use anything he can to malign us. As John and Maud's cousin you have a right to stay here and keep the farm. With my help we could make it a success. It is not as large as Jim Calder's, or my old farm, but we could have a good life here Clara. I will work hard for you.'

'Can I think about it?' she asked timidly.

'Yes, that is wise. It is a big step to take. Think about it as long as you want. I hope I did not frighten you; I want the best for you.' He got up. 'I will go to the barn. Goodnight, Clara, sleep well.' And he was gone.

Clara sat in the dark for quite a while. Helmut was a nice man. Not as clever or handsome as Perk, but he was always respectful. He would not treat her roughly like her father had treated her mother. He might, one day, treat her like John treated Maud. That would be a dream. The reality was that she would be a married woman. She could write her father that she was the mistress of a farm, with a tall husband, and maybe later children of her own. She would never have to see Cornelia and her nasty brats again. As she thought of what Helmut's suggestion would look like, it became more attractive to her. Yet, there was Perk!

Ah Perk! What happened to you? I fear I will never see you again. Like Helmut had said: it would take a miracle. Miracles did not happen in Clara Stack's life. Maybe Helmut was right, maybe marriage was a good thing. She remembered how Maud's parents had laughed together; in her mind she saw how Uncle Connor would put his arm around her aunt, and how, in response, she would smile up at him. They did not marry for love, yet that had come later, as they lived and worked together. Could that happen to Helmut and her? After all she always had liked Helmut, and he was a gentle man. She knew she could live with that.

At breakfast the next day, Helmut was shy. He did not look at her, and while she put the porridge in his bowl, he mumbled a soft 'Thank you', but said no more. In silence they ate their food and drank their hot tea.

Finally, they started to talk, both at the same time. The coincidence made them laugh. Then Helmut said in a decided tone: 'Me first.' He held up his hand to show he wanted her to listen: 'I want to say I am sorry if I spoke out of turn, last night. I have been thinking about all this and last night, in my bed, I came to the conclusion that what other people say about you is not a reason to take an important step like marriage.' He looked a bit miserable.

Clara sighed; was this chance for a future pass her by as well? She could answer nothing but a disappointed 'O,'

'You must have been thinking too?' he concluded.

'Yes, but quite the opposite,' she ventured.

'You mean, you don't think it is a bad idea?'

'No. I think it gives us both an opportunity to look at the future. We should look forward... because we cannot change the past.'

He looked thoughtfully. Then a kindly smile lit his face.

'I think you are a wise woman, Clara. Then, you will marry me?' he asked unnecessarily.

'Yes Helmut. I think that is the best for both of us.' She stood up to put away the breakfast things, thinking the subject was closed for the day. He came to her and put his hand on her shoulder: 'Thank you, Clara, thank you for trusting me. I promise you that I will do my best to take good care of you.' Then he bent over and kissed her gently on her mouth, then he went out to the barn to get his tools.

Clara had never been kissed before. She could not remember her mother ever kissing her; her father had not been affectionate in any way. And Maud had hugged her, but never kissed her. She stood in the kitchen for a long time, feeling a sense of exhilaration at the touch of Helmut's lips against hers. She felt like running after him and tell him to do it again. She chided herself for being silly. But the thought struck her that it was possible that Helmut, like all the other people she loved would not come home; that he would disappear like all the others. She ran to the barn, calling his name. He looked up in surprise. She walked up to him, suddenly noticing he was not only tall and blond, but also very handsome.

'Helmut, can you kiss me again?'

'But why?' he asked in total wonder.

'Because it was the first time anyone has ever kissed me.' she said, wondering where her audacity sprang from. 'And I am afraid that you will leave me just like Perk, Maud and John.' He smiled at her and stepped closer. She lifted her face up to him and he kissed her again gently at first, then, as she put her arms around him with more passion. After a while he lightly pushed her away. 'Clara, I need to go to work, the field will not water itself, and the fence needs to be mended at the north side. I will come home to you. I promise.'

CHAPTER 18

By the sixth day of their journey, John had befriended the captain of the *Sea Eagle*. They had a few mutual acquaintances in England and what the captain lacked in noble blood, he made up for education and experiences. Though they were careful to address each other by their rightful titles, in their conversations they treated each other like equals. Hirst was sincerely sorry for the plight John had left his family in and had asked John what he could do to help.

'At the first port we stop to take on victuals and water, you could put me on the first ship back to the Colony,' said John with a hopeful grin.

'No, I am contractually bound to bring you all the way to Southampton,' the captain responded, regret colouring his voice. 'After that, there are other agencies who will, by force if they have to, bring you to your father's sick bed. I am telling you this to help you understand that your family in England has made desperate attempts to call you back home. According to your mother, you have not reacted to any of her pleas to return. This has led her to apply these forceful methods. I am sorry, my lord, but there is no way out.'

'Thank you for speaking so candidly with me. I have been preoccupied with my farming endeavours. You see, at heart I am not a peer of the realm, I am a simple man, wishing to live a simple life. I love my wife. I am about to become a father. My relationship with my elder brother was strained. So, you see, I have my own reasons for leaving England, and the people in it, behind, wanting none of them to spoil the life I have chosen for myself. I have not been interested to pick up any correspondence that now lies waiting for me in a drawer in my lawyer's offic. That was the only venue I left open for my mother to contact me, and I have neglected to make use of it.'

The captain nodded. Too well he knew how family could impact the plans you made for yourself.

'Would it be helpful if we send your servant back to the Colony? Is he trustworthy enough to let him sort everything out at your farm, help your wife to sail for England, while you take care of the estate in Somerset?'

It was a helpful offer for a possible solution that might satisfy all involved, but John reacted sharply: 'Firstly I want you to understand that James Perkins is not my servant. If anything, he is my partner, but foremost he is my friend.' John let that sink in. Then he continued: 'I take it your first stop would be Cape Town. By the time he would return, my first crops would be spoiled, my first child would been born and heaven only knows how my wife and her cousin would have managed.' He had to stop himself from becoming agitated thinking of the situation he had left behind. 'And to know that I could have prevented all this,' he added regretfully, 'if only I had not been so stubborn to entirely cut myself off from my family in England. I could at least have told my mother I was married.' He left the captain to go in search of Perk.

John had made an attempt to draw Perk into his connection with the captain, but Perk had resisted the alliance, preferring the company of the crew. Jeremy Hirst was thankful that he did not have to hob-nob with the likes of Perk and did not understand that John insisted on sharing his cabin with him. Yet, to John, Perk was the only link he had with his farm; with the happiness he had experienced with Maud. Moreover, they shared hope that one day soon, they could to return to the Colony.

He found Perk with one of the crew, who was trying to teach him to lay some of the most intricate knots in the thick ship's rope. He looked on for a while, noticing the enjoyment Perk got out of the parley with the sailor. When he finally asked Perk if he could have a word to him. Perk did not hesitate one moment: 'Yes Master, did you convince the captain to let you go?'

'No, I am sorry to say the captain is not going to accommodate us.' As they walked off John became aware of the distaste the crew had for him, while they had a soft spot for Perk. He had seen the disapproving squint of the sailor's eyes when he saw Perk jump up at the request of his friend. He had seen the pressing together of lips in animosity at the term 'Master', used by Perk.

When they were out of the sailor's hearing, John addressed the problem.

'Perk you have to stop calling me Master. You know who I am, and what I want to be. Please, be my friend. There is no one I trust more than you. You are even more to me than my brother.'

'Knowing how you love your brothers, that is not a compliment,' Perk quipped, circumventing the real issue. John laughed at this, but did not leave it there.

'Do you consider me your friend, Perk?'

'Yes, I do, Master. But one has to be realistic. Once you are in England you will be My Lord and because I do not have a title I will eat in the kitchen.' Perk looked at John to see if he too had realised that in England things would be different. John's silence said it all: he also had realised that his mother would not have Perk at her dinner table, or in the house, unless he was serving as a butler, or valet.

'What I would not give to be back at *Maere Green*, this very moment,' he whispered sadly. Then he shook his head to clear out the cobwebs of wishful thinking.

'Perk, how would you feel about travelling back to the Colony from Cape Town? I have discussed it with Captain Hirst and he agrees that it would be the best solution. What do you think?'

'Anything,' Perk grinned, 'as long as I don't have to go back to God-forsaken England.'

'You could take over the farm, with Clara. And send Maud to me.' He stopped there and after a moment, added: 'Maud and the child.'

Perk was so excited he shook John's hand.

John laughed at his enthusiasm. 'There is one condition,'

'Of course,' Perk's eagerness was not going to be dampened. 'What's your wish, Master?'

'You need to call me John the rest of the journey.' John was not prepared for the reaction of his friend:

'I love you like a brother, Master, but I cannot do that. You have always been my Master, and I like it that way.' He looked at John with an air of challenge.

'But Perk, it sets us apart in the eyes of the crew. I can feel it.' John was unable to order his friend what to do, but he could argue the point.

'Eyes be damned, Master. You will always be my best friend. And I will run your farm well.' A crooked smile crept over his face. 'With Clara, if she will have me.'

'So be it then,' conceded John. 'I know I can trust you. Thank you, my friend. It seems that our life-long partnership has almost come to an end. I will sign the farm over to you. I wish I could say I will come to see how you get on, but I know that my future must lay in England.' The last was said with sad resignation. 'Of the two of us, you are the happier.' John had to walk away; the loss of his friend was already too heavy to be borne.

And so it was done.

On the very day that Perk boarded the steamship *The Castleton*, to travel back *to Maere Green,* far away in the Colony, Clara was married to Helmut.

She had put on Maud's Sunday dress, and Helmut had bathed in the creek for half an hour before he considered himself ready for matrimony. Clara suspected that during that time, he had had a serious conversation with Constance. Saying 'Goodbye' to his first wife, before he started out on a new life with her.

The preacher had been helpful; he thought they were wise to tie the knot. Liza had made a garland of flowers from her garden, and braided it through Clara's hair.

When Helmut saw her, he told her that she looked beautiful. Nobody had ever told Clara she was beautiful and she felt like the Queen of Sheba. She beamed up at him; some of the women who noticed this nudged each other, saying how wonderful it was that Helmut had found himself another adoring wife. A few ladies in the congregation had brought in plates of food: cakes, ham and cheese, and other sweetmeats. Liza had made a large canteen of lemonade. It was a happy wedding feast.

When Helmut drove his new wife home, she told him that her wedding had been so much better than Maud's; he only half listened when she explained why. Finally, she realised he was much quieter than usual. She asked him if he had had a good time.

'Too many people around,' he said shortly.

'But they were all people from our church; I did see you talk to quite a few of the men.'

'Yes, they all said I can be happy now I have a wife again, but you are not Constance, Clara, and I am not James Perkins.' He sighed, 'Ach, but we must make the best of it.'

It was as if Clara had been slapped in her face. She did not speak again until they were home, then she took off her nice dress and brushed the flowers out of her hair.

When at night Helmut lay fast asleep, next to her, in the bed that John had made, she silently cried. Her mother's words sounded in her ears: 'I hope you don't get a rough one like your father." No Helmut had not been rough, but neither did she feel loved. Her heart ached for Perk and his funny ways, the manner in which, without saying a word, he had shown her that she was special to him. She remembered the way he had looked at her, and his impish smile. Knowing she would never be another Constance for Helmut she decided to take his advice and make the best of it. Like Constance was Helmut's, Perk would always her best memory of love.

The days seemed endless for Maud. In the dark lock up there was not much room for movement and it was difficult to know what day it was. In complete silence Werner brought her two meals per day. She begged him to let her out to get some fresh air, but all she got was a grunt and a disgusted mumble when he picked up the bucket, to empty.

'Philip, I need my baby's clothes, please let me out. I cannot possibly give birth here.' she would plead. There was no answer from her gaoler. When she would ask why he left her there and why she was locked up. All she would see was his sardonic smirk.

Maud was past crying. In the end she just sat in a corner, her backside hurting, her discomfort so great, that she did not try to remedy it anymore. She knew she did not have long before her child was born and the only worry she had, was that he would leave her to fend for herself. Now she was sorry that she had not asked more questions about childbirth. She had been certain that Liza would be there with her, to guide her and take care that the birth would end in a safe delivery. She called out to God, and tried to remember times in the Bible where He had intervened to help His people. She thought about Mary giving birth to baby Jesus in a stable, with only Joseph to help her. And there was Hagar. Hagar had been noticed by God when she was in dire straits, and God had been faithful to console her and give her peace. She was sure God saw her. Only He knew the situation she was in. Only He knew the fear she had for the future and the desperation she felt when she thought of the birth getting closer and closer.

'Dear God, I pray for somebody to help me with the birth of my child.' was her daily prayer.

Meanwhile, painfully slowly, the days crept past.

CHAPTER 19

On a particular hot day, Maud heard voices outside. Besides the voice of a woman, she recognised Werner's voice. They were speaking in a language, that Maud supposed was German. She knew that the voice did not belong to Gerda. There was a raucous laugh as they came closer and Maud felt a wave of terror flow through her.

The door opened and a fat, blond woman came into the shed.

'Wird sie hier gebaren?' she asked Werner in astonishment.

'Philip what is happening?' Maud asked terrified.

'This lady will help you when the child is born.' he explained. 'She does not speak any English so you cannot tell her any of your nonsense.'

'How will I tell her what I feel during the birth?'

'Just shut up and she will show you what to do.' was his gruff reply.

Without so much as by your leave, the woman started to poke Maud's body, not taking any care if it might hurt her.

'Ja, gib ihr noch zwei tage,' she nodded, then walked out into the sunlight.

Werner followed her, at the door he turned and said: 'Your baby will be born in two days. Helga knows what she is on about.' Then the door closed again.

Two days!

Maud had looked forward to the day she could hold her child in her arms, but now she thought of the place she was forced to live in. To have her baby here would be cruel.

Jesus was born in a shed, he survived. Maud kept on telling herself even though it did very little to reassure her. *He had a loving mother, and so does your child.*

For the hundredth time she wondered why Clara did not come for her. Did Liza think she had just walked off? They knew she had been on her way to the Werner farm. They knew Werner and his reputation. She had trusted him only because he had paid before taking the crop.

Like a demon he had planned this hell for her.

But why?

The questions rolled through her mind, as they had for days on end. And all she could do was telling her Heavenly Father how much she needed Him.

The next day Philip brought some nappies, and two little blankets. He just put them neatly in the corner close to the door. Then he sat down on a small stool he had brought in from outside. He looked at her as if he had a lot on his mind.

'Tomorrow your baby will come. Helga will come as soon as you start having labour pains. She does not know who you are. I have told her you are a poor woman I am trying to hide from a cruel husband.' He stopped for a while thinking how to go on. Maud wanted to ask a question, but as soon as she began to talk he stood up walked towards her and slapped her hard in her face. She tumbled backwards. As she wiped her mouth she saw the blood on her hand.

'You will not say a word.' he threatened. 'Not now, and not tomorrow. I will stay just outside the shed and I will hear it if you speak. If you say one word to Helga, or mention one name, I will kill your child.'

Maud began to shake with fear. This was far worse than she had ever thought possible. Philip Werner was an evil being. And she was at his mercy.

'After the birth, you will stay here,' he indicated the shed, 'until your bleeding stops; after that you will move into the house and at night you will spread your legs for me, just like you did for John Beauchamp. The child you will give to Gerda to rear as her own. If she has a child she will not bother me with her complaints. Remember you will say not one word.'

Maud could ot help herself. She whispered: 'Why?'

Now Werner stood over her and started yelling: 'It is easy for you. You did not have to marry a hag for the sole reason that her father wanted to get rid of her. It was the only way I could get money from that man to buy this farm. You married a normal person, not a monster. You and your husband shared a bed, like all married people. My wife sends me to a room of my own, because she can't stand the sight of me, just as much as I hate the very sight of her. I want a women for my own, and I want a child of my own, and I will have one: you will give it to me. You hear? That is why. And remember,' Werner's voice became menacingly soft now. 'If you do not please me, your child will die!'

With that he walked out and locked the door, leaving Maud in tears.

Oh John, this should be the happiest time of my life, and now look at me. She started to pray, John had always said that when he was desperate, he had turned to Heaven and had never been left without a response from a loving God.

As she prayed for John she saw him, how he had read the Bilble on that last day. They had talked about the reading. It was from the Book of Micah.

They had been sure of themselves, believing the text was not for them at that moment. Now, Maud knew it had been:

Do not gloat over me, my enemies.
For though I fall I will rise again,
Though I sit in darkenss, the Lord will be my light

Now the text had come to her she was reassured that there would be a way out, even though, at that moment, it seemed quite impossible.

Helga was wrong. It took another five days before Maud's son was born. Helga was a great help, without speaking she was able to reassure Maud and make her as comfortable as possible. The birth was not a difficult one. Maud was proud of her healthy boy, who was in posession of a good set of lungs. When she held him, immideately after the birth, for the first time since many long weeks, she smiled.

'Hello Hugo. Here you are, and you look just like your father.' The tears came easy after that, but she caressed the child and suckled it.

Helga disappeared straight after the birth and was not seen again. For six weeks Maud and her son were alone. Maud told him all about his father and enjoyed her child as much as she could. The day Hugo smiled for the first time was the most terrible day in Maud's life.

For Clara and Helmut life fell into a quiet rhythm of work and rest. During the day Helmut made no gestures of affection towards her, but Clara tried to show what affection she had for Helmut, by putting her hand on his arm, or calling him with a term of endearment. Helmut did not react to these in any way, but at night he was an ardent lover, which Clara deemed a promise, that in future he would come to love her. She tried to hone her cooking skills by asking Liza and other ladies in the neighbourhood for recipes, to make life for Helmut as comfortable as possible.

Liza had convinced her husband that Helmut was not his property, and anyway, to have him as a good neighbour would profitable or him. She knew Helmut ahd Clara would do anything to help them if necessary. She had also assured Jim that he had still many years of health and strength in him and that worry about what was to come was neither Godly, nor healthy for him.

Whenever Clara and Liza visited with one another, they remembered Maud.

'The baby would have been born by now,' Liza would say.

Or Clara would remark how she felt guilty sleeping in Maud and John's bed, while she did not know what might have happened to them.

The men would be more down to earth: 'There are many rascals around; I have not much hope for their wellbeing if they have been set on by bad bloods.'

Another would agree: 'Yes, if they can tackle two grown up men, they certainly would not have any difficulty with a pregnant woman.'

Another would blame the people who lived on the other side of the creek. 'Oh no,' some one else would say, 'that German fellow up the hill took care of them.'

And so the people around would explain away the disappearnace of their neighbours. They would put extra locks on their doors, train their dogs, and have their guns loaded, ready for their own defence.

When Perk arrived back in Sydney Town his first port of call was the sollicitor. John had written a letter that Perk handed him as he came in.

The letter instructed Mr Scrivener to pay James Perkins an allowence of a certain amount of guineas, each month, starting from the day this letter was handed to him, and to transsfer the ownership of the farm, by name of *Maere Green* to said Mr Perkins. After a clear and concise explanation of the facts, my Lord wanted the solicitor to return forthwith, all correspondence from Lady Eleanor to Cheltenham House in Somerset.

Perk made it clear to the man of law that he had very little time to waste in the city, as it was imperative that he travel to *Maere Green* at the earliest possible moment.

Mr Scrivener, who was au fait with the unusual actions of John Beauchamp, shook his head and mumbled how extraordinary the behaviour of a scion of such a highly regarded house, was. But to Perk's relief he opened the safe and gave him the first installment of his money.

Perk did not linger at the solicitor's offce, but bought himself a horse and started out on the road out of Sydney Town. As he did not stop very long during the night, he made good time and arrived at *Maere Green* in the middle of the next day.

His excitement when he neared the farm was hard to contain. He would see Clara again. He would have a house of his own. He would be a man with a name and a place in the neighbourhood. He had arrived where he always wanted - no dreamed - to be.

He jumped off his horse tethering it to small tree. He called out to Clara, then to Maud, in the end he whistled for Baz.

There was no answer. He was surprised to see the door open. He went in calling out but no one answered. The place looked neat. He went into the bedroom. The bed was made, but there were man's boots under the bed and a few female garments hanging on the hooks.

He was puzzled. Where was the crib that John had made. He looked up in the attic. There he found the crib filled with the baby clothes, neatly folded. Did something happen to the child? He fervently hoped that Maud had not met with the same fate as Constance, and died in childbirth. The master would be heartbroken. Perk reasoned if that were the case he would marry that lady that his mother had in mind for him, and never love again. He was as dedicated to Maud as he himself was to Clara.

He looked around and followed the path to the vegetable patch and the creek. He found it all well kept, but of Maud and Clara there was not a trace.

Liza Calder! The girls could be visiting Liza and Jim. He took the eastward path to the Calder farm, where he found both Liza and Jim at home.

Liza came running out, arms wide open, she embraced Perk and welcomed him:

'Oh how wonderful to see you, We all thought the worst, and see, here you are hale and whole. What a blessing!'

Jim was a bit slower, but shook Perk's hand with gusto.

'Perk, may I say: welcome home. We thought the worst. Is John also...' He stopped mid sentence, as something caught his eye. 'Dear God! That is smoke!' Alarm coloured his voice. Liza and Perk turned around and cried out in alarm.

'That looks like the Werner farm! Liza, bring the water cart over the ridge. Thank God, I filled it only yesterday.' He started to run through the bush, Perk hard on his heels. Now his body was telling him he was not a young fellow anymore and he frequently had to stop, gasping for breath. Perk overtook him, and did not wait, but hurried through the thicket, taking the shortest way in the direction of the fire.

On the far field Helmut had taken a breather from the repairs of the fence, to sit with Clara, who had brought him cool water and freshly baked bread with butter. As they sat in the shade, they too noticed the smoke coming from Philip Werner's farm.

'Mein Haus!' Helmut cried out. 'Come Clara, we must see what we can save, before it will burn the whole....' He did not finish his sentence but started to run, leaving his lunch behind. Clara followed him.

CHAPTER 20

Kurt stood in the doorway of the toolshed. Through her tears Maud looked up at him, her eyes begging him to give her child back. Only moments before he had tied her up with ropes, so she could not follow, then he had taken little Hugo from her and laid him in the arms of Gerda Werner, who was waiting in her trap, ready to leave. Gerda had driven off. Without saying a word.

'Please, he is my son, why have you taken him from me?' Maud sobbed. She pulled at the ropes to no avail.

'Orders of the mistress,' Kurt answered without a skerrick of mercy.

'What will she do to him?' Maud asked.

'He'll be her son from now on; he will be spoiled rotten and he'll be as rich as Croesus. Don't you worry about him. She always wanted a child; now she has a boy. Her father will be proud of her.' He started to walk away; she called out to him.

'Kurt, tell me what's going to happen with me? Where is Philip?'

Kurt laughed riotously.

'That's another one you don't have to worry about. I know he had great plans with you; treating you like his slave and making him feel like a real man. Yes, he told me all about it.' Kurt snorted mockingly. 'Ha, he won't do anything of that sort now. The mistress hates men and Werner is a viper. She fed him schnapps - loads of it. He is in his bedroom, sleeping it off. If he wakes up before he is dead, I will be surprised. I have to go; I am taking all the mistresses' possessions back to her father's house, where she will return as a widow with a child. I bid you good day. I am leaving this hell hole; I am going back to Melbourne.' His cackling laugh getting fainter as he walked off.

Maud shook with fear. She was bound so tight she could hardly move. She started to writhe to try and break free, but Kurt had known how to tie up a person permanently.

For a moment Kurt disappeared into the house and when he came out climbed on the cart laden with cases and furniture, and drove off.

All Maud could do was cry for her child. There was no way that she would catch up with them, even if she was able to free herself. In her distress she repeated over and over again: 'My boy smiled at me, oh God, my baby smiled at me.'

In her despair, it took her some time to notice there was an acrid smell in the air. When she finally became aware of it, she looked up and she saw smoke billowing from the farm. She realised that Kurt had set the farm alight and that Philip Werner lay legless in one of the bedrooms. Through her own grief she felt no pity for him. But slowly it dawned on her that she herself was in danger too. The fire, if not contained, could jump to the trees and it would be only a matter of minutes before the tool shed would be alight. Is this how it all would end? At least Hugo was safe, she realised. Even if she would burn to death, he would be brought up in safety. John's son would be safe. That is the thought she held onto while she tried, with more zeal now, to undo the ropes that held her. In her will to live, she told herself that Kurt had left the door of the shed open so she could see the fire. So she would have a chance, so she would be able to tell the story. She realised that Kurt did not like his mistress, just as much as he disliked his master. She looked around if by chance he had left something for her to cut the ropes. But she did not see anything lying about. She renewed her effort.

Suddenly there were voices. She heard male and a little later female voices. She tried to call out, but the sound of the fire and the people screaming orders at each other drowned out her calls. She had to wait and while she waited, she revived her fight to break free.

Perk was the first to arrive at the burning farm. He looked around if he could see any people or animals. He called out to see if anyone was in the house. No answer came. Then he tried to see where the Werners kept their water supply. When he found the water barrel, he started to bucket the water into the window of what he thought was the living room. As he was doing this, Jim caught up with him.

'See if their carts are here, they may be out. I tried to see if anyone was home, but had no reply,' he yelled at Jim. Jim did as he was bid.

Helmut came to the farm and as the builder of the house he knew what to do. He had installed a pump that could spray the water with great force into the building. It was hand operated and the men took turns manning it. Meanwhile Liza had arrived with the water truck and was gladly received by the men who started to use her contribution too.

As they were working together, Clara reached the farm and stood as one nailed to the floor watching the effort of the men. At first, she did not know who the fourth man was, but as Perk yelled a request for more water to the others, she recognised him.

"Perk!' she whispered in wonderment. 'Where did you spring from?' Had he been here all the time, just leaving them to fend for themselves?

She had to stop herself from running to him and asking him a thousand questions. Then he saw her standing in the shade. The grin that covered his face was enough to break her heart, but she could not move. All the love she had ever felt for him flooded over her. Yet, she could not go to him, she did not dare to come closer; she knew she had forfeited the right to him.

He stepped up to her. With long strides, eager paces, to gather her up in his arms and tell her the good news that he was back, that he loved her and that they could marry. As he came closer, Helmut saw him move toward Clara. He jumped down from the pump, ordered Jim to take over from him and ran to his wife.

Both men reached her at the same time. Perk with a question on his face, wondering why she did not come to him and Helmut putting a possessive arm around her waist, his face challenging Perk to come one step closer.

'Perk, I have married Clara; she is my wife.'

'Clara?' The question hung heavy in the air between the three; the disbelief in Perk's voice cut like a knife through Clara's conscience. She hung her head for a moment, unable to stand the look in Perk's eyes. Then she turned to Helmut and said: 'Let me have a few minutes to talk to Perk, Helmut.' It was not a question; she was telling him that she needed to talk with Perk, come what may.

Just then the pump stopped working and Helmut was summoned back to help out.

Clara and Perk walked away from the house a little. Clara was careful not to get out of Helmut's sight, just in case he would come back for her. As long as they were seen talking, she knew he would not interfere.

'Clara is it true?' Perk 's voice cracked. Here she was, his girl, thinking about her had kept him sane on the boat, when all he had dreamed about was their reunion, the opportunity to tell her his plans for the both of them. Especially on *The Castleton*, when he knew *Maere Green* would be his, and he finally would have something to offer her. Happiness had come so close to him that he could almost touch it. And now she was snatched from him.

She nodded silently. 'Maud and I thought that you and John had been murdered. We found Baz with his throat cut.' Her eyes begging him to understand, she looked at him. 'Perk, we did not know what to do. Then Maud disappeared…'

'What?' Perk had not meant to yell but it all seemed too horrible to be true.

'Yes, she had gone to Werner to get the cart back… No, let me start from the very beginning.'

He stopped her, realising he needed to process the news before he wanted to hear the rest of the story. He said: 'Let me first help with this fire, then we can take all the time to tell each other what happened.' He walked away to take his turn at the pump.

Soon the fire was out. It had been well lit: there was very little left of the house. In silence, overcome by a feeling of loss, they all stood stunned by the ruins of the once beautiful farmhouse. They all looked worse for wear and a profound weariness burdened their bones.

Liza was the first to suggest they all needed to wash and have something to eat and drink.

Helmut shook his head and said decidedly: 'I first want to make it safe. As it is now, the walls will collapse on anyone who tried to enter. Let's break them down. The women can get us some drinks. Clara,' he turned to his wife. 'Can you get the bottles of ale I brewed? Put them in the wheelbarrow so there will be enough for all of us.'

As the women walked away, Helmut walked toward the tool shed to see if there was an axe he could use. As he entered, he heard someone cry out. When his eyes were accustomed to the dark, he saw Maud, bound on the floor. He ran outside to call the women back. 'Quick girls, come back; I have found Maud!'

Everyone came running while Helmut knelt down to loosen the ropes.

'Lay still, Maud, we are all here to help you. Hell and damnation to the person who did this to you.'

Then they were all around her, asking the questions they had wondered about in the last four months. Helmut suggested forcefully to let Maud out first. Unable to walk, she stumbled, so Perk carried her into the open. She squinted against the light. She cried with relief, but everyone fell silent when, with a heart-rending sob she whispered: 'Gerda took my baby. Gerda took my Hugo away.'

CHAPTER 21

On arrival in Southampton, Captain Hirst allowed John to walk freely down the gangplank. He knew John was a man of his word. Knowing that Perk would put Maud and the child on the first ship going to England, John was assured that it was only a matter of time before they would be reunited.

The second leg of the voyage had been a rough one, with wild storms, that resulted in a shattered mast. John was impressed with the addition of a modern steam engine to the ship. This recent invention ensured that even the event of the broken mast, did not have much impact on the duration of the journey. As he said his farewells to the captain, and invited him to stay at Cheltenham House, any time he was on furlough, John realised Hirst's thoughts were already taken up with the repair works.

A coach with four horses was ready for him and as he nonchalantly threw his duffel bag on the seat, he saw the coach man blanch. He smiled to himself, thinking that he might have to mend his ways, and try to behave like My Lord John. Yet, he was loath to leave John Beauchamp behind, so he decided to throw all caution to the wind and instead of climbing inside, to sit on the comfortable seat, he told the coachman to move over as he was going to take the reins.

This was how, two days later, his mother saw him drive up to the steps of his ancestral home. She stood at the window, and in disbelief, closed her eyes for a moment.

'I will have to teach that boy to mind his manners. Cressida will not marry an uncouth person, acting like a hireling, even if he is a peer of the Realm.'

She went down stairs and met John at the door.

'My son, how wonderful to have you home,' she gushed.

'Mama, you look well,' he bent down to kiss her as she offered him her cheek. 'You and I need to have a serious talk, as soon as is practicable. But I first will see Papa.'

'He is in his room, my dear. I will let you have a tete-a-tete with him. But first, please, take off those things you are wearing, and get dressed properly'. He looked at her for a moment, before the John Beauchamp in him decided: 'No, I will see him straight away.' He started to walk onto the stairs that led to his father's bedchamber. His mother hastened after him and took his arm.

'John, you cannot possibly come to him in your travel… clothes.' The pause clearly indicating that if he took his clothes off, she would burn them so she would never have to see him wear them again.

'I can and I will, Mama. I have made my own decisions for the last eight years. I have been never happier; I am not going to stop now.' Gently, he took her hand away from his arm and continued towards his father's room.

Lady Eleanor watched him go up, thinking that it would not be easy to render him fit for society. She would have to warn Cressida.

John entered his father's bedroom without knocking and found him sitting in front of the window, cossetted in blankets.

'Good afternoon, Pater. I see you are well taken care of.' He kissed his father and drew up a chair. When he had a good look at his sire, he noticed the hollow cheeks and the greyish, paper-thin skin on the aged face. He was moved to put his hand over his father's, regretting how he had missed him.

'John,' the feebleness of his father's once booming voice shocked John. 'You have heard Charlie had an accident?'

'Yes, Papa, I was told. Quite distressing for you. I've come to help you.' The tenderness in John's words reflected the admiration he had always had for his father.

'And Will is a fop. He cannot possibly run the estate.'

'That is why I am here, Papa. Don't worry.'

'And Annabelle still needs a husband; she is very choosy; she won't have young Beresford. She has said so in no uncertain terms and now he has gone off her.'

John laughed: 'Yes, I remember she always had a will of her own. I will take care of that too, Papa.'

'But what will become of her?' The old man was becoming agitated.

'We can always send her to the Colony,' John quipped.

'Oh no, John has gone there, and he has no plans to ever return.' John realised that his father had not really recognised him and that his mind was quite muddled. Whatever he said was either rehearsed or a repetition of his mother's words. He stood up and returned to his mother to ask what the doctors said about the illness of Sir Gervaise.

'They have no hope that he will ever think rationally again.' Lady Eleanor sighed when asked about her husband's state of mind. 'That is why you were so badly needed at home, John.' Her voice begging him to understand, she turned around not to let him see her tears. 'He used to be so strong, so wise, so dependable. Now, he is no more than a child."

'I wonder that Charlie did not take over when he was needed.'

'Charlie did not understand why he it was necessary for him to be at home. The accident happened when he was on his way back to the city, to have fun with his friends. He was angry because I had asked him to stay at the Park, to take over the responsibilities that were his. He was quite rude and screamed at me that he would not lift a finger until he had the title in his pocket. Then his horse rolled over him and crushed him. I think he jumped the rock wall on the high side, and no horse has ever been successful in that feat.' She let out a sob. 'Poor Charlie. Of course, Pennington is a great help. You remember old Pennington? He was your grandfather's ground keeper. His son has been in Pater's employ for the last five years. A capable man, but not the same as family of course.' She walked towards John now and put her hand on his arm. 'You see how desperate things were here and why I employed the measures that were... let us say, somewhat unorthodox.'

'Mama, I wish you would have sent a man to explain this all to me. I could have left Perk and Clara in control of my farm and travelled home with Maud. And ..'

'Maud?'

'Yes Mama, I am a married man. I have the most beautiful wife and by now I am a father. I cannot tell you if I have a son or a daughter, because when the child was born, which I am sure it is by now, I was bound with ropes, yes Mama, with ropes, on my way to England.'

'Married! Oh, but how will I tell Cressida?'

'Cressida be damned, Mama! What about Maud? She has no inkling of what might have happened to Perk and me. She might think that we are dead. I left my corn crop near ready to be harvested. I left my wife close to her due time. *That*, is something you should be worried about.'

Lady Eleanor hung her head, whispering an aghast: 'Corn crop?' Then she straightened up, facing the issues at hand.

'I have not handled things very well, son. I am sorry for that. Naturally we need to do what is necessary to take care of the woman and the child. But you need to keep in mind that a chit from the colonies may not be suitable to become the next Lady Cheltenham.' John looked at his mother in disbelief.

'What exactly are you saying Mama?' his voice was icy calm.

'Well, your marriage may not be binding if it is not ...' Her voice, almost hopeful, she did not get any further, as John held up his hand to make her stop.

He stood up and walked away a few paces, then he turned to her and said in measured tones: 'Let me make this clear: I am married before God and witnesses. I love my wife. I will, myself, sort things out with Rutherforde and Cressida. And when Maud comes here, you *will* treat her with all the respect due to the next Lady Cheltenham. You plucked me from my life in the Colony because you wanted me to take over the running of this place, and so help me God, I will!'

With that he walked out of the door, before he lost the last bit of precious self-control that he had barely held on to. In long, angry strides he went in the direction of the front door; he was in desperate need of fresh air and long walk to rid himself of his rage. A footman came running to open the door for him, but he motioned him away. Glorious sunlight streamed in as he unlocked the door; it reminded him of the Colony. Down the driveway he could see a carriage approaching. Not feeling he could cope with visitors, he went back into the house and loped in the direction of the kitchen.

There he was greeted by a number of well- known faces:

'Master John, we heard you was come home.' Cook wiped her hands on her apron, her face breaking into a wide grin. 'Trust you not to forget us. Welcome, welcome. I remembered your favourite dessert, and you will have it at tonight's dinner.'

The hearty salutation was a salve on his wounded mind. 'Mrs Tupper, I could never forget your kindly deeds, if I turned a hundred.' The rotund lady had made the semblance of a curtsey, but while speaking John had given her a quick hug, making her glow with gratification. 'Thank you for your generous words. I am glad to be here and look forward to your many surprises.' Around them the other kitchen staff observed with pleasure that Master John had not changed. He was as personal with them, as he always had been.

'Oh Master John, you are too kind, what will your mother say, hob-nobbing with the likes of us.' In answer to that John sat down on one of the stools.

'Mrs Tupper. Can I let you in on a secret?'

Everyone stepped closer, not wanting to miss out on any news that Master John would tell.

'I am a father, I am married, to a wonderful lady, and when I left the Colony, she had almost reached her due time. I cannot tell you if I have a son or a daughter, but let me tell you, I cannot wait for my wife and child to join me here. I am sure you will like her.' At that announcement a babble of felicitations broke out.

'Congratulations Master John. If she loves you, I am sure she will be a great Lady Cheltenham. And we will all be happy to serve under her.' Lucy Tupper looked around to the others in the kitchen, who all nodded agreement.

'Thank you, Mrs Tupper.' John got up. 'And now I need to go and have a bit of a wander; I think the herb garden will be the right place for me.'

He walked out of the back entrance under a hum of greetings to which he responded with a wave of his arm.

Outside he reflected about the difference between his mother's reaction to his marriage and the cook's delight to hear of it. He could not picture Maud in the state of Lady Cheltenham; yet he could see her helping cook out, and laughing and joking with that lady. He could not imagine her in the clothes she would be required to wear, he could see her with an apron and a headscarf.

But then, so many times, in so many ways, Maud had surprised him. One thing he was certain of: she would be loved by all and sundry. If he could bring his mother to forget about Cressida Rutherforde, she would see how much he and Maud loved each other. A painful longing to his wife took hold of him. If only he could rush time and have her with him. The only remedy was to keep busy. He was certain there was much left to do, after all Charlie had been gone for some time and his father was incapable of taking care of business.

He went inside. In the blue parlour he heard many excited voices. He saw his image in the hall mirror, He was still wearing his travel clothes. He decided he would not put his mother to shame, and asked one of the footmen to send his father's valet up to his room. He would have to wear some of Charlie's clothes.

CHAPTER 22

Slowly Maud learned to walk by herself again. After not being exercised for so long, the muscles in her legs had weakened to the extent, that she needed help with every move.

That first afternoon, they had gathered around her, to hear Werner's atrocious treatment of her. They were horrified by the tale. After her story was told, Clara helped her into her bed, and being reassured that, with the help of the Sydney Town solicitor, little Hugo would be easily found, Maud had fallen into a deep sleep, comfortable for the first time since months.

In silence Clara had provided drinks of ale or lemonade to all, and made a platter of bread and meat. They ate greedily; the dousing of the fire and subsequent breaking down of the still smouldering walls, had been physically and mentally draining. They had found the charred corpse of Philip, but they had left it under the glowering black timbers, to turn to ash. None of them had talked about a Christian burial; no one had mentioned his name.

Now, each of them sat in remorse of having done naught to save Maud, to leave her to rot under Werner's control. They knew that they had taken the easy way out: No one had checked where she had gone, why she had not returned. They knew Werner's malevolence, his hateful selfishness, yet they had believed him, and not tried to investigate his motives, or tested his words. Each of them thinking that if only they had, Maud would still have her child, and all would be well.

Clara was the first to talk: 'To think, that I got married, while Maud lay rotting in that hovel. To think, that we had a better wedding than her, while she gave birth on the bare floor. I don't know how I can live with that.'

'I agree with you,' said Perk, sharper than he intended. The meaning of his remark clear to all present. Clara closed her eyes in shame. She knew he meant her eagerness to marry someone else instead of waiting for him.

Helmut spoke up for his wife.

'Perk, I am sorry how things worked out, but no one knew what had happened to any of you: John, you and Maud. By the way, what did happen to you, and where is John Beauchamp?'

It was then that Perk explained the reason that they suddenly had disappeared.

'Do you mean to say that Maud is married to a nobleman?' Clara interrupted him in the middle of his account

'Yes,' confirmed Perk. 'She will soon be Lady Maud Beauchamp, Duchess of Cheltenham.'

'That is why you always called John 'Master'; we thought it was because you had been a convict. Even Maud thought so.' Perk had to laugh at that.

He continued his story. He described in detail how he had tried to free John, how they had been held in the cellar in Sydney Town, how John had almost made it out of the cellar, but for the silly lawyer's clerk, who recognised him, and how they were put on the ship. He told them about Cape Town, where he had to wait for ten days before he could board a ship to take him back. He related the strange things he had seen and how on the way back he had made a new friend who had told him about the gold that was to be found, further inland of the Colony. He finished with: 'I don't know how Master John fared on the rest of his journey, but I can tell you, that the family in Somerset will be treated to a changed son and brother. I would give my left arm to be witness to that reunion.'

He pulled some papers out of the bag he had brought. 'The master gave me the ownership of this farm. I was to live here with Clara,' his voice turned melancholy now. 'He thought I could arrange to have Maud and the child to travel to England and then make a life for myself here.' Silence followed that remark. All present wondering what would happen to Helmut and Clara now Perk owned the property.

Perk got up and asked Helmut: 'Helmut, can I have a private talk to Clara please?'

Clara's husband nodded and Perk motioned for Clara to follow him to the far end of the garden, where they were not visible to the others.

When they were alone, Perk asked her: 'Did you really think we were dead?

'Yes Perk, we thought a few things could have happened, but in the end, we thought you had been either murdered by Werner, so he could have the land; or that you were tired of working so hard and had just gone back to the city.'

'Clara, would I ever leave you? Do you think I could? I cannot tell you how the thought of coming back to you, and living here with you, kept me sane and hopeful for a future. My own farm, with a family with you, that was the only thing I dreamed of, the only thing that kept me going.'

'But Perk, you never said anything. If you had given me a hint, - no that is not true- 'she interrupted herself, now not wanting a lie to stand between them. 'I *did* know that you would speak to me, sooner or later, but we worked so hard and we were so tired, that I think we did not think straight. Did you know, that we got the crop to market?' Then it was her turn to tell him what had eventuated on *Meare Green* since he had gone. He was full of admiration for the women and said he had known that they both of them were extraordinary ladies. The very reason why he was so disappointed that she had been taken away from him.

'Do you love Helmut, Clara?' he asked, tension straining his voice. He did not want to hear that she had given herself freely to someone else.

'I married him to stay alive, to have a home; so I did not have to go home to my father's house and be a drudge in my step-mother's household. After all, I did think that you were lost to me. But we seem to have become fond of one another. He is a good man, James.' Again, she hung her head, knowing she was hurting him.

Realising that for the first time she had used his proper name, he took the unwelcome news stoically.

'So be it then,' he said finally.

She took a few steps closer to him. 'Perk, I am so very sorry,' she begged him to understand her predicament. 'If I could change it I would.'

'You could if you wanted to,' he said hopefully, putting his arm around her waist and pulling her close.

'But I am married before God and witnesses; I cannot walk away from my vows. It would not be right.' She did not pull away, but her words sounded final. He let go of her, knowing she was doing the honourable thing. He repeated: 'So be it then.' He walked back to the group in front of the house. There he stood before Helmut.

'Helmut, I am leaving this farm to you and Clara,' he declared. 'There is one condition: You will treat Clara like a queen, you will love her and take care of her. You will make a success of this place.'

Helmut looked non-plussed for a moment, then he got up and shook Perk's hand.

'You are a fair man. I regret that things are as they stand. I promise I will take care of Clara. And any time you want to come and check up on me you can; you will never find her wanting, Perk. You are a good man! The best I know. What will you do now?'

Perk had to think, but it did not take long before he had made up his mind.

'I have to arrange for Maud to journey to England. The master is waiting for her. Then I need to go and chase after Gerda Werner, to get little Hugo back and bring him home, too.' A smile stole over his face. 'After that I will come back to the Colony to join my travel friend and go inland to look for gold.' As he put his plan into words he was overcome by a hunger for adventure. 'Yes,' he said as if he had to convince his inner self. 'That is what I will do.'

Once the word was out that John had returned home from his travels, Cheltenham House was inundated with visitors. First the relatives came to hear the latest news and see for themselves that the lost son had been restored to the family fold. After that came the curious: the neighbours and members of the Somerset nobility, many of them impoverished, mostly mothers with daughters, hopeful for them to become the future Lady Cheltenham. Family members John could abide, he would treat the matchmakers with cruel honesty:

'It is lovely to see you Amelia, I think my wife has a dress in that same colour' or 'Mrs Hempfield, I believe your daughter plays the pianoforte almost as well as my wife does.' The ladies would inadvertently blink and cut the visit as short as was polite, much to John's satisfaction.

He dealt with his sisters in the same familiar way as he had with Clara. Their partners were pleased that the future lord treated them with a relaxed informality that made the atmosphere at the manor a pleasure to reside in.

His conduct bore no distinction between the duke and the squire's son, treating them both as equal family members. Annabelle was happy to realise that her brother was in no hurry to marry her off to anyone, and that he would allow her to travel, a wish that had been vetoed by her mama.

'You can travel with your husband, when you have one,' was the dictum under which she had lived for a long time and against which she had rigorously argued.

John, who understood his sister's adventurous spirit changed this to: 'Make a plan of where you want to go, and I will book your passage. But wait till Papa has passed, so you will be able to support Mama in her grief.'

The staff rejoiced in having a master who genuinely was interested in their well-being; who understood the effort they put into their jobs and who would at times lent a helping hand. It was very unusual for a servant to have the master take a shovel and dig the hole for a new rose bush, or roll up his sleeves to help unload a cart of wine or vegetable delivery. Yet as he talked to his workers, he always joined in their activities, and had a joke or compliment for them.

The only person in the house who regretted his return was Lady Eleanor, whose management of John's return was barely forgiven, and who had lost the domination over the family; a power that she had enjoyed for a long time. 'Life would have been so much easier if only I had let William have the title,' she would lament to her confidantes. 'He would not have cared one way or the other, and I would have still had the reins in my own hands. John has very modern ideas. I am afraid I am not looking forward to meeting my daughter-in-law. To think that he found her in a baker's shop. A baker's shop!' Abhorred by the idea she would close her eyes. 'I ask you: Who *is* Maud Stack? And that kind of person will inherit my rubies and the Beauchamp diamonds!' They would all agree and express their sympathy.

'To have a low born female rule the house, it is not be borne.' said Lady Patricia Cloverfield, who knew the distress of a misalliance in the family.

'Mayhap Maud may have died in childbirth,' Mrs Fotherling suggested, scratching an itch under her widow's cap.

'Ships often have to cope with foul weather, she could be swept overboard.' offered another of my lady's friends.

Those thoughts would comfort her, even though she argued against the horrors that could befall Maud.

CHAPTER 23

The meeting with Rutherforde and Cressida had been easier than John expected. Riding to Colyton Lodge on his newly acquired steed, Paris, he prayed that he would have the wisdom to tell them of his marital status without having to hurt Cressida. Knowing his mother, she would have told them all the wonderful things that would be waiting for the baronet's daughter. It would be a big step up the society ladder for the girl. John reasoned that she must be quite a beautiful lady, with pretty manners, to have impressed his mother.

On being announced into the library of Colyton Lodge, he found a relaxed Rutherforde smoking his pipe, while reading the *Hunter's Digest*. John felt rather brutal to have to disturb the man's peace by changing the prospects of his young daughter so radically.

Rutherforde, a portly gentleman with a shock of white hair and an impressive moustache, stood up, put aside the publication and welcomed him with a firm handshake and a wide smile: 'John Beauchamp, what a pleasure it is to see you with mine own eyes. I had heard of your return from the Antipodes. Welcome home, My Lord! I know why you have come, so without keeping my little beauty waiting, I will summon her.'

'You are too good, Sir, but I would think, I need to have a few words with you to explain....' He did not get further, my Lord Rutherforde, too hasty in his conclusions, would not give John the chance to say anything else, as he feared there would be a change of heart.

'No, no, no, my lord, I know why you are here and I will not be in the way any longer than is necessary. My Cressy is eager to meet you, and I know the keen nature of the young.' He shook his index finger at John. 'I was once young too, you know! No my lord, I will not stand in the way of you two young ones. Ah, here she is.'

As soon as John had been spotted nearing Colyton Lodge, my lady had bid her daughter to come to her. She had checked for creases in her dress, wayward locks of hair and pouting of the mouth. Thus, she was at the library door, and entered as soon as her father called her name, ready to meet her future husband.

Admonishing her by: 'Hold your head up high, smile, and do not look him straight in the eye, smile, but modestly, my dear, modestly!' my lady pushed her daughter into the room.

John looked up at the girl his mother had chosen for him. She was indeed a lovely lass; his mother's good taste was evident. Tallish and with a proud stance, her blond hair tied up prettily with pink ribbons, a lace wrap falling from her shoulders, she walked up to him. He pictured Maud next to her and smiled. My Lord Rutherforde saw this as a good sign and rubbing his hands together, he left the room saying: 'I will leave you two to talk by yourselves; I'll wager you will have much to discuss.' And the door closed softly behind him.

John smiled at Cressida and noting that, in his eagerness, her father, had not properly introduced them, said:

'Good morning, I am John Beauchamp, I am charmed to meet you.'

Against her mother's counsel, she looked him square in the face and replied: 'I'm delighted, My Lord, I am Cressida Rutherforde,' With a mischievous grin, she added, 'but I am sure you were well aware of that.'

John was taken by the flamboyant smile and the jolly remark. He liked her straightforward manner. He grinned at her and said: 'Yes, I would be a fool to think you would be the valet's daughter.' To which she reacted with a nod. His face turned serious when he continued: 'You may be under the impression that I have come on my mother's ..erm.. errand. That I mean to propose to you.' John was rambling but he could not stop himself. 'And I must say when it comes to choosing a spouse for her sons, my mother is seldom wrong; you certainly are, in every way suitable. But I must tell you that here is one acute incumbrance to our ...' she would not let John go on. She had been standing before him, but now she sat down on the settee and motioned him to sit as well. 'Sir, there are more than one incumbrances.' For a moment John felt a slight disappointment; it seemed the lady was not as willing to marry him as her father had suggested.

'Yes,' he admitted stiffly, 'You and I do not know one another at all. But more importantly ...' again she interrupted him.

'I do not love you. I love another man. I am sure you will find *that* an incumbrance hard to ignore, even if my parents do not.' Her eyes and her direct tone of voice challenged him. Again, he had to smile. She took this to mean that he would overlook the fact and that their marriage would be one of convenience. So when he said: 'Then we understand each other. I am sure ..' she would not let him finish and interjected: 'I will not marry anyone else but Mr Beresford.'

After this statement here was a silence in the room.

'Mr Beresford is a lucky man,' John said finally. 'I hope you will be as happy with him, as I am with my wife.'

She looked up at him her eyes flashing. 'And you come here to propose to me, while you have a wife. Do you think I would marry you if you had a wife in the Colony?'

'No, neither would I. Had I been able to make myself heard, by you, or your father, the first thing I would have told you is that I am a married man. And I have a child. But in your father's enthusiasm to marry you off to me, and your enthusiasm to repel me, I did not get that chance.' She started to laugh, showing a row of straight white teeth and dimples in her cheeks.

'Oh dear, Papa and Mama will be so angry, they had it all arranged with Lady Eleanor,' she giggled girlishly.

'My mother told me as much, but I did prefer to tell you and your parents of my marital status myself, instead of hiding behind her skirts. In defence of my mother, she did not know that I have a wife and child when she made the arrangements with your parents. I have been very much occupied with my property in the Colony, and I did not tell her. I accept the blame for this debacle. Though, I think it frees you to marry the man of your choice.' He stood up and walked to the ornate mantlepiece.

Cressida sighed and looked far from liberated.

'There are other problems. I think your mother has arranged for Annabelle to marry Patrick. They knew each other long before Mr Beresford and I met and fell in love.'

'I take it Patrick Beresford loves you?'

'Yes, but he is promised to your sister, and he is a man of honour.'

John laughed. 'I think Annabelle is going to travel; do the grand tour of Europe, or some such thing. The last thing on her mind is marriage. I think you and your Patrick should make use of her absence. I know for a fact that my sister is not interested in marrying Mr Beresford.'

Cressida's eyes lit up. She cried out: 'What a wonderful brother you are to your sisters, Sir. Thank you for making me the happiest girl in the world!' In her exhilaration she flew to him, satin and lace rustling, as she threw her arms around his neck. At that same moment Mr and Mrs Rutherforde re-entered the room.

'May I be the first to wish you happy, my boy,' Rutherforde asked, walking toward the couple. 'Cressy, you are a lucky maid.'

At the door lady Rutherforde stood wringing her hands, meowing: 'My little puss will be a countess; Lady Cressida, how wonderful that sounds.'

Before Rutherforde reached John, Cressida had let go of him and now flung her arms around her father's neck. 'Father I am so happy, I am going to marry Patrick, John is married. Did you know he had a child?'

'What is this? Is this true?' John nodded. Rutherforde pushed his daughter away and accosted John, turning a dangerous red. 'Sir, you have a nerve, to come to offer for my girl. and you a married man! I don't hold with bigamists. I do not like them at all. No, my lord, not even when they have a title. I take it, your estates are mortgaged and you sought to replenish your coffers with my money?'

'No Sir. Not at all,' said John, who with difficulty restrained himself from bursting out in laughter. He reckoned the situation was a hilarious comedy of errors. 'Sir, had you but let me speak, the first intelligence I would have furnished you with, would have been, that I am a married man. But you were altogether too impatient for me to have my say,' Rutherforde opened his mouth and closed it again. Still standing at the door, Cressida's mother changed her warble to: 'Oh my poor little girl, oh my poor dear little puss.'

Meanwhile the dear little puss pranced through the room too relieved, too happy with the day's work.

Somehow Cressida reminded John of Maud. She seemed to have the same indomitable courage to fight for what made her happy. It left him feeling with a great longing for his wife. He made his farewells soon after that, reassuring dear Cressy that he was sure she would make a great friend for Maud when she arrived in England.

Maud was unwilling to leave the Colony. She stubbornly refused to even talk about stepping aboard a ship that would take her further away from her baby. Perk tried to convince her that she could do nothing to get Hugo back: she needed to leave that to him. He stressed that at this moment her place was at John's side.

'Maud, you need to go to him, he is lonely.'

'Perk, my child is brought up by a strange woman; you have no idea how vulgar Gerda is. I need to find him first.'

Perk reasoned that Hugo would not remember any of his time with Gerda and as soon as she was on the way to Cheltenham House, he could wholly devote his time to find the boy. In the end he accused her of not wanting to go to England and keeping him from starting his search for Gerda's whereabouts.

'But I can't go to John with empty arms, Perk!' she cried pitifully. She had been bound up by Liza, and her painful breasts made her incapable to either think straight or to cope well with her quandary.

'Oh Maud, I cannot tell you how he is looking for the day that he will have you back again. And Hugo will follow,' he promised. 'I will hire a nurse to carry him to you, as soon as I find him; just let me go and do what the master has ordered me to do.'

Finally, after a week of arguments and debating, Maud gave in and she prepared to take her leave from Clara and Helmut.

Clara had written a letter to her father which Maud would deliver when they were in Sydney Town. In it, she told her father that she was married.

Dear Father,

I have settled well on Maud's farm. Maud is going to live in a large house in Somerset, as John is an earl and she is now a real lady. John has left the farm to us and we are growing corn and other vegetables. We also have a cow that I milk to make butter and cheese. I am married now. I have a very handsome and strong husband. His name is Helmut Gross. I hope you are well. Maybe I will come to visit when we have to come to town, to see how you are.

Yours affectionately, Clara Gross

She knew her father could not read, but maybe Cornelia could. Or one of her children, after all they all went to school. She secretly knew her father would ridicule her letter, saying things like: 'She thinks she is better than us, now that she can write.' and 'La-di-dah, the mistress of a farm, no less. I hope she remembers who her parents were.'

Saying goodbye to Maud was heart-breaking. Together they had known hardship and happiness. They had fought together for their lives and livelihood, and their sufferings had forged a strong band between them. In the end both women wept as the cart took Maud away.

CHAPTER 24

With trepidation, Maud boarded the *Cormorant*, an old-fashioned sailing ship. She had never travelled and as she was on her own, she felt very alone among so many strangers. As she walked onto the ship, she saw a woman with three children standing at the railing. One babe in arms and twin boys about seven or eight years old, trying to climb dangerously on the ship's ropes. She nodded to the woman and noticed the drawn face. She put her luggage in her cabin, glad that she had a room all to herself. Then she went back on deck, where she introduced herself to the lady.

'Good day, I am Maud Beauchamp. Are you going all the way to England too?'

'Yes, I and my children. I am Mary Gibson. These rascals are Tom and Toby.' She smiled proudly at her two sons. 'And this here,' she held up the little girl, who was peeping out from a woollen wrap, 'is Evelyn.'

Maud looked at the infant through misty eyes. 'She is very little, how old is she?'

'A little over three months,' said Mary, 'I had to wait for her to be born, before Martin allowed me to make the journey home. He is in the army and was stationed first in Hobart and later in Sydney Town.' She pulled her shawl tighter around her. 'This wind is very chilly, but I am afraid to go down to our cabin. On the voyage to the Colony, I was so very seasick, and it is so stuffy down there.'

'Give me little Evelyn, I'll hold her while you go and walk about the deck a little. I think we are not long from departure. And just think, that wind is going to bring you to your husband faster.'

Maud did not see Mary walk away, two little boys at each side of her, holding their mother's hand. All her attention was centred on the baby in her arms. She talked softly to the little girl: 'You know, my Hugo is only a little younger than you. He is such a handsome little fellow. Did you know he smiled at me on the day Gerda took him away? He smiled. Like he knew me. I am very homesick for my Hugo…' and on and on she poured her heart out to the child, who seemed to be listening intently to her voice. When at last Evelyn showed her toothless grin, she held her closer and rested her cheek on the soft baby head. She felt alarmed at the strong sense of ownership of this child. Her desire to take little Evelyn to John and claim her as their own shocked her. She chided herself: how could she consider to afflict the same pain on Mary as Gerda had done to her. Was she going mad? Was this what happened to people who lost someone dear to them; that they wanted a substitute of any kind? She followed where Mary had gone and returned little Evelyn to her. She would go down and read her Bible. This, she had found, was the only remedy that was effective to assuage her grief.

During the journey she became good friends with Mary, for whom travel by sea was torture. She taught the boys their alphabet when their mother was sick, while rocking little Evelyn, who was quite used to her now, on her lap. She read the children stories from her own books. The same stories that her mother had read to her. Being her only link with her parents, these were the only belongings she had taken with her, leaving the small desk with Clara.

She tended to Mary, who did not travel as luxuriously as she, having to share her cabin with her three children. They comforted each other, having to spend so much time, away from their husbands. For Mary the voyage was made more agonizing by the many storms they encountered. The doldrums caused everyone to lose their patience: sailors complained that they were never going to work again on a ship that was not fitted with the newly developed steam engine, that could improve the speed of the ship and reduced the time to reach their destination. Altogether the mood on the ship between crew and passengers, was lamentable.

When the ship finally docked in Southampton, Mary and her children were eagerly awaited by Lieutenant Martin Gibson. Maud looked on while the soldier embraced his wife, admired his new daughter and shook hands with his sons. It took a little time before Mary remembered her compassionate companion. She turned around and introduced her husband to Maud who shook hands with him.

'I must thank you for taking care of my wife. I remember well how she suffered in the way to the Colony.'

'And Mistress Maud taught us to read, Father. I have read a whole book on the ship. All by myself!'

'I've always thought you were very clever Toby, you may display your reading skills to me when we are home.' He patted the boy's curly hair. 'But let us not stand in this chilling wind too long. Mistress Maud, may I offer you some refreshments in the inn. I have bespoken a room for us, I would like to show my gratitude, by offering you a proper meal, knowing that the fare on board a ship may at times not be as tasty as one would want.'

Maud gladly accepted his offer, and they all walked toward the inn, where an inviting fire lit up the tap room and the warmth embraced them.

There was a smell of fresh bread that reminded her of her uncle's bakery in Sydney Town and a plump host welcomed them heartily.

During the meal, which was delicious, Martin asked where she was going. When she told him he clapped his hands: 'What providence! I am stationed now at Land's End. Cheltenham Park is on our way. Will you do us the pleasure of your company and travel with us?'

'Oh yes, please do,' chimed in Mary.

'That would be wonderful. Perk told me someone would take me to Cheltenham, but as no one asked for me, I think they may have gotten the day wrong. The voyage has taken so much longer than was expected.'

When the meal was finished, they piled into the carriage, which took off just after lunch.

The children travelled well; the books that Maud had lent to them kept them amused. Maud found much to look at; the many sights were so different from Sydney Town. Maud was impressed by the quaint villages they passed and the beautiful greenery, the variety in trees, so different from the Colony.

On the way they stayed in a country inn, where Maud shared her room with the two boys. There were so many new impressions, that she did not have much time to think of what she had left behind. It was only in the night that thoughts Hugo and John kept her from sleeping peacefully. She prayed for her little boy, that God would protect him and that he might come to her soon.

In the late afternoon of the second day, the carriage stopped at a magnificent manor.

'Here you are,' Martin said, 'please do not forget us, we hope to see you again. Please feel free to come and visit us. We would like it very much'. They said their farewells, the ladies both shed a tear; the boys and the baby were heartily kissed. Then the coach drove off again, leaving Maud, holding her canvas bag, in the middle of the drive.

As she walked up the broad steps of the Cheltenham Park, she felt uncertain that John should be here. She dared not be excited. A footman opened the door and she asked after John Beauchamp.

'Yes miss, who shall I say is calling?'

Before she could answer the butler came running: 'Excuse me miss, you have the wrong entry!' Then, turning to the footman, he said in a reproaching voice: 'Show her the kitchen door. Potts. Really, you have a lot to learn!' His irritation was unmistakeable. Without a word the footman took Maud's arm and took her down the steps and around the back of the house. He was not happy by the rebuke given to him, in the hearing of an underling, nor by the cold he had to bear while showing Maud to the kitchen entry. He went in before her. Then he disappeared into the butler's office without telling her where she could find John.

As the preparations for dinner were underway, the kitchen was a bustling place. Mrs Tupper bellowed out her orders to the kitchen maids, who ran hither and thither to obey her. Everyone seemed to be too focussed on their tasks to bother with her. Maud looked around and saw that much needed to be done. She shoved her bag under a corner table, rolled up her cape and put it on top of her bag. She went out to the scullery where a lonely maid was trying to keep up with the washing of cooking utensils. She picked up a towel and started to help the maid.

'Hi I am Maud? Gee, is this place always this busy? How many for dinner tonight?' Without looking up the girl introduced herself: 'Sally. Him upstairs expects the missus. Everything has to be just so. Newspaper said her ship docked in Southampton yesterday.'

'Does John Beauchamp live here?'

'Yes, he certainly does.'

'I am his wife,' Maud told the girl.

'Sure, and I am the queen of Sweden.' Sally said with a cheeky laugh

'Sally where's that whisk you promised you'd bring to me?' Mrs Tupper yelled. 'What is that dratted girl doing in there?'

Sally handed Maud the whisk with: 'You bring it to her, or she'll whip me one.'

Suddenly, there was a hush over the kitchen. Maud came out of the scullery with the implement, just as John entered the kitchen and addressed the cook:

'Mrs Tupper, can we hold back dinner for an hour? It seems my wife is late in arriving.' As John stood with his back to the scullery door, he was unable to see Maud, who had the widest smile on her face and with difficulty stopped herself from running up to him.

Mrs Tupper curtseyed and said: 'Of course, My Lord, I will see to it.'

'Thank you. I know it can't be easy. Thank you.' He turned to go, almost bumping into Maud.

His first reaction was to ask what she thought she was doing, then he recognised her.

'Maud? Is it really you? Oh Maud!' To everyone's stunned amazement he wrapped his arms around the girl, lifted her off the floor and twirled around. When he put her down, he asked 'How long have you been here?'

'No longer than half an hour. The footman brought me to the kitchen and it was so busy, I helped out. I did not know where you were.' She held out the whisk to Mrs Tupper who quicky relieved her of it.

He shook his head, 'Come, we need to get you out of your travel clothes.' It was then that she noticed the way her husband was dressed. Before she could say anything, John remembered where they were, and that the servants could well do with some kind of explanation.

'Listen every one.' he cried out, quite unnecessarily, as all and sundry had not taken their eyes off the couple. Especially Mrs Tupper, had looked at her master with a first-rate understanding.

'This is my wife,' In the scullery Sally dropped a plate. 'Someone must have misunderstood and sent her into the kitchen door instead of the main entry. Maud this is your kitchen staff. And,' pointing at two footmen who had come running when they heard something was up in the kitchen, 'those are our footmen.' Maud recognised Potts, and drew up her eyebrows at him. He tried to slink away, while others curtseyed and bowed.

'Come my dear, we will see you dressed for dinner.'

'I'll get my cape and bag,' Maud said, while she tried to walk away to get her belongings. But John held on to her hand, nodding to one of the men: 'Potts, the luggage to my lady's room, please.'

In the hallway, John held on to her hand tightly. But as soon as her bedroom door closed, he drew her to him and covered her with kisses. She laughed out loud with happiness and finally said: 'I have kept my Sunday dress clean for such a day as today.'

Then it was his turn to laugh. 'My dear, your Sunday dress will not do for dinner. It will not even do for a walk in the garden. But no matter, I will ask Annabelle to dress you. But first tell me about our child.'

They sat on the bed and John heard the sorry story of Maud's confinement and the subsequent theft of the baby. He cried when he heard of the treatment Werner had dealt Maud. 'Three whole months in the shed. O my darling when I hear this, I cannot forgive my mother for what she caused us to experience. But you are here now. The worst is over. You called him Hugo? A good name, my love. I am sure Perk will find Gerda and get our son back.'

CHAPTER 25

Annabelle was the first of John's relatives to meet Maud. She was a sweet, plump girl, with a head full of dreams. Maud found that her sister-in-law had an insatiable thirst for the adventures that were to be had in the Colony. She wanted to hear all about *Maere Green* and the peoples who lived on the other side of the creek. Maud was very careful with the information she gave the girl, yet the stories about the snake and Lowanna fell on fertile ground. Annabele declared she would not marry until she had seen the farm in the Colony, shot a snake and had met with all the people Maud told her about. At only seventeen she had already had several suitors, but so far, she had been able to convince her mama that she would be deeply unhappy with any of them. As so often happens, the youngest child gets their way more often than the older ones, who are told to put their duty before their wishes. In managing her mother with hot tears and sweet embraces, Annebelle had the power to get her way in many things. Now Patrick Beresford was lost to the family, Lady Eleanor had left Annabelle to John to manage.

She did not flinch at the dresses that Maud had sewn and worn with pride. She found some of her own dresses that almost fitted Maud; she tucked them in, here or there, bound an extra ribbon at the waist or pinned a corsage over a fold. Between the two they tittered and giggled, and within the hour Annabelle had Maud dressed to impress her mother-in-law. Faye,

Annabelle's maid brushed Maud's hair and bound it up with ribbons in the same colour as the dress, and when Maud saw her image in the glass, she hardly recognised the girl from the bakery.

John had fled when the twittering got too much for him, but when he saw his wife, he kissed his sister and said she had wrought a miracle.

'Mama will be impressed,' he praised her.

'Please, don't tell her that I did it.' said Annabelle, 'she is always saying that I should have been a boy and I want her to keep her thinking about me like that.'

Then, there was the gong for dinner and Maud walked down, holding her head high.

When she met Lady Eleanor, the two married sisters of John, and their husbands, she made a small curtsey and though her brother-in-law led her into the dining room, she went to sit next to John at the dining table. His mother shook her head. 'No, my dear, you cannot sit next to your husband; sit over there, next to Cornelis.'

But Maud would not have it and directed her speech to the duke.

'I am sorry if you feel shunned, Your Grace,' she smiled sweetly at the Duke, 'but I have been forcibly separated from my husband for many months, and nothing is going to prevent me from sitting close to him now.'

There was a tense silence, finally broken by Annabelle, who cried: 'Bravo!', and clapped her hands.

Lady Eleanor did not flinch, but with an icy smile pronounced that she and Maud needed to have a serious talk together.

John held his breath.

'I am looking forward to that, Lady Eleanor,' Maud answered, unassumingly. 'There are a lot of things I need to learn.' Again, Maud had surprised him. He put his hand over hers and gave her a grinning nod. He whispered in her ear if she knew how to use the cutlery in front of her and she sweetly answered: 'Of course I do.' Again, she astonished him by having the perfect table manners. Later in her bedroom she would explain that whenever her father had gone out, she and her mother would play 'ladies' and do things like ladies do.

'Was your mother a lady's maid?' he had asked.

'I don't know anything about my mother's life in England. She never talked about it.' Because she had frowned, he had not asked more.

Dinner was a family affair, and Maud listened more than she spoke. Nobody asked her about her travels; no one asked her about life about life in the Colony. No one mentioned little Hugo. It seemed that these subjects were taboo. When Annabelle declared that she was happy that dear Cressy was going to marry Mr Beresford, Maud saw that Lady Eleanor pressed her mouth into a thin line. She would ask John about that later.

Maud was appalled by the fact that she and John had separate bedrooms. John explained that it was the norm, but he assured her that he would seldom sleep in his own bed. He held her close and said: 'Already I have been without you too many nights, my love. I don't care what anyone says. I still think, with some melancholy, of our little bedroom on the farm. Those were the happiest times of my life.' He undid the worn ribbon that tied the simple night gown she had brought with her, and added: 'I remember this one well.'

They talked all night, filling each other in about the time they had been apart. John was full of admiration that they had harvested the corn field and he was amazed at the money Werner had given for the crop.

'Of course, that was all part of his evil plans, but it was a gamble he took. You might have come to get the cart with Helmut and then, what would he have done?

'I was silly enough to go by myself,' Maud admitted. 'I have cursed my stupidity many a time.'

They talked about Hugo and John promised that the next day he would show Maud the nursery, where he would be sleep and play, when he came to England. He held her tight when she cried for her child, knowing not how to comfort her.

They discussed the new invention called the telegraph, by which, in the future, you could send messages to a faraway place via a cable.

'How wonderful it would be if you could send messages between the Colony and England. Perk could tell us how he is progressing with his search for our son.'

'That will not be far off, but at the moment it is not helping us. Can you imagine what it would cost, if they had to bring a cable all the way to the Colony' John remained rational.

When morning was almost dawning, John and Maud finally fell asleep, wrapped in each other's arms.

Late that night, in her downstairs room, Mrs Tupper put on her night-cap and tucked her hair underneath its band. It had been quite a day. She smiled as she thought of the master's face when he noticed who had been helping out in her kitchen.

'Oh Master John, your eyes lit up when you saw my lady. I wish the footmen would tell me how Lady Eleanor received her new daughter-in-law. But you were right, dear sir, you were right, when you said that I would get along famously with your Maud. I like her a lot. Yes sir, I like her a lot.' Then she blew out her candle and went to sleep

The next day while Maud was taking a bath, Lady Eleanor summoned John. He set his face, knowing that there would be a lively discussion about the conventions Maud might break or change in the household.

Lady Eleanor started the conversation in her direct manner: 'John. you need to rein in your wife.'

'Mama, even if that were possible, I would not want to do that.'

'She will not fit in; do you want me to live in constant fear for what she will do or say next? I have the family name to uphold.'

'I think it not unreasonable if people fit in with the future Countess of Cheltenham, Mama. And as far as I can tell, she has in no way sullied the Beauchamp name.

'To go against my good counsel and refuse to sit where I placed her!' His mother became agitated. 'To effectively and publicly blame me for pulling you two apart! It is beyond the behaviour of a real lady. Maybe you should remind her that rank not only has its privileges, it also has its obligations.'

'Mama, you have admitted you did not handle my homecoming well. It is because of your madcap management that we are without our child. You have no idea what Maud has suffered.'

'Yes, and I would like to know what happened to your child.' The remark suggested the clear doubt Lady Eleanor had of the verity of Maud's story.

John sighed. His mother would never understand or believe what had happened. She had no idea what kind of persons they had to deal with on the farm. He wanted to brag about his wife: the fact that the girls had brought in the crop; that they kept the farm going while suffering so much worry and so much uncertainty. His mother would not comprehend what damage she had done to his family. He was not prepared to explain that fact to a woman who had been taken care of all her life, who had never lifted a finger to feed or clothe herself. A woman whose only concern was that her peers should have a good opinion of her.

'Hugo was stolen from us, Mama. A woman who had no children of her own took him from her by force. She had her henchman bind Maud and left her to die in an old shed. There will be changes to the way the house is run. And do not be mistaken: I want them as much as Maud does. Only remember this: her firstborn son is lost to her; as you have lost Charlie, you should have some understanding of what she is feeling.'

'What about my feelings? You do not care what my friends will say about this? How we will be the laughing stock of all of them?'

'Frankly? No! For some years now, I have lived free from the need of the good the opinion of others, good or bad. You should try that, Mama; it is a liberating experience.'

Considering the subject closed, he walked towards the door. He heard his mother's sob, no doubt the mention of her eldest son had brought this on.

Before he could go, his mother reminded him that Maud needed to meet with his father: 'Will you take her to him on the morrow, John?'

John stopped for a moment, assured his mother that he would, then her left the room, not wanting to be manipulated by her tears.

In the morning as they walked to Sir Gervaise's quarters, John explained to Maud that his father's brain was slightly addled, and not to take it too much to heart, if he said something improper.

'Don't fret, my love. It will be fine, I will be a good daughter-in-law,' she smiled his worry away. Hand in hand they walked into the room. Sir Gervaise sat, as before. in front of the large window, wrapped in many blankets. As soon as they entered his face lit up.

'Charlotte! My dear, you have finally come back to me. I knew you would return one day, my dear heart.'

'Papa this is Maud, she is my wife. Will you say hello to her?

'Oh nonsense!' was the irritated answer his father shushed him with. He turned his face to Maud and said: 'Come my dear, sit with me, it has been so long. My dear Charlotte, where have you been? I waited and waited. But never mind, you are here now, my darling girl.'

Maud did as the Earl asked and he held her hand and beamed at her.

'You are too kind, my lord,' Maud said. 'Are you comfortable? I think they have almost buried you under all those blankets. With the fire going, methinks one will suffice,' she pulled the blankets away from him and folded them, then she sat down next to him and asked him if he felt like a drink.

'Caring for me, as ever you did, dear Charlotte. I have missed you; you know. Where have you been?' the old man repeated.

'I come from the Colony, my lord.' Maud smiled.' It is a long way away from here.'

'Yes dear, I know. Did I tell you I missed you, my darling girl?'

Maud had to smile, and nodded. The door opened and the countess came in. Seeing Maud so cosy with her husband made her jealous and she said that Dear Papa had to take it easy and too much excitement could spell the end for him.

'You take too much upon yourself, my lady!' the earl rumbled. Maud, who wanted to keep the peace, stood up and said that she would come and sit with him a little each day. She kissed him on the forehead and walked out, John followed her. The last thing they heard him say was; 'This is not the first time you are taking my Charlotte away from me, Eleanor.'

As he rode away from *Maere Green*, Perk tried to rationalise his disillusionment. It was in vain. The feeling of loss was too strong to be reasoned away. His girl had been stolen from him. Curse Helmut! Let the devil run away with him! He wanted to go back and take Clara by force. Together they would be able to start all over. Yet, he knew Clara was bound by loyalty and honour.

The master had given him a yearly stipend, so they could live well even when there was a drought or the crop failed for some reason or other. Now he did not have the farm the money was his, to do with as he pleased. It would be enough to lead a simple, yet comfortable life. He could take it easy, if he wanted. Once he had found Hugo, he would be free to go wherever he wanted. Wondering where he would start to find the boy, he went into an inn. He ordered a rum, thinking he needed – no, he deserved a stiff drink to fight off the feeling of rejection. One followed the other, and thus began a week that, later on, Perk could hardly remember. Through a haze of alcohol, he spoke to many mates, who would share his rum and listen to the woes of his love-life.

One morning he woke up and saw his funds seriously depleted. He decided to mend his ways and travelled to Melbourne. He was sure Gerda had gone back to her parental home. Whenever he spoke to anyone during his journey south, he heard about the goldfields, and the ease of striking it lucky. What a laugh it would be if he found a plump nugget, making him rich beyond imagination. In his dreams he saw himself standing on the steps of a great mansion, while Helmut knelt in the dust begging for work. Clara with a babe in er arms standing next to him her eyes beseeching him to give them something to eat. Of course, there was something wrong with the picture. The hard work on the farm would age Clara. And if they had a couple of children, she would lose her youthful bloom within a few years. She would look old and haggard.

Yet after he had had his revengeful thoughts about his lost love, there was always the undercurrent of regret: My sweet Clara. Why did she not wait for me? How long had he been away? Little more than five months. And she had not waited for him.

For shame! For shame!

CHAPTER 26

On his last stop before he reached Melbourne, Perk stayed in an inn, where he happened to meet with a group of gold miners. They had come from the big city where they had sold the gold from their lease. After all the hard toil, they had spent a great deal of their money on grog and prostitutes. Now they were on their way back, to resume mining for more of the yellow treasure.

'Tell me honestly now, how hard is it to find a goodly nugget?' Three men explained the ins and outs of a miner's life. The more they talked the more they drank. As the drink addled their thinking capacity, they painted a life to Perk that held all the adventure and riches he ever dreamed about.

'Why don't you join us?' the one called Davey asked. 'You look like a man who can use his hands and is not afraid of a little hard work.' He sounded like a true-blue Irishman. As Perk had been out of patience with the English most of his life, and he and Davey seemed to have a common enemy, he did not have to be asked twice.

'I would not mind broadening my horizon a little, just you tell me what you want me to do. I suppose I can spare a few weeks of looking for the end of the rainbow, before finding my master's brat. I'm sure Gerda doesn't move about much with a young 'un on her hip.'

'You jes' come wif us, work our lease and we'll share whatever we find, equally.' Davey's friend Gordy said with a sly grin. Davey and Sean, the third man, nodded vigorously.

And, so it was done. Perk changed his travel plans; instead of travelling to Melbourne, he went to Ballarat, where the foursome worked Davey's lease.

It was hard work, but Perk kept his head clear from the whiskey and rum, and soon knew all the secret ways to coax the earth to give up her valuable treasures. Each day they found little nuggets, which were stored in a jar, zealously guarded by Davey.

The work was relentless and conditions were grim. Life for the miners was deplorable: Men, women and children, as young as six years, worked the digs, all day long. There was poverty all about, there was illness, there was starvation and there was thievery. Because of Perk's money, the men never went hungry, though he refused to spend more of his money on grog, he considered food a necessity and he was a faithful customer of Fung Zhu the local greengrocer. Fung soon became his friend, and some nights, when the other men were in their cups, Perk used to chat with the Chinese gardener.

'Them men no good, Perk.' Fung would tell him many a time, 'You watch your back. You not first man to be …' In quick motion, Fung wiped his finger across his neck, indicating a slit throat. 'They thieves. They sell other family gold. They thieves!' he repeated, with emphasis, wagging his finger at him.

'Ah Fung, they are my mates, we work together,' Perk laughed at the nervous man. 'I trust them.'

In frustration Fung would shake his head: 'You fool! You not listen to warning!' Then he would walk away in disgust.

After they had a decent number of nuggets, they decided that before the Sunday they would ride to Melbourne to sell it, have a good time and get some better tools. Perk, was planning to withdraw some of his money for his expenses. To access the allowance from John, he had been appointed an agent in Melbourne. He did not remember Hugo or Gerda until the last day of their stay in the city.

'I need to attend to some business here, Davey, you need to excuse me. I must find my master's child and send him over to his parents.'

Davey clapped him on the shoulder: '

'Allus the dutiful Perk, hay? You do what you gotta to do, my boy. I will hold the fort and have me some fun wif these two here,' he bobbed his head at Sean and Gordy. 'Have a drink with me now, and we'll call it a night.' he sniggered. 'I found mesel' a woman to keep me warm tonight; you won't hear a peep outa me.'

They bought a bottle of rum and after the fourth cup, Perk got up, to go to his room. With great satisfaction, Davey looked on how he sank to the floor, his legs unable to hold his weight.

'Oi, you two, help our friend,' he called out.

Sean and Gordy got up, put their boot into Perk's ribs and confirmed that 'Old Perky had had enough and would not refuse a pleasant voyage to far away and exotic shores'. Between the two they unceremoniously dragged the limp body out to the back, where he was inspected by a large bearded man.

Davey, who had followed the ensemble greeted the beard and said: 'This one will work for two. Have a look at the muscle on him!'

'But will he sign up?' the beard growled.

'That is somethin' you have to ast the man hissel.'

The beard nodded: 'Righto then, I'll give you the same as for the others.'

Davey held up his hand and received a thin roll of guineas.

'Allus good doing business wif ya,' and he walked off, back into the inn, leaving Perk in an unconscious heap with the bearded giant, who hoisted him over his shoulder and walked off.

Maud had been taken to Lady Eleanor's modiste, to be fitted with proper clothing. She was appalled by the amount of money she had to spend to satisfy the countess.

'We might order some black dresses as well,' Lady Eleanor had said, 'I think we soon will need mourning clothes, as my lord will not last long now.'

Maud could see that the seamstresses were all in a dither because of the many dresses that needed to be created, as Lady Eleanor ordered all gowns to be ready before a certain time. Knowing what was involved, she understood that it would be a Herculean job for any establishment. She told her mother-in-law that she disliked too many embellishments on her dresses and as long as Madame would make the dresses, she would add the lace and ribbons herself, to her own preference.

When the finished garments began to arrive, her mother-in-law wanted to examine the handiwork. When she found fault with all of them, Maud had to speak up.

'Mama,' she found it difficult to call John's mother 'Mama', but, choosing her battles carefully, she had bitten the bullet. 'Mama, these imperfections are too small to send the dresses back. I will rectify the buttons and hems; I think these are beautifully made.' She held up a soft pink dress with short puffy sleeves. 'I am happy with them and do not want them sent back.' Because she could see the anguish of the seamstresses, she spoke with undeniable authority; in response Lady Eleanor lifted her head haughtily, turned and left the room without a comment.

Later she complained to John that Maud had behaved like a common customer; she advised him that he needed to teach her that his wife's future rank demanded a high quality of raiment. Higher than she was obviously accustomed to.

'If she accepts shoddily made dresses now, I fear what they will deliver at the next order. You cannot let those trades-people get away with low quality work.'

Yet when John saw his wife in one of her new dresses, he only had the highest praise for the finished article.

'Is this one of the dresses Mama considered put together in a slapdash manner?' he asked.

'Yes, my dear. I did add the ruches and the little corsage at the waist, but this makes me feel like the queen.' Maud twirled before him. It reminded him of the day in the Colony, when she had made her Sunday dress, and the happiness it had given her. He put his arms around her and whispered: 'You are going to be the most beautiful countess in England!'

When she came to dinner that night Annabelle complimented her on the simple style of her dress. Much to the displeasure of Lady Eleanor, her youngest daughter asked if Maud could teach her to embellish her dresses in the same fashion. And much of the dinner was spent in discussion of gauze ruches, lace overlays, and the positioning of posies.

It did not end there. Yet more disagreement was waiting. On Sunday mornings the family attended the village church. The family always arrived late and disturbed the service by entering in a stately procession: the countess first, then John and Maud, followed by Annabelle and any guests they might have, then a few maids. The family would sit at the side of the altar, while the maids stood behind their pews. Lady Eleanor would proudly tread forward, holding her head high, looking neither left nor right. She had recommended Maud to follow her lead, but Maud could not possibly ignore the people who she had come to know by name or by sight. She nodded and smiled at those she recognised, all the while feeling ashamed for being tardy. After the service she would talk to those she knew had sick children, those who she had met in the street, and those she had bought items from. This always resulted in an awkward ride home.

'I do not know why you have to bother with the likes of Collins; he is our butcher, not one of our acquaintances.'

'I wanted to compliment him on the leg of lamb we had last week. It was exceptionally tender. Mrs Tupper remarked on it.'

'That is his job: to provide us prime produce. I would not expect anything less.'

'I like to give credit where it is due, Mama; and this way he will do his best to repeat his good service.'

The countess was not to be mollified: 'Or think we can do with second rate meats next time.'

After a few weeks of last-minute entry to the church, Maud accosted John: 'I would like to come to the church a little before the service starts, John. I hate to disturb the first hymn and every one waits for us to be seated before they finish the song. I think it is quite rude.' Though she thought it, she made no remark about the fact that the countess was full of her own importance, and that her pride was not a good example of Christian living for the congregation. 'Even if Mama wants to go late, I want to be in time. And on your arm, like we did in the Colony.' John agreed to talk to his mother. Buoyed by this, she had another request: 'John, you never read the Bible anymore. Can we read a chapter in the mornings, at the breakfast table? And pray as well?'

Pensive, John stood looking at her. 'You are right, Maud. I am grateful you reminded me of my duty. I will bring this also to Mama's attention.' But Maud was not content with that.

'What if she vetoes it, John? What will you do then?'

'We might have to wait till my father passes away and I have the title. Then I will have the power to change things here. And so will you. Will you have patience until then?

'No,' Maud was not going to give in that easy. 'Please call on her Christian obligation to be a good example for all the staff. And for her daughter. I think Annabelle has very little knowledge the Bible, or what it means to be a Christian.'

John tipped his finger on her nose. 'Well, my dear, while you are teaching her to beautify her dresses, there is another task for you: talk to her while you sew. I will talk to my mother, and you can teach Annabelle your favourite Bible stories.'

'Deal,' she smiled at him. Knowing that, while she was able, the countess would reject her ideas, she expected Annabelle would be an appreciative listener and this was where her influence might be fruitful. They had become great friends. With her two older sisters married, Annabelle enjoyed having a sister again, especially one who was, like her, at odds with the strict rules that her mother set on the household.

The next morning John surprised Maud by asking the footman for the family Bible to be brought to the breakfast room. Before his mother could excuse herself, he walked to the end of the large table where the Good Book had been placed. He opened it and asked for silence. To the amazement of his mother, he read the first chapter of the Book of James. He closed it with the words: 'Each day I will read a chapter from God's word. We are a Christian family, and we will live accordingly.'

In accusing silence his mother walked out of the room. John knew that later that day, he would be summoned and asked what that was all about.

To Maud he said: 'My Dear, I decided that I would read the Bible without Mama's consent. I think we need to take one step at a time.'

Maud was proud of her wise husband.

'You are right John. It must be difficult for her; she knows she will soon lose her command over the way things are done. I will ask for her advice for running the house hold. Then she may realise she will not quite be bereft of the power she now has.'

John smiled at her: 'Thank you for understanding, my love.'

CHAPTER 27

In the first two months Maud lived in Cheltenham Park, she shared her maid with Annabelle. Faye was an able lady, but even though Maud was not demanding, she found that taking care of two ladies on a permanent basis was too much. At dinner time when both women needed their hair rearranged and buttons done up, shoes buckled and jewellery unlocked, Faye was running from one room to the other, trying very hard not to mix up requests. Maud thought that between the two of them they frustrated the maid unnecessarily. She put her dilemma before John.

'You need a maid of your own, my dear; hire anyone you think is suitable.'

She went down to the kitchen and, after excusing herself for taking up precious time, asked if Mrs Tupper had five minutes to spare. Mrs Tupper was all smiles as she invited Maud into her sanctum.

'I always have time for you, my lady. Come into my parlour where we can talk privately.'

Once seated the housekeeper waited expectantly for what was to come.

'Mrs Tupper, I have two things to discuss with you.' The white cap bobbed up and down as Mrs Tupper nodded to her ladyship.

'I need a maid of my own. I am sharing Faye with Mis Anabelle, but the poor lady cannot possibly keep on doing the work of two.'

'Do you want me to advertise for a suitable lady's maid, My Lady?'

'No. I want to teach Sally to be my maid.' Mrs Tupper almost fell off her chair.

'And her only a scullery maid!' she exploded.

'I know, yet, I think she would be able to be taught quickly.'

'But, my lady..'

'I have quite set my mind on it,' Maud said.' Will you fix her up with an appropriate apron and shift, please? I will speak to her myself, so if you could send her up to my room in half an hour, I would be grateful.'

Mrs Tupper put on her stubborn face. She was not at all happy with the promotion of the young girl, who she thought was incapable of doing anything right.

Stiffly she asked: 'And what was the other thing you wanted to discuss with me, my lady?'

'Your job,' said Maud. Mrs Tupper blanched.

'My Lady, I am trying very hard to…'

'I know,' Maud interrupted her, 'that is why I think you must choose. Do you want to be the housekeeper or do you want to be the cook? I realise you are doing the job of two people and also, I want to help you. I think you are doing both jobs equally well, so you need to tell me what you like doing best.'

'You mean you would hire another cook, if I was to hold the position of housekeeper?'

'Yes, that is my intention. I have no complaints about your cooking, but I can see that there is never a time you do not work. How old are you Mrs Tupper?'

'Forty-one, My lady,'

'It is time that you get some time for yourself. Do you have family?'

'I have a sister who works for the Beresford family and two brothers who work in London; they have a tea salon in Kensington.'

'And how long since you have seen them?'

This question stumped Mrs Tupper. Maud smiled at her.

'Too long by the sound of it…' Maud suggested.

'My Lady, if I may be so bold to ask, what will Lady Eleanor say when you do this?'

'Think on it,' Maud ignored the question. 'Think on which part you want to play in our household.' Maud got up and walked to the door. 'Send Sally to me, please.'

As Mrs Tupper walked down the stairs to the kitchen a gamut of emotions wrangled within her. She did not know what to make of Master John's lady. Things certainly were going to be different when she was the lady of the house.

Shyly, Sally came to Maud's room, eyes wide with fear. Maud asked her to close the door behind her. She shuffled a little closer, not knowing what to expect.

'Sit down Sally.' Maud indicated a chair close to her. Sally hesitated, had she heard it right?

'Come on, I do not bite.' Maud smiled at the girl hoping she would feel more at ease.

'Sally what are the hopes you have for your life?'

Maud waited for an answer, as Sally tried to make out what it was the mistress wanted to hear.

'I have a proposition for you, Sally. You need to tell me if you like it or not. I want you to be honest with me.'

Sally nodded and whispered: 'Yes M'lady.'

'I am in need of a maid. Do you think you could learn to be a lady's maid, Sally?'

'Me M'lady? Me? A lady's maid?'

'Yes, I think you might learn quickly enough, what do you say?'

'Oh M'lady, Oh!' she got up and took a few steps toward Maud. 'Oh M'lady, I could kiss you!' She clapped her hand over her mouth in horror. 'Oh I'm so sorry my lady. It will not happen again.' Maud giggled, and repeated her question.

'Does that mean you would like to learn to be a lady's maid? You have to tell me!'

'Yes M'lady. I would like it above all other things.'

'Good, Mrs Tupper will organise the proper clothes for you, and I will speak to my husband about a reasonable remuneration.'

'Thank you M'lady,' Sally curtseyed. Maud nodded for her to go; she felt she had made two people happy; a good morning's work.

In the afternoon she had to explain things to her mother-in -law, who was livid that Maud had hired Sally without her knowledge.

'A common scullery girl? Have you no sense of decorum?'

'She can learn, she was the first person who was kind to me in this house, and I can see her potential.'

'How would you meet a girl like that?' her mother-in-law wanted to know. Maud told her the story of her arrival. Lady Eleanor was disgusted with the footman and the butler. But Maud told her that she must have looked like a person who was meant to be in the kitchen, it was a logical mistake.

'Mama, I came fresh from the Colony, fresh from the ship, I had my travel clothes on, and I came with a hired coach. If I had arrived in a carriage, it would have been amiss of them, but in this case, I can fully understand their actions.'

'I still do not understand you. Why would you have a simple girl with raw hands touch your clothes and hair? Not to mention your jewellery. How do you know you can even trust a girl like that?'

'She will not have rough hands for long, when she stops doing the dishes.' Maud reasoned.

Mama-in-law had one more complaint: 'You always seem to have an answer, what is wrong with trying to please me for once.'

Maud went over to her and sat on the floor at her the countess's feet. 'Mama, I have not had a mother since I was ten. I have had to always think for myself, jump in to do things others did not do.'

'What do you mean by that?'

Maud then told her about her wedding, and when Maud repeated the words that Uncle Elliot had threatened her with if she did not marry John, she cried out: 'Oh, horrid man! You poor child!' At the report of the work that had to be done after John and Perk disappeared, Lady Eleanor was horrified by the things that had happened in the Colony. She asked questions about neighbours who could have helped and about the uncle in Sydney Town. Could they not have asked for help of him? Maud smiled at the naivety of her mother-in-law.

'But in the end, it turned out well; it took a little while but John and I came to love one another. The only sadness I have is missing Hugo, my little boy. Mama, I have cried so much for him, but at this distance, I am unable to hurry Perk's search for my son.'

'Tell me about the boy.'

Maud told her all the things that happened after John had gone missing. Lady Eleanor could hardly believe her ears. At the end of Maud's account both the Countess and Maud were in tears. Maud felt relieved that, finally she had spoken of her life before she came to England. It had been treated as something that never happened.

'This is why I always run to the post-tray as soon as the mail is brought in,' she explained to the countess. 'I so want to know what happened to him, where he is, if he has been found. But Mama, my baby smiled at me just before Kurt took him away from me; Hugo smiled so very sweetly.'

'Oh, my dear, what a lot of suffering have you had to endure. '

At this juncture John burst in. Annabelle had filled him in about what Maud had done and he was worried. He was certain his mother would have something to say about the business, and it would be nothing good. It surprised him to see Maud sitting at his mother's feet, encircled by his mother's comforting arm.

'What has been done to get your son back, John?' she demanded to know. 'Maud has just told me the full story and why is it that I was not told earlier of this? It is hard to believe that such evil persons have crossed your path'.

John smiled at the turnabout of his mother's opinion of Maud. He told his mother how he had sent Perk back to the Colony to find out what had happened to the boy. So far, he had received no communication at all from Perk, but his agent in Sydney had communicated to him that Perk regularly took money out of the bank account in Melbourne. The logical deduction from that would be, that he was working hard to get the child out of the clutches of Gerda Werner. The lawyer had not heard anything from him for some time now, and he was going to Melbourne to check out the progress Perk had made.

Maud sighed. Sometimes she regretted leaving the Colony; she should have looked for Gerda Werner herself. She often felt that without trying, she had left Hugo behind. She was so comfortable now; she wondered what his life was like. If he was not found soon, she would miss his first steps, maybe his first words. Each night she prayed that Gerda would treat him right, and that he would be able to learn. She did remember Kurt's words: 'Don't worry, he'll be as rich as Croesus'. At least he would not live in want.

Two important events happened in the cold month of February: Lord Cheltenham passed away, making John the new Lord, and Maud discovered she was pregnant again.

Annabelle refused to wear mourning clothes, not even on the day of her father's interment. Which caused quite a stir.

'I despise black dresses. I will only wear black when I am over sixty.' John and Maud told her to wear the darkest green or blue. Her mother did not speak to her. Lady Eleanor bore her grief and her frustration in stoic silence.

That same month two letters from the Colony arrived at the Park. One was from Clara and one was sent from Melbourne by the solicitor.

Clara's epistle was welcome; it told John and Maud of their friends of their old life.

Dear Maud and John,

I hope that Maud is now safely in England, and you have been united. We have not heard how Perk is going. I hope he has found little Hugo and you are a nice little family now. I will have my own child soon. Liza says it will be born sometime in March. I am using the crib that John made for Hugo. I hope you do not mind. Maud you are a lady now; do you have beautiful dresses and a horse? Jess broke a leg and Helmut had to shoot her. We had to buy a new horse to pull the dray. Things are going well. We have two cows now and Helmut has made a fenced meadow. The grass is not very good, but they still give milk. Jim Calder has a bull, so maybe we will have some calves in the future. Helmut grows food on the land of his old farm as well. We have tried other crops. Some work and some don't. Helmut works very hard. Maud, I do miss you. We had such a good time together. My father has been here on a visit and Cornelia liked the farm.

Have to stop now. Jim Calder is taking the letter to Sydney Town to post it.

Your cousin Clara

The solicitor's letter was upsetting:

My Lord,

I hope this missive finds you in good health.

There have been certain developments that may be of interest to you.

A band of miners have been arrested. These villains have lured certain persons to the gold fields of Ballarat, and after winning their trust have sold individual persons to the captains of the merchant navy, as addition to the crew of their ships.

According to witnesses, to wit Mr Fung Zsu, who knew James well, Mr James Perkins has fallen victim to these outlaws and though they have been apprehended, the whereabouts of Mr Perkins remains unknown. He had withdrawn money on a regular basis, but the latest withdrawal was made in August, as your balance sheets will show.

I remain your humble servant, etc, etc.

Jacob Stiegel

When Maud read the letter, she sank to the ground; distraught she cried: 'Hugo! Oh Hugo, my little boy, when will I ever see you?'

John carried her to her room and put her gently on her bed. He too had tears in his eyes. In one moment, he had lost his trusted friend and his young son. It seemed that their son was never searched for. The craving for riches had been too strong, and Perk had not kept his promise to return the boy. And now all was lost. Gerda had him safely in her life; he would only know her as his mother.

The next day John put an advertisement in the courant for men who wanted to go to the Colony to find a lost child. As the salary was generous, there were many applicants. In the end John hired two former members of the gendarmerie. They were two burly, no-nonsense men, whose families lived in the neighbourhood. Besides the money they needed to look for the boy, their wives and children would be looked after financially, which was an attractive arrangement. They carried a letter to Jacob Stiegel, who would be their supervisor and who would report back to John every month.

CHAPTER 28

For a couple of weeks after the funeral, *Cheltenham Park* was thrown in chaos: Lady Eleanor insisted that John and Maud would take the part of the house that was usually inhabited by the titled head of the family and his lady.

Both John and Maud protested that, while she was alive, Lady Eleanor should keep the apartments, but there was no gainsaying her. Her ladyship insisted that she was going to live as it behoved her. She sorted through all the cupboards to see what she wanted to take to the Dower House, that was situated at the South side of the Park

'But Mama, you will be so lonely. Why will you not stay with us?'

'I could not possibly stay, when there is, by rights, another Countess in the house. I have been so used to making the decisions, and now I have lost the right to do this, I gladly hand over the reins of the household to your wife.'

'Is it because you think I will make changes that you will dislike?' Maud asked in her forthright manner.

'My dear, you have already done this on many an occasion.'

Maud hung her head.' I would hate to be the reason you are moving,' she said meaning every word, 'I know I have a lot to learn.'

'My door is always open, Maud; you are always welcome to visit if you need advice.' She pulled on her black pigskin gloves and, with her head held high, strode out of the manor, followed by her maid and Potts, who had been chosen to serve the dowager in her new abode.

Life without the parents was considerably easier. Annabelle enjoyed the relaxed atmosphere and freedom that Maud allowed her. John sometimes pulled in the reins a little, but she was unfashionably free to do as she pleased. Surprisingly, she reacted by becoming more circumspect and mature.

Because of her father's illness and the customary mourning period, her mother's wish that she be presented at court had been delayed. Annabelle did not miss parties or balls; she missed wearing the comfortable clothes she liked so much.

Her main suitor seemed to be similar to her. He had heard the stories of the adventures in the Colony and he declared that his greatest wish was to visit there before he settled down to marriage and a family. Together Roger Ballantyne and Annabelle made plans run away and travel to the great Southland. Yet, at the very last moment she was unable to treat her family in such a shabby manner, and the plan was abandoned.

'Maud will get in so much trouble, Roger; Mama will tear strips off her and blame her for my misdeeds. I cannot possibly do this to her, now she is so close to giving birth.'

Mr Ballantyne, who was very much in love with Annabelle, saw this as one of her many virtues.

'I can see that you let your heart speak for you. You would not be happy if someone you loved as much as you do your sister-in-law, would bear the brunt of your actions. I adore your high principles.'

'Oh, stuff and nonsense, Roger. If I had any principles I would not even be planning to run away to the Colony.'

In the end Maud overheard them talking and asked John if it was possible to send Annabelle to stay with Clara and Helmut.

'She needs to see the reality of life in the Colony, John. I do not think she will like living in a small house like *Maere Green*, and having to do the heavy work that needs to be done. If she goes, she will get those dreams out of her system and will be able to settle to marriage here in England and count herself lucky.'

'Marriage with Mr Ballantyne?' John had asked sarcastically.

'Marriage with whomever she wants to, Mr Ballantyne or no.'

Thus, letters were written and arrangements were made for Annabelle to sail too the Colony. Clara was overjoyed by the prospect of having Annabelle staying with her. She had given birth to a boy who would celebrate his first birthday while John's sister would be with them. Little Gunter was such a perfect little boy. Very much like his father. He had already outgrown the crib that John had made and Helmut had built an extension to the farm house: two extra rooms, one of which would be for Annabelle. In all her letters it was clear Clara was proud of her husband, who made beautiful furniture, and her boy, who, on hot days, loved to play in the creek.

Reading Clara's letters made John and Maud homesick for the simple life. For two days after the letter arrived, Maud especially, would be quite melancholy.

Mr Ballantyne did not go with Annabelle. At the last moment it was he who could not bear to leave the safety of England and his very staid family.

'He was all talk,' said Annabelle who was thankful she had not fallen totally for his charms.

It took the Dowager two days to get over the fury brought on by John's decision to let Annabelle go; after that she saw the wisdom of it:

her youngest daughter would benefit from the experience of life without comfort and servants.

Little Louis was born two months after his aunt left for her adventure. He was a beautiful baby, with a head full of black hair and a dimple in his chin.

'Is he very much like his brother, my dear one?' asked John as he looked, besotted, at his son.

'No, Hugo was different.' Maud's face crumpled into a frown; tears began to stream down her face. 'Oh John, I have forgotten what Hugo looked like,' she cried in panic. 'What kind of mother forgets what her child looks like?'

'Hush Maud. You forget that you were always in the dark with him. You only saw a glimpse of him when he was taken away. I shouldn't have asked you. How would you know?' He laid Louis in Maud's arms and put his arm around both of them.

'Look at this little fellow, he is the most precious child, and he is safely with us. Don't tease yourself; sooner or later Hugo will be found, and when he comes home, our family will be complete. You know the reports we get from the lawyer are positive. The men have found out where Gerda's father lives. Even if she does not live with him anymore, I am confident that soon they will find her. The men in the Colony work hard and they are highly trained. Now enjoy our son; Louis is the joy of the household. Mrs Tupper is beside herself, and Mama finally has a grandson who she can hold in her arms.' The babe slowly opened his eyes and observed his mother. She started to sing and he closed his eyes again and within a moment or two he was asleep.

'See, you are a natural mother,' John said. He kissed her and left both mother and son to rest.

In the time that followed, changes in the household were made to suit the family and staff. Sally, loved being a lady's maid, but found that however hard she tried, she made too many mistakes that her ladyship needed to correct. She was much better at taking care of little Louis. She asked Maud if she could be the nurse for the baby boy, and other children if they were blessed with them. Maud was relieved that she had a more suitable job for Sally, who came from a large family. As the eldest of ten siblings, she had taken care of children from the age of eight. Faye, who after Annabelle left was without a position, was happy and able to become Maud's maid again. She had been asked to go to the Colony with Annabelle, but could not leave her ailing mother, who lived in the village.

When Mrs Tupper became the housekeeper, John hired a French chef, making the dishes that came to the table not only more interesting but also exquisitely tasty. Ettienne d'Orczy did not only create food as an art, he also created a stir in the kitchen. His saving grace was his passionate love for Sally, who now was learning French and often acted as a buffer between Etienne and the rest of the staff.

Potts who kept connection with the big house staff well oiled, reported all these things to the Dowager. She recognised that she desperately needed someone with whom she was able to discuss the "capricious goings on" in her son's household. To this end, she invited her late husband's sister to come and live with her for a few months; there was no other person in her acquaintance she could abide for more than one afternoon. Thus, her choice was limited. The dowager and her sister-in-law had never been close friends, but as Henriette was available and, for a limited time, easy to tolerate.

Mrs Henriette Hamilton-Griffith was a no-nonsense family member, known to speak her mind in all things, not caring if she insulted or abused. Most of her nieces and nephews loved her, but her sister-in-law had always been careful not to spend too much time with her. Now however, the Dowager thought the two of them could agree about the preposterous habits of the next generation. Added to this, they had the common denominator that they both were widowed that year.

Just as much as his mother was looking forward to show Henriette how low the House of Cheltenham had sunk under Maud's management, John could not wait for Maud to meet Aunt Henry, as she was known in the family

'Imagine, Henriette, he found her in a baker shop! I must say I admire the girl for what she has experienced, but I think she has no notion of what is expected of a countess.' Living alone in a lesser home, the acrimonious thoughts about Maud had returned to the Dowager.

'Let me meet her first, Eleanor, and I shall see what I make of her.' answered her sister-in-law, leaving The Dowager feeling like her story was too exaggerated to be true.

On her first visit to the big house, Aunt Henry was very quiet. Whereas they were used to hear her strong opinion about everything, she now listened more than she spoke. Her nieces and nephews put it down to the loss of her husband and brother in the same year and, amongst each other, they lamented her loss of spirit.

The next visit she made on her own, as the Dowager did not feel up to a walk through the grounds on a day that promised drizzle. Away from the eagle eye of the Dowager, the old Aunt Henry, they all loved and adored, returned. She demanded to have a tete-a-tete with Maud, who was bemused and a little anxious about the request.

When they were cosily settled in the blue salon, with the tea tray between them, Maud remarked that it must have been a strenuous year for the elderly lady. She asked how Aunt was coping.

'I might well ask the same question of you, my dear.' Aunt Henry answered, without a hint of sadness. 'Surely you have had your share of difficulties of late. Your mother-in-law tells me you have a son, still in the Colony?'

Maud nodded, not wanting to talk about Hugo, as lately, there had been very little good news in the monthly letters of the lawyer. Aunt Henry seemed to understand so she tried another avenue: 'How did you like my brother Gervaise? Did you know him when he still had his senses altogether?'

'I am sorry to say that, when I met him for the first time, he was quite muddled. He seemed to like my company though, so I sat with him each day for half an hour or so. But he never seemed to understand who I was. He called me Charlotte.'

At that, Aunt Henry's head shot up. She squinted at Maud and said cryptically: 'Yes, I can see how he would think that. Charlotte, eh? Well, well, well. Did your mother-in-law have something to say about that?'

'No, before I went in, she had warned me that his mind was quite befuddled, so I expected him to be nonsensical. I just played along. I did not want to add to his confusion.'

'You are a good gal.' Aunt Henry patted her hand and observed her again. 'Maybe I can shed some light on the reason why he called you by that name.'

'I would like to know some of the history of the family. The Dowager seems to be hesitant to speak of it.'

Aunt Henry smiled. 'Yes, but I am here to enlighten you.' she said. 'Maybe we should ring the bell for something stronger than tea,'

After Maud had tugged at the bell-pull, she explained that Aunt Henry could have any drink she liked, but that, because she breast-fed Little Louis herself, she would have tea only.

'Oh dear, you feed your child yourself? How quaint! I can see that your mother-in-law would not agree with that at all. I can hear her say "How bourgeois!".' Aunt Henry imitated her sister-in-law so precisely that Maud had to laugh, making her feel guilty. When she said as much, Aunt waved it away: 'Nonsense child, Eleanor has put strict rules on her house ever since she became a duchess. I can see why she moved to the Dowager House. She could not cope with the freedoms you are used to. I have always been an outcast of my family because I married for love, quite unfashionable you know, and because of that, beneath my rank. It would seem you and I have a lot in common, my dear.'

CHAPTER 29

'I think my brother was happy with Eleanor,' Aunt Henry started her story. 'She certainly was a remarkable countess for him. And to top it off having three sons and three beautiful daughters....' She stopped looking wistful for a moment. 'Yes, he could not have done better.' She moved the folds of her luminous skirt, sighed and went on.

'He was the second son of my father. Our eldest brother fought a duel with the husband of one of his mistresses. Alphonse was mortally wounded and died a week after the fight. Swords! What fools some men are!' Maud nodded in agreement. To her the history sounded like some legend from the Middle Ages.

'Gervaise never wanted the title; he loved the quiet life, here in Cheltenham, where he could simply be Gervaise Beauchamp; where he could hunt and keep horses and dogs. That is why he and Eleanor seldom made use of the London house. But as Alphonse was not married, there was no son to follow in his footsteps, so Gervaise became the fifth earl of Cheltenham, with all the falderal that goes with it. Eleanor was overjoyed with her new status; being the youngest daughter of a baronet, you understand.'

Having never been educated in the peerage of England, Maud did not understand, but she nodded anyway. It seemed like there was so much more to John and his family then she ever guessed.

'John must take after his father,' she suggested. 'He does not like the falderal, as you call it. He would have been perfectly happy to stay in the Colony all his life.'

'Would you have been happy? I heard you lived in squalid circumstances.' Aunt Henry asked, wondering how anyone could tolerate life in the Antipodes, as it was always described by those she knew.

'They were the happiest days of my life.' Maud whispered, the memories bringing a melancholy smile to her face.

'Then you must have married for love, like I did,' said Aunt Henry.

'No, I had not set eyes on John before I married him.'

'Impossible!' exclaimed Henriette.

Maud told her of her wedding day, extolling John's patience with her and how the love between them had blossomed later on. she completed their history of the subsequent, disastrous events, till the time they both had arrived in England.

'How extraordinary! How romantic! I never heard such a thing.' Aunt Henry declared at intervals. 'Eleanor told me some of the incidents that took place on your farm, now it is good to know the whole of it.'

'But John never told his family he was married.' Maud excused her mother-in-law's management of affairs. 'Not because he did not want them to know, but we were so busy on the farm. You cannot imagine, Aunt Henry, how tired he was when he came in from the fields at night.'

'From what I have seen you still have to get used to a few conventions, but I must tell you that I am surprised that you have taken to your new situation so well.'

'I want to please John; I don't want him to be ashamed of me.' This, Aunt Herny could understand.

'Making Sally your maid was a mistake; Eleanor told me you had a few hair mishaps.' Both ladies giggled; Maud at the memory and Aunt Henry at the mental pictures her sister-in-law's stories had painted.

'I bet she played high and mighty downstairs, lording it over the very people who ordered her about before.' Suggested her aunt.

'No.' Maud assured her aunt. 'No, Sally and I talked about this. I told her I came from a humble family and that she should never look down on anyone. I think that is why she understood that she was given an opportunity. When she realised she was not good at being a lady's maid, she accepted it, and asked to do a job that she knew she was able to do better. I think they respect her for that ..er.. downstairs.' Maud was ill at ease with the downstairs versus upstairs aspect of her present life. 'Anyhow, it worked out very well in the end.'

'Of course. Now, where was I with my story?' asked Aunt Henry.

'Your brother became the fifth earl,' Maud reminded her.

'Ah yes. But my story was really about how he got to be married to Eleanor. You see he was head over heels in love with Charlotte de Rochefort. She was the eldest daughter of the Duke of Valois. A beautiful girl. But with a head on her shoulders. I mean she was clever, and headstrong.' Aunt waited, to let that sink in. 'Now, my father and the duke had both fought on the Continent against the Bonaparte. When they came back, their friendship had soured. Something must have happened that made them detest the very sight of one another. All contact between the two families was broken. The lovebirds were meeting clandestinely but were betrayed by one of the sisters, who was jealous. My brother was a very dashing young man in his day. The duke had five daughters to dispose of. Actually, only four were marriageable. The youngest Esther, was close to a half-wit. Never saw such a silly gal in all my life!' Aunt Henry grinned at the memory.

'When Gervaise and Charlotte were discovered, the duke and my father forbade them to ever see each other again. Charlotte, had she been anyone else would have fallen prey to the dismals, but not she! She packed her bags and travelled to the Colony. She was a wise girl; she knew that nobody would ever offer for Esther, so she took her sister with her. The family never heard how they fared. The other three married well, but their mother mourned the loss of her girls for a long time. Never was the same after.'

Maud sat still. Her sympathy for the duchess with five daughters was palpable. She knew how it felt to have a child in a faraway country, not knowing what had happened to them.

'That is a tragic story,' Maud said at last. 'My father-in-law was lucky to marry Lady Eleanor then….'

Aunt Henry shrugged.

'But don't you see? You must in some way remind him of his first love. Why else would he call you Charlotte?'

'His mind was so disordered, maybe it was because I am young. He must have really loved her, his Charlotte.'

They sat in silence, mulling over the sad love story. Then Maud said: 'My mother came from England too.'

'What was her name dear?'

'Lottie Stack.' Maud said.

'What was her maiden name?'

'I never knew. But I think she took some story books with her, maybe she wrote her name in one of those. I took them back; they are the only reminder I have of a wonderful mother and a very happy childhood.'

Together they went to the nursery where Louis lay fast asleep and Sally was folding his clean clothing. On a shelf were some well-read books. Maud picked one up a volume of fairy-tales and opened it up to the title page. There, in beautiful writing, was written: This book is the property of

Charlotte de Roch… The rest was illegible, as the frequent use had bleached the ink off the page. The ladies looked at one another in amazed wonder.

When they were safely back in the salon, they could speak freely about their discovery.

'My dear,' Aunt Henry said to Maud, 'you are the granddaughter of the Duke of Valois! Wait till I tell Eleanor! This will certainly change her tune.'

Maud was quiet. Her mother, her wonderful mother, had not been able to marry the man she loved, yet she had loved the man she married. And she had made a home for her family, and she had sung hymns for them and taught her daughter to behave "like the ladies do" and had taught her to speak properly.

'In a way it explains why you have so readily taken to your newly found rank.'

That remark set Maud on the defensive:' My father was a blacksmith. And a very good man.'

'Of course my dear, But we do not have to mention him, surely?'

'I cannot forget the things my father taught me. He doted on my mother… and she on him. They were happy together, and wonderful parents.'

Aunt Henry tried to change the subject: 'Your mother, my dear, was she a handsome woman?'

'She was beautiful, she could sing like a nightingale. She could do anything she set her heart to.'

'Tell me what happened to her? I know her sisters very well and I would love to tell them they have a niece, who apparently is very much like their sister, your mother."

'Diphtheria. It was going around where we lived. Many people died. I only just turned ten when Mother succumbed to the disease, and then my father, a few weeks later. Aunt Essie died the same year, that is why I lived with my uncle, Elliott Stack, He was the baker who made me marry John. Clara is their daughter, so she would be their niece as well. She is a lovely girl; we were good friends on the farm. She and her husband Helmut are running *Maere Green* now. They have a son called Gunter.' Maud knew she was just running off at the mouth but it all was too much to take in. She wished she could tell John, it was so inconvenient that, especially at this time, he was visiting the cottages on the other estate, ten miles away.

'I would love to meet my aunts. My other aunts I mean.' Maud stammered.

'And so you shall. I'll be bound to tell you, that they will be on your doorstep as soon as they hear of your existence.' She thought a while. 'Maybe not Gwendolyn, she has been feeling her age lately.'

Maud wanted to know all about her aunts and any other family she had.

'Gwendolyn is the second eldest, she married a man quite a few years her senior and has been a widow since she was forty; you have two cousins there: Gerald and Francis. Elizabeth has for ever been at court; she and your uncle James have only one son: Oliver. And the youngest of the brood is Georgina; she married Mr Calhoun, a very rich man with properties in the West Indies. They have three children: Charles, Anna and Beatrice. Beatrice is not out yet; she is fourteen or there abouts.'

'Oh! All those people are related to me?'

'Yes, through your mother.' Aunt Henry could not resist the urge to stress this fact. 'I hope you will meet them all. They are worth knowing, if you want to take your place in society.

'I doubt if John will want to do that, and frankly, I would prefer to stay here too, and live happily ever after. That is, once Hugo is brought back to us.'

'What is that latest news on that front, Maud? Who have you sent looking for him?

Maud told Aunt Henry about the two policemen and the lawyer's monthly reports, ending with: 'They have found the whereabouts of Gerda. She has taken back her maiden name and is now called Gerda Braun. She lives in Melbourne. The house where she lives is constantly guarded by dogs. It is as if she knows we are on her trail. Either that, or she is just a very suspicious person. Hugo never comes outside without a guard. You know he is almost three years old.' Maud ended with a sob. 'I have missed all of his infancy already.'

'And you have sent two burly policemen you said?'

'Yes, John thought they could pry him away from Gerda, but it seems an impossibility.'

'And you are paying for all this?'

'Yes, and keeping their families.'

'That is an expensive exercise. I think I have a better idea.'

'Wait till John is home and discuss it with both of us.'

Aunt Henry returned the following day with the Dowager and an impressive looking person, who she presented as Arnold Guldstein.

John had been amused by Maud's ancestry. His reaction to the disclosure had been: 'Of course! After seeing you fulfill your role here, I did not have any doubt you were of an impressing lineage.' He hugged her and turned to Aunt Henry: 'Aunt, my lady never ceases to surprise me. First in the Colony, and now here.

'Yes John, you made a fine choice marrying her.'

His mother looked the other way; she had always looked down on Maud, now she was annoyed that the tables were turned: Maud came from a ducal house, while she was the daughter of an impoverished baronet, the lowest of the peerage ranks. The dowager's jealous resentment of her daughter-in-law grew.

When they were all seated Aunt Henry presented her plan.

'My good friend, Arnold Guldstein, is a man of many passions and talents. He is proficient in the German language and has, as you have noticed no doubt, a lot of charm. He is also a member of a famous theatre company. I propose that we send him to the Colony, to charm Gerda and make her trust him. Once he is allowed into her life, he can aid the policemen to take Hugo home.'

There was a cacophony of reactions from everyone, mostly opposing the very idea. Aunt Henry tried to gainsay them all. The only one who did not react was Maud. She sat staring quietly into thin air. When this was noticed, they all turned to her and asked what she thought of Aunt Henry's ludicrous proposal. She blinked, looked at each of them and said:

'It is the most preposterous scheme I've ever heard of. And it is also genius! This is exactly what we need to do. Are you prepared, Mr Guldstein, to go to the Colony?'

CHAPTER 30

Gerda proved to be a hard nut to crack. The monthly missives John received from Mr Guldstein remained the same for a long time: 'I have been able to meet with Gerda in a "mutual friend's" house, but she will let no one into her own place. It seems to be too much of a sanctum for her and the boy. I am taking her out to tea, and carry her parcels home for her, but she leaves me at her front door. I have heard the boy play in the garden. It has a high wall about it and no chance to see over it.

Then six months after he had left England there finally was a step forward: he had been in the house and had seen Hugo.

'Gerda has called him Peregrine, a name she read in a book. No one is allowed to shorten it to Perry. She has told me her son (that is what she calls him) speaks mainly German, but has an English tutor. I am disgusted with this woman. She wants me to make love to her, in order that we may marry one day in the future. It seems, her friends have made derogatory remarks about women who live by themselves, and she wants to be accepted by the elite of Melbourne. This is why she needs a husband Please let this be over soon, there is only so much acting I can do.'

Two months later Arthur Guldstein stopped writing his reports. It seemed that he had given up the pursuit. Mr Jacob Stiegel did not know where he was; it seemed like he had disappeared from the Melbourne scene. Maud was in despair.

'Will we ever see our son back, John?'

'You need to focus on Louis, my love; he needs you. And what's more, I need you. I can see you are becoming obsessed with Hugo. You are changing, you never sing anymore, you hardly play with Louis. We have one son right here, he needs your attention. I need your attention'

'You have given up on Hugo, haven't you?' Maud accused her husband. 'Just because you have never seen him, does not mean he does not exist.'

'Maud, please don't be unfair to me. It has been more than four years and you need to face the fact that we may not see him before he is grown older. You must admit I have done everything in my might to find him for you. You will never get his childhood back, but maybe when he is older, he will come of his own volition, when he hears the truth.'

'Who would tell him? Who would tell him about his real mother and father? Tell me that, John. Certainly not Gerda!'

It was the first time in their marriage that they did not see eye to eye.

In anger Maud ran to her room, threw her mantle about her and fled out of the house.

As she walked down the drive, she saw Sally come back from her walk, with Louis in the perambulator. She turned around and walked the opposite way so she would not have to say hello to the boy and his nurse. She stepped briskly over the lawn to in the direction of the village. As she neared the first houses, the wind was getting quite fierce. For a moment she had the urge to go back and see if Sally and Louis had made it home in time. Then she reminded herself that Sally knew more about wrapping children up against the cold than she did. She walked on, not looking at anyone she met in the street. There was a small teahouse where, at times, she met with Aunt Henry. Today she went past it, without greeting the host, who, when he saw her approach, came out to welcome her. On she walked, stepping out her anger and sorrow. The first drops of rain started to fall when she was at the other side of the village. It was then that her tears came; they mingled with the lashing rain. She did not care if anyone saw her; she wept and wailed out loud, the noise of the storm cancelling out her cries of woe.

The rain hurt her face, her coat was soaked and her shoes were clumped with mud. When she began to shiver with cold, she turned around and slowly walked back. As she passed the church the Vicar came out with an umbrella. Observing her bedraggled state, he took her into the church, not caring that the flagstones wore the dirt of every footstep.

'Come My Lady, you need to get dry. Come and sit inside, while I summon Mrs Proud to get you a hot drink. Tea will do you the world of good.'

As he walked away, she called him back:

'Vicar, let me sit by myself for a while. I need to collect my thoughts. Later I would love a hot cup of tea, but I need to think first.'

'As you wish, My Lady.' He discretely left her.

Maud sat in the warm church thinking about the things that had happened that afternoon. Her anger had dissipated, rinsed away by the storm. Only her misery remained.

John was right, he had done everything that he could possibly do. It would not help even if he went to the Colony himself, and demanded Hugo back. Gerda would just call the police and he would have no proof that Hugo was his child. She held all the cards. Unless they used stealth, they could not get their son back. Hugo would not know them. He would try and speak German to them and they would not be able to understand him. Her own son. Her own boy!

In her mind she suddenly saw Sally pushing the perambulator. With a jolt she saw her own actions. She had ignored her own child and his nurse; no, she had avoided them. Purposely! She looked back and saw how often she had let Sally do the mothering. She had not bothered with the son she had borne a little over a year ago. Again, John was right, she was not the mother to Louis she should be. She only thought only about the son she could not sing to, or cuddle; the one that seemed lost to her.

Because she wanted the son she could not have, she was neglecting the one she did have.

She hung her head in shame. Poor, Louis, she had not seen his first smile because she hardly ever looked at him. She fed him and then gave him back to Sally to burp and change. She had heard Sally sing a lullaby to him and she had walked away. Louis would know Sally as his mother, just like Hugo knew Gerda as his mother.

'*Oh God, I am such a fool.*' Now tears of regret streamed down her face. She sank on her knees and prayed for forgiveness. '*Heavenly Father is it not enough that I lost one son, that I do not care about the second son you have blessed me with. Lord I am not worthy of your love, but grant me your forgiveness. You are a merciful God, great in love and slow to anger, I have sinned greatly to you and my husband. Forgive me and help me be a better wife and mother.*'

Wife! She had put John to shame. She had walked the full length of the village not greeting anyone. Showing the world her anger and her resentment. 'Oh John. I need your forgiveness as well,' she whispered.

The vicar came back carrying a mug of steaming tea. And a saucer with a scone.

'I have taken the liberty of bringing you something to eat as well. Drink up, My Lady, it will warm the cockles of your heart.'

'Just what I need, Vicar,' said Maud with a faint grateful smile. 'Thank you so much.'

He sat next to her and was silent while she drank her tea. He thought that if she needed to talk, she would; otherwise, it would be none of his business. Maud bethought herself of Louis.

'Vicar, our son has not been christened yet. May I ask you to do this in the next service?'

The vicar beamed: 'My Lady, it would be an honour. Will you and My Lord come by to give me the particulars?'

'Yes, I will come tomorrow, I will take the young man with me as well, so you may meet him too.' She smiled. Maud looked around wondering where the baptismal font was. When she asked the vicar, he pointed at the back of the church.

'But why is it situated at the back. Can we move it to the front, so the whole congregation will be a part of the ceremony?'

'My Lady there is not enough room,' He looked at the pews that filled the front.

'We can move those pews, and put them along the sides,' She got up and paced the length out. 'Yes, they would fit here,' she enthused.

'But... but My Lady, that is where your family sits.' The vicar looked uneasily at Maud. She returned his gaze and started to laugh.

'Oh Vicar, I hate the way we sit away from the rest of the people. I want to be part of the congregation. The christening would make a wonderful excuse to move the pews closer.'

'What would the Dowager Countess say to that?' the vicar asked, uneasy with a change like that.

Maud shrugged. 'I say we move the font. And put the pews to the side.' She smiled sweetly at him, 'I am sure my husband will agree with me. It will not bother me, if you want to wait for his consent.'

'No My Lady, I did not mean that, I will do as you said. It will give a stir though; the family having had their own place in the church for as long as I can remember. But I can see your viewpoint. It will be done. I will ask Mick Colton to help.'

'Yes, that is a good idea; I will send a few men from the Park as well. And now I'll leave you. Thank you so much for the tea, it did warm me, like you said. I am mostly dry now.'

'You cannot possibly walk home, my lady. There is a storm outside that will drench you to the bone. I will get the buggy and convey you home.'

'That is very kind of you, thank you, Vicar.'

The buggy did have a roof, but it was open on three sides and the wind whipped the rain inside. The vicar had covered Maud with a blanket, over which he draped a piece of oil cloth, to keep most of the rain out.

Half way to the Park, they heard hooves clattering on the cobblestones. Someone was in a hurry. Yet the rider stopped in front of the buggy.

'Ho,' he ordered his horse. 'Vicar, well met! I am looking for My Lady, the whole house is in uproar, she has been out all afternoon - in this weather!'

'I am here, Bellfry. I am safe. The vicar took good care of me.' Maud called against the wind.'

'Thank God!' the man cried out.' My Lady, everyone is looking for you. I will ride back to the house and tell them you are on your way back. It will set their mind at ease.'

An hour later Maud felt a lot better. She had had a hot bath and wore a long-sleeved dress. The fire in her room had been lit as soon as it was known she was on her way home and the room was cosy and warm. With her hair brushed and bound in a shawl, she went to the kitchen first and called all the staff together.

'I am sorry that I put you through a lot of extra work and worry,' she began her apology. 'I need to tell you that I appreciate your care for me. I have been out of sorts lately and have been a little grumpy. As you can imagine. I worry about my eldest son. But that is not an excuse to be unreasonable, so I ask you to forgive me, and I promise I will mend my ways.'

When she stopped speaking there were a few voices that reassured her that they would do it all again for her sake, but Mrs Tupper stilled them all.

'My Lady,' she said in a dignified manner, feeling the importance of her position, 'you need not be asking our forgiveness. You have a lot on your mind and we do our best to make life easy for you.' Then she nodded her head as if to say that that was the end of the issue.

Talking to John was much harder. He had been looking for her and came back to the house as cold and bedraggled as she had been that afternoon.

He had put dry clothes on and came to the dining room where the table was set and the fire burned gayly in the hearth.

Maud rushed to him, rested her forehead against his chest and told him her thoughts:

'John, I have been such a beast to you, and I am so very sorry.'

He embraced her. 'Maud, you had me worried. In this storm something terrible could have happened to you.'

'No my love,' she told him, 'I have acted in such a silly way. You were so right: I have thought about all the things you said and how all I could do is accuse you.'

'My dear, I only want you to understand one thing: I do want Hugo back as much as you do. Never again tell me that I do not care about him.'

That brought Maud to tears. 'I was a fool to say a thing like that. And John you were right: I need to love Louis as much as I love Hugo. I need to mend my ways. I have talked to the vicar, John; don't you agree that Louis needs to be christened? Tomorrow we need to go and arrange it with the vicar. Will you come with me?'

CHAPTER 31

our weeks after the storm, the christening of Louis took place. John wanted all his family to attend and make it a family reunion. He was eager to show off his beautiful wife and healthy son. His sisters Frederica and Marrianna thought it was a splendid plan, even though Annabelle would be the only one unable to join them. William came under protest: 'What do I care for a slobbering kid? Did my brother visit me, when he came home from his adventures? No! He just came home to take away my chance to live the life he now enjoys. He robbed me of the chance to bear a title. I do not care for my family. I do not care if I never see any of them again… ever!' Yet his curiosity got the better of him and as his friends encouraged him, he deigned to stay at Cheltenham Park for a whole week.

It was the first time Maud met with John's youngest brother. He was the first guest to arrive and Maud welcomed him with her usual amiability. He looked her up and down through his lorgnon, noticing she did not follow the current fashion. Though her dress was well-cut and the material of an excellent quality, the omission of a crinoline was almost unforgivable, he mused. It was clear that the new duchess had no idea what was due to her rank. When he uttered his opinion to his mother, when, shortly after his arrival, he visited her, she could not but agree with him.

'Deplorable!' she emphatically stated in sympathy with the son, she had deemed too effeminate and too selfish to run the estate. 'There are new rules in the house that are absolutely revolting. And not only in the house either. She has ordered the removal of our seats in the church.' She waited for his reaction, when he only pressed a handkerchief to his mouth, stopping him from crying out, she explained: 'We now are expected to sit with the hoi-polloi, where the vicar can keep an eye on us.'

'And you let this happen?' William had asked, amazed that his mother had given up her control so easily.

'It was done before I knew about it. Imagine my abhorrence when I came to church and the baptismal font was in the front of the church, instead of our seats.'

'That is quite underhand, I must say. You did not think to order the change to be reversed?'

'I must bow to the new countess, William. A mere baker shop skivvy.' She shuddered. 'The joke is, that she thinks she is the grand-daughter of George de Rochefort! Can you imagine that?'

'Heavens, she cannot possibly be Lady Elizabeth's niece. Wait till Gwendolyn hears of this; she'll put her straight soon enough. I know all the offspring of Rochester's three daughters, and she not one of them. The nerve! What gave her that idea?'

'Your Aunt Henry. Seems they concocted the plot together. I am sure it was all to vex me, in which they have succeeded, I must admit.'

'That a vulgar miss is now living on the capital that should, by rights, be mine! I find this unbearable.'

'Oh, she is far from vulgar. She has all the manners and language of the nobility, but as I understand it, her father was a common blacksmith. With a name like Connor Stack, it would not surprise me at all if he was from Irish descent. I presume I her mother was a lady's maid, who was sent to the Colony for some petty theft and taught her all the fine ways.'

William convulsed at the thought of these suggestions.

'Why, oh why did John ever come back? It defies all logic,' he declared, gesticulating wildly with his hands. Here, his mother had no answer suitable for his ears.

'Do not upset yourself William, it does not suit you. I guess he preferred England and its comforts over the hard work in the Colony.' she suggested, feeling a slight pang of shame at the lie. 'Remember he was nameless there. A common settler. Only his lawyer knew who he really was.'

'Utter madness!' William pronounced. 'I am glad that at least Somerset will attend. His Grace will lend a little respectability to the company.'

'Oh but you forget. Aunt Henry has made it her business to inform Lady Gwendolyn and her two sisters to be present at their newly acquired great-nephew's christening. There will be enough gentility to give the occasion the distinction Maud must crave.'

When he returned to the Park, his sisters were cosily in conversation with their sister-in-law. Marianne and Maud confiding in each other's experiences during their pregnancies, confinements and talking about their offspring. And Frederica, who had just discovered she was expecting also, listening with much interest. William gave his sisters a quick peck on the cheek and excused himself with: 'You ladies will not mind if I join the gentlemen in the library?'

'We will see enough of you at dinner time, Will.' said Frederica, waving him away.

'I knew you would understand Freddy-dear.' He closed the door behind him, glad to have escaped the females of the family.

He found John, Cornelis, duke of Somerset and Mr Richard Swanson in heated debate about the latest riots in Belfast. When he realised what they were talking about, he tried to change the subject to the events concerning the Royal family.

'Blast the Irish,' he declared, 'uncouth folk, not worth worrying about. Did anyone of you gentlemen have a chance to visit the Victoria and Albert Museum? Her Majesty was prodigiously gracious when she opened it in June. I attended with my good friend Lord Busenthal; he arranged for us to have very prominent seats. Did you hear she gave her husband the title of Prince Consort? She dresses so well, I had the felicity to see her in the gardens in the start of this month. With the right kind of connections, you see real history unfold, don't you know?'

Three men stared at him in astonishment. John was the first to react.

'Thank you, William. How did you find Mama?'

'Not at all happy with the situation here at Cheltenham Park, John. You might have had a little more feeling in handling her affairs. To fob her off to the Dowager House is beyond all that is filial.'

'She went on her own volition, brother. As soon as Papa was buried, she withstood all invitations to hold on to her apartments and stay.'

'You can see that that was an impossibility, with the house being ruled by a woman of the populace.'

'I think you have the wrong end of the stick there, William,' Richard Swanson said pleasantly. 'Maud has quite a respectable ancestry.' William cast his brother-in-law a condescending look through his glass.

'Yes Richard, you would think that. But you will agree that Mama has a better understanding of how the land lies.'

'Come now, William, I don't think that you know the whole of it. I was present when both Maud and John tried to convince the dowager to stay in her own apartments.' His Grace spoke soothingly, as to a spoiled child 'A multitude of events have taken place while you were in London, and they make up the full story. I can assure you that Maud is a worthy mistress of this house and,' here he smiled at John. 'I have never seen your brother happier. That must account for something, you will admit.'

'Please tell me, Cornelis, that you do not hold she is one of de Rochefort's granddaughters.' William said peevishly. 'I've never heard of such a thing! You know that family well, I have no doubt.'

'Yes, that I do, but you seem to forget that he had five daughters.'

'Impossible! Someone would have told me.'

'It is obvious they did not. The oldest Charlotte, and the youngest Esther, travelled to the Colony, where they married. Maud is the daughter of one of them.'

William sank down on the couch, confounded by what he had heard. He decided he would ask John the rest of the story when they were alone, after this wretched family affair was over.

The next morning, he had the opportunity to speak with Maud. As the men were out on a morning ride and the sisters had not come down yet, they were left alone at the breakfast table. After the usual matutinal pleasantries he offered her his services.

'I was wondering why you do not follow the fashions, Maud. I'm known to give solid advice to ladies in matters of style and what is in vogue. Would you like me to help you with choosing a new modiste, maybe, and show you how to dress to your advantage.'

Maud cupped her face in her hands, leaning her elbows on the table. She observed her brother-in-law with a smile. 'You are very kind William,' she said. 'I know that I sadly lack in style, but I have a very simple taste and I like to please myself in how I dress.'

'But the mere addition of a crinoline would be such an improvement. And an overskirt with a little flounce, maybe.'

'Not for me, I have tried to wear a crinoline once and I found it dreadfully cumbersome.'

'All the ladies I know, bear the burden for the sake of looking their best. It would not be a costly price to pay to look your best, for John's sake,' he pressed.

'I have not an ounce of vanity, I must admit. I am a lost case when it comes to fashion, William,' she confessed.' I am the despair of your Mama's modiste. And I have resisted visits to London, which is another imperfection laid at my door. I hope I do not put you to shame, William. You must forgive me.' her eyes begged him for the clemency, that was difficult for him to grant her. He himself was dressed immaculately, outer appearances being the pinnacle of importance for him.

'What about jewellery? You hardly wear any; there must be a few good pieces lying about.' He said reproachfully, looking disdainfully at the small silver cross hanging on a red ribbon, close to her neck. Her hand flew to the pendant.

'This cross has value for me because it was my mother's. My father gave it to her when they were wed.'

'That is a paltry gift; I understand you are under the impression that she was the daughter of a duke. I think he could have done better.'

'He was a blacksmith,' Maud's voice reflected the pride she felt for her father. 'He taught me so many wonderful things.' She stopped there, realising that William would not take friendly to being told about the garden she had planted with her father. With a smile on her face, she considered telling him about the day, not long ago, when a storm was expected and the lawn half mowed. She had put on her *Maere Green* dress, borrowed an old hat of Sally, and had helped the gardener rake the clippings. He had asked if Mrs Tupper had sent her, which she had denied. When they were almost done, he had finally recognised her and his face had been something to behold. For a full five minutes, he had excused himself for taking her for a common help. But she had felt alive, working in the open air. For a little while that day, she had imagined she was working on *Maere Green*.

No, she would not regale William with that story; he would be shocked and he already was upset with her for not wanting to present herself in a way he thought a countess should. She looked serious again, lest William should misconstrue her intention and think she was laughing at him. But he only shook his head, not understanding why she would not make full use his instruction of how to spend the riches that were hers.

The christening was a happy occasion. The only sour face was that of the Dowager, who disliked her new placement in the church. Master Louis behaved beautifully, so that even Uncle William was agreeably impressed with his nephew. There was a luncheon set out in the large dining room and there was ample time for everyone to converse and joke. Maud looked around the table and found that the atmosphere was relaxed and cheery.

John had been disappointed that Maud's aunts had declined to come. They found the travel too precarious at their age. Besides, severe autumn storms were predicted and they feared the roads would not be at their best. They sent letters with kindest wishes and pretty presents for Louis. The letters also contained invitations to come and stay with each of them. When John asked Maud if she was saddened by their absence, she answered that it was better this way: 'I have so many new people to get to know. I expect, I will visit them in the future, then I will get to know them, at my leisure.'

CHAPTER 32

I n Melbourne, The Duke of Wellington Inn, in Flinders Street, was humming with a happy throng of cheering Germans. Birthday celebrations for their monarch, King Friedrich Wilhem IX were in full swing. The festivities were held in a public house where they were able to lift their mugs to the King's health and sing German songs. Half of the carousers attended for the love of their Prussian Heimat; the other half just wanted an excuse to get intoxicated.

It was on this occasion, there was a chance encounter between Kurt and Helga.

Kurt was the first to recognise the midwife who delivered Maud's son. He had to look twice to be sure, for the worries of the last few years had not been kind to her.

'Hey, you were in the neighbourhood of Windsor town about five years ago, weren't you? What are you doing here?'

'What's it to you? I have not yet met one man that I can trust, so don't expect me to tell you nothing,' she bit at him.

'No? I think you can't be trusted yourself. I am sure that you used to know Gerda and Philip Werner.' With satisfaction he noticed that she blanched.

'What's that to you?' she repeated.

'I used to work for him too, you know.' He looked around to see if anyone could hear them. When he considered it safe, he added: 'They were bad, very bad people. Absolutely evil!' For one moment Helga hesitated, then she decided they were the victims of a similar fate.

'Yes, I remember having to help that girl having a baby in that hot shed. He did not want her in the house because, he said, the baby was his, and did not want his wife to know. She was such a brave girl. But as soon as the baby was born, he sent me away. Only paid me half of what he had promised. He was a nasty creature. I was glad when I could leave. He gave me enough money to travel to Melbourne, to my sister. But when I arrived here, she had died.'

'Spare me your life story. That same baby was taken by Gerda, after she put a match to the farm.'

'You mean the girl died?'

'I don't know what happened to her, but I am sure that Philip did. He lay in a drunken stupor inside, while Gerda and the baby left. They live here now. In pure luxury. Her father is Bernhard Braun.'

'I have heard of him. There she is, living it up, while we are poor as street rats. There is no fairness in this world.'

'We could ask her for money. After all, she has more than she can spend.' Kurt's eyes squinted at her, trying to gauge if Helga would be a help or a hindrance in the plan that had kept his mind roiling in the years after his return to Melbourne.

She looked away pensively. 'So she is rich, eh?' she said again.

'Yes, money like water.'

'I would like some of that, do you think she would give us some?'

He rubbed his chin. 'We could convince her that it is wise if she did.' He watched her slowly grasp what he meant.

'Mmmm, I would not want much. Just enough to get by you know.'

'I would ask for a goodly sum. You never know how it might end up.' he warned her.

'Can you write?'

'Yes, but only in German.'

'That is good, she will be able to read it.'

When the festivities were over, they sat till deep in the night to put the letter of demand together. When in the dusky morning hour, they finally went to sleep, it was with a head full of dreams of how they would spend the money Gerda would hand over. They were convinced that she did not want it known that her Peregrine was not her natural child, and that, the less was known about the lot of her husband's death, the better.

The letter reached Gerda Werner Braun in the afternoon of a particularly frustrating day. It was fortuitous that she had sent Peregrine to play in the yard, in the shade of the large jacaranda tree, where his nurse kept a sharp eye on him. Thus he was unable to hear her outburst of wrath. The letter of demand, though badly written, contained a threat to her very comfortable and happy life. It seemed two of the people from the worst time in her life had conspired together to rob her of all that was dear to her. She could not apply for help of her father, who was convinced that Peregrine was her child and that Philip Werner was his sire. She had returned to the riches of the Braun family home, with the tragic story that she was widowed. Her father, who did not like his surly daughter around had bought her a house on the outskirts of Melbourne, where she and her son could live. Father and daughter did not frequent each other's places often, and when they did it was of short duration.

Now however, Gerda was torn: should she give in and pay the price of her blackmailers' silence? What difference would a hundred guineas make to her? Would it be enough? If she gave in, there was the danger they would come back for more at a later date. The alternative was not brilliant either if she went to the police and used a counter attack as defence, her father might hear of it and suspect the truth. Too often he had made remarks about the black hair and the lack of likeness to either of his parents. The love for Peregrine and her reluctance to share her riches fought within her.

In the end the money won.

The next morning saw her pour her sad story out in the ears of a sympathetic constable.

'Not only did I lose my husband,' she concluded her sorry tale, 'now these awful people want to take my child from me as well.' She threw the letter on his desk and he shook his head in disbelief as she translated the scrawled note to him.

'It is wicked what people will do for money,' he said. 'We will find the culprits and give them their just desserts. Leave this with me. I will let you know what progress we make. Now go home to your son, Mistress Braun, and don't you worry.' His fatherly manner comforted Gerda no end. 'You may have to give evidence when we put them on trial. Our first concern is to catch the felons, and that we will. I promise you that we will.'

For three months Gerda went to the police station every week, to see if there were any developments. Then, when she had given up all hope of being able to see her nemeses locked up, or even better, hung, she received the good news that both of them were apprehended. Yet, she was not ready for what followed. Neither Kurt nor Helga denied that they had blackmailed her, but they held fast, that all they had written in the letter was true. They gave the names of other witnesses who in all probability were still living North of Sydney Town.

The newspapers grabbed hold of the story. The Age and The Argus both reported the case in their front pages, asking the question: "Who is the real culprit?".

John's lawyer, Mr Jacob Stiegel, followed these reports with interest. He now regretted sending the Earl of Cheltenham a missive, advising him to halt all pursuit of Gerda Werner Braun, as he despaired of ever being able to prove Hugo was not her son. John had responded that after five years of hope, theirs appeared to be indeed a hopeless case and to send the two police men back to England. As more details came to hand, the case of Gerda Werner Braun was a topic discussed in every pub and at every dining table in Melbourne.

In England the mail delivered several letters to Cheltenham Park. There was one from Jacob Stiegel, Liza Calder and Clara Buchholz.

John read Jacob's letter first:

Dear Lord Cheltenham,

> *Here in Melbourne developments have taken place which must be of the highest interest to you. There have been reports that a Gerda Braun, formerly Gerda Werner, was blackmailed by two fellow Germans. It seems that in defending themselves they have laid bare the history of your son. If reports are true, it seems that she did, indeed, take Hugo, after burning her husband's farm, with him inside. I do not know what other facts will come to light, but when all is said and done, you may have your son back in England before next Christmas. I am careful not to build your hopes before we have certainty, as desperate people will tell desperate lies. Yet I am optimistic that the mystery will soon be solved.*

> *I remain your faithful servant*
> *Jacob Stiegel,*
> *Attorney of law.*

John laid the letter next to his plate, not knowing if he should let Maud see it. If this was another dead end, it would be cruel to let her hope again. Yet, he had not counted on the letter that was written by Clara:

Dearest Cousin Maud,

I have news that will set you by the ears: Police constables have been in this area to interview people and find out what happened more than five years ago. Is it really that long since you left for England? They have been to our house and also to Liza and Jim's. We have told them of the horrific things that went on and we told them you moved to England to be with John. They were surprized that you went without Hugo, but we told them that we did not know where Gerda had gone and that we left Perk to find out where Gerda had taken the boy. They were impressed that we all told the same story. But that is because it is the truth, I told them.

Maud held her breath. Hope was swelling in her heart. Gerda was found out. They would soon discover that Hugo was not her son. Tears of joy ran down her cheeks. After she had lost all hope, Hugo would come home after all. The letter went on:

How are you? I heard you have another little boy now. I hope you can enjoy motherhood to the full now. I have a girl; she was born only last month. We call her Heidi. Gunter loves his little sister. Mols has died, but we have 10 head of cattle now. Helmut works very hard and he has made a special cabin for Annebelle. The son of Jim and Liza has come home to take over their farm after all. Noah and Anabelle have become great friends. I would not be surprised if a romance is brewing.

My father has died, and Cornelia has sold the bakery. She lives in a small house in Parramatta. I did not go to the funeral; I was just pregnant and very sick. I was lucky to have Annabelle here with us. She is a hard worker. Just like you.

This is a long letter. Please write back to me. I would love to hear how you are going.

Your cousin, Clara Gross

Liza's letter contained the same information. And she also made mention of the connection between Noah and Annabelle.

There was a silence after they had both read the letters. Maud 's teary face told John that she had hope of seeing her son again. She might not realise that they had to wait till the trial was over and it was proven that Gerda never had a child. When he mentioned this to Maud, she reacted wonderfully cheerful.

'Don't you see John; they will find out that Hugo is not hers. He had black hair and lots of it,' Here her memory made her smile. 'He was very much like you. Both Philip and Gerda are blond with blue eyes. Only his looks would tell the tale. Besides there are so many trustworthy witnesses, who found me in that shed. I am sure it is only a matter of time now,'

It took another six months before a trial put Gerda in goal. Even the money of her father could not save her, or take away the misery she had caused. Maud wrote a letter with a bid for clemency for Kurt and Helga, stating that Helga had only been helpful and kind to her, and Kurt had done what he did, under duress. Annabelle offered to come home for a year, to bring Hugo back and to show off her beau, Noah Calder. It promised to be a Christmas they would never forget.

CHAPTER 33

For the first time since she had moved to England Maud felt like Christmas would be the feast it was supposed to be. Hugo and his aunt Annabelle were expected to arrive a week before Christmas Day, and an excitement got a hold of her that she found hard to shake. She talked animatedly to Louis, told him how wonderful it would be to have his big brother with them. She bought a mountain of presents for everyone. For the first time she took the lead in decorating the tree in the large salon. She even organised the tree and decorations in the church, where she hung a large advent wreath with four thick candles. Each week of the Advent one candle more was lit. The congregation loved the count down to the birth of their Saviour and the vicar smiled each time he lit those candles. My lady had undergone an unexpected transformation; she was a different person from the lady who had walked through the village in the storm of her anger.

Even John made a remark about the change that had taken place in his wife. She had listened to his Bible reading each day, passively, without comment. Now she actively discussed the reading. She had asked if they could again pray together, like they used to do in the Colony.

'Maud, my Maud, you are back. I have had the feeling you had abandoned life and left it in the Colony.'

'I did, it stayed there with Hugo. But now he is coming back to us.'

'Maud why is it not enough that you have me and Louis? I want Hugo to come home too, but so much of yourself you have locked yourself away from us, for the sake of him.'

'I know, and I am sorry. Please understand, Hugo was the child I bore when I had nothing - absolutely nothing left.'

'Surely you did pray when you were locked up in that shed? God is always with you; that is His promise.'

'I know but … I find it hard to explain,' she said, trying to find the words for what she had felt.

'I cannot imagine what it must have been like.' He admitted, trying to excuse her. 'Even when I was taken away from *Maere Green*, I always had Perk for company and food and some degree of comfort. You were there by yourself. All alone in the dark. No, I cannot imagine what it was like, I think no one can. But my Darling, you make me happy, now I have all of my old Maud back.'

On the first Sunday of Advent, she went down the kitchen and called all the servants together.

'I would like to read part of the Christmas story to you. But I will not make you listen. If you want to, please stay. If you would rather do something else, I will not stop you.'

Most of the staff stayed and she read the story of Zacharias and Elizabeth.

To her surprise there were questions about the story. And broader questions about God and the Creation. For over an hour, she sat at their kitchen table and discussed things of God. She told them about some of the times that God had been obvious in her own life and of times she thought God had forgotten about her. In the end she remembered her mother-in-law was coming for dinner.

'Oh dear, this is very cosy, but the Dowager is expected. I'd better change and get ready. Thank you all, I think we can learn a lot from one another.'

'My Lady, will you come again and teach us from the Bible,' one of the younger kitchen helps piped up. 'I do listen to the vicar, but he muddles up all the stories, and then I do not know what he is talking about.'

Mrs Tupper chided the girl for being forward, but Maud had to laugh.

'No, Mrs Tupper, Sandy is right. And yes, if you like, I will come next week and up until Christmas.' There were many reactions like: 'yes please' and 'thank you, my lady'

Dinner was late that evening, but no one complained. The Dowager noted with satisfaction, that, finally Maud had adopted a more fashionable time to dine.

Maud had the feeling that now the door had closed on her sadness. With a smile she welcomed her mother-in-law that afternoon. They discussed the return of their children: The Dowager looked forward to see Annabelle again and secretly made plans to talk her out of returning to the Colony and marrying a commoner, a mere farmer. Maud talked about the room she had readied for Hugo, and how wonderful their reunion would be. John had bought him a rifle so that he could teach him to safely handle fire arms.

'Never was a child more eagerly expected than my boy. He will be so happy to have his own family here.'

'Have you thought of hiring a tutor for him?' asked the Dowager.

'Yes, John has advertised, but we are not in a hurry to put him into a study regimen. I want to talk to him and ask him all kind of questions. I do not know what his likes and dislikes are. Oh Mama, I cannot wait to have him in my arms. And introduce him to Louis.'

'Yes, yes, but I do think you get over-exited, Maud. Be careful, in case the reunion falls flat.'

'But how could it possibly?'

'My dear, you forget that Hugo does not know you. He is taken from a familiar world into another, with people who are strangers to him. I am warning you not to overdo it. Give the boy time to get used to his new surroundings and his new family.'

Though Maud knew her mother-in-law was right, she could not hold back her impatience.

When the day finally came Maud sat in the window seat, peering down the drive. John had to ask her to stop pacing so often, that the three-year-old Louis picked up the refrain:

'Mama, come and sit down with me, help me with this puzzle,' he asked, stopping her for a minute, after which she went to the window once more.

In the carriage that finally rode up the drive, Annabelle encouraged a surly six-year-old: 'Not long to go now, Hugo, and you will have your own family back. The boy leaned heavily into Noah, whispering: 'Uncle Noah, I want to go home.'

'This is your home, Hugo. Look there, that big house.' Vehemently, the boy shook his head.

'No! I want Mutti. I want to be Peregrine, Hugo is a stupid name, how often have I already told you that? I want to play in the garden with my Nelly.'

'Remember what we talked about on the boat? Mama, is your real mother, Mutti is a friend who took care of you.' Noah was careful not to talk badly of the person the boy had loved as his mother.

'This is a stupid country. Look how bare it is outside. I want to go back to Melbourne. You said I would like England, but I don't. I want to go back.'

'Papa will teach you to ride a horse,' Annabelle tried. 'I told you that he has many beautiful horses.'

'Bah, horses; they stink!' Hugo said with passion.

Annabelle looked in despair at her fiancé. He shook his head; they had tried everything to make England attractive for the boy, to no avail.

Noah had been able to reason with Hugo best as he could; which on the boat, on a sunny day with a stiff sea breeze, had been successful. But now they were on land, in the winter snow, the boy's homesickness for what was familiar to him, returned with a vengeance.

Annabelle shrugged. 'Let John sort him out, Noah. Once he puts him on a horse, or lets him run with the dogs, he'll be alright,' she said. This was the mood in the coach as they stopped in front of the steps.

Maud came running down, her shawl fluttering in the wind; in a very un-lady-like way, she did not wait till the footman had opened the door, but beating him to the carriage, she tore it open to reach out for the son she had last seen when he was only a new-born. Forgetting all the good advice of her mother-in-law, she lifted him out of the carriage and pressed her to her heart. With tears streaming down her face, she repeated the German sentence she had learned by heart to make him feel at home: 'Wilkommen, mein Liebchen; welcome, my love,'

Hugo, whose world had always been small, and already felt uncertain in an alien world with foreign people, started to cry: 'Ich will meine Mutti. I want my Mummy.'

'I am right here,' Maud said holding him tighter and stroking his hair while she carried him up the steps. Noah who had come out of the carriage surveyed the spectacle playing in front of him and shook his head. He sensed that Maud's actions would have dire results. As he helped Annabelle down the step, he said:' I think we are in for a turbulent time, my dear.' He held on to her arm. 'Let's wait till they have dealt with the boy.'

Inside Hugo's wailing resounded through the hall, bringing alarmed servants to the arriving party. Hugo, distressed by the echoing sound of his cries and the stunned faces of those around him, intensified his effort and made such a spectacle of himself that John lost his patience. The first thing he did, was sending everyone away, so that he and Maud were alone with their son. As Hugo had kicked wildly, Maud had set him down, holding on to him, only by his hand. In a few strides John had moved to Maud and her boy. He looked at his son and said in an icy tone; 'Hugo, you will stop crying. You are not a baby!'

Being silenced, bar an occasional hiccup, by the authority of a man, Hugo looked up at his sire. John gazed at his teary face, and felt like he looked in a mirror. The boy was the spitting image of him. His anger melted away and he took the boy's free hand.

'Hugo, I am your father. We have waited a long time for you.' he said very gently.

'My father was a bastard; may he rot in hell,' the boy hiccupped.

Maud moved as to protect the two from one another, but John said to Maud: 'That is Gerda speaking,' then he turned to Hugo: 'Hugo, here we do not speak of other people like that.'

'Not Gerda, it is my Mutti.' sobbed the boy.

John put his arm around Maud, knowing how devastated she must feel when this long-awaited moment was so spoiled. 'We need to give him time, my love. Before too long he will know that we are his real parents. But remember, he is only a child.'

At that moment Annabelle and Noah entered the hall and Hugo flew to the people who were most familiar to him.

'Uncle Noah, take me back. I don't like it here.' he begged.

Noah knelt down next to the boy. 'Hugo, you are going to stay here. This is your home; this is your real family.'

'But I don't want a real family; I want Mutti.' Hugo wailed. Maud stood like a statue; she stared at her son, who was as unhappy to be with her as she was happy to have him back.

'This is getting us nowhere.' John said, impatience taking a hold of him. 'Take him into his room, Maud, and show him the things you have prepared for him.'

She took Hugo's hand and led him up to the nursery. His sobs had diminished, his crying now was almost pitiful. In the room there was a friendly fire burning and the toys of Louis were spread all over the floor. Louis sat in the midst of them, playing with a wooden drawbridge. He looked up and smiled at his mother. Just as he was starting to tell her about the bridge and the horses that were crossing it, Hugo stepped forward and kicked the bridge over. Louis looked more surprised than angry.

'That was not very nice, boy.' he said quietly to his brother. Maud pulled Hugo back and demanded why he had kicked his brother's toy.

'It is a stupid toy.'

Louis offered to share it with him, saying that he could march the soldiers over the bridge.

'Louis, Mama is going to show Hugo his bedroom, will you wait a while, so I can have a talk with your brother first.?' Louis nodded. Here Maud witnessed the obvious difference between the two brothers. She was certain that it would take them a long time before they could undo the effect of Gerda's pampering of the boy.

In Hugo's bedroom one of the maids was unpacking his trunk. Maud saw that there was a need to buy many more suitable clothes for her boy.

She talked softly to him, about his new bed, the Christmas tree with its presents, and about her love for him. He listened with a surly face, not reacting to anything she said. Then she left him with Sally, who had been told that he probably needed to learn a lot of manners.

Downstairs John was waiting for her. He took her is his arms and asked how Hugo was coping with his new surroundings.

'Oh John, did you hear what he said about you, my love?'

'Gerda taught him to hate his father. What he was saying was meant for Philip, not for me.' he assured her. 'Come let's go and hear the latest news of *Maere Green*. Did you know Clara had another baby?'

CHAPTER 34

I n the middle of the night, John woke up to find the side where Maud
slept, empty. He smiled to himself, because he knew exactly where he
could find her. He tiptoed to the nursery, and found his wife sitting
next to Louis' bed, staring sweetly at her son. He sat next to her on the bed
and held her hand.

'Look how peaceful he sleeps.'

John nodded, 'I thought I would find you in Hugo's bedroom,' he
whispered.

'I prayed over Hugo, but I had the urge to sit with Louis. Hugo is like a
stranger to me, John. Does that make me a bad mother?' She looked up at
him, anxious questions in her eyes.

'Of course not,' he soothed her. 'He is a strange boy though. Obviously
spoiled to the core.' He put his hand over hers. 'We will love him into
loving us.'

She nodded. 'Yes. Louis is so patient with him. He is the sweetest child.
I hope Hugo learns to love him first.' She tucked the blanket over her son,
who mumbled in his sleep and turned his back to them.

'Come to bed, Maud. Before you know it, it will be daytime. Tomorrow
is going to be a big day.'

Maud followed her husband to their bedroom. While she undid her
robe, she said: 'John I think I am pregnant again.' He came to her and took

her to his heart. 'My love, that is great news. What a wonderful Christmas present for me.'

She looked up at him and he kissed her. 'I am glad it makes you happy.'

'Are you feeling fine? Aren't you happy as well?'

'Oh yes. I hope this one will be a girl. I would love to have a daughter.'

Sally was worth her weight in gold. Her experience with children meant that Hugo, while under her management, did not get away with teasing Louis or being cheeky. Yet as soon as Maud entered the nursery, he began to play up and display the most atrocious behaviour.

'Sally how do you do it?' Maud asked her on the third day that Hugo was with them. 'How do you make him take heed of what you say?'

'I do take away his privileges, My Lady. I think you want to love him too much and spoil him; he knows that you are disinclined to punish him.' Sally said, anxiously watching if she had been too presumptuous in telling Maud what to do.

'But I am his mother, and Louis likes it when I hug him. I have missed out on Hugo for so long. And he knows it hurts me when he will not listen to me when I call him Hugo. He will always remind me that he wants to be called Peregrine.'

'Louis is a good boy. I do not listen to Hugo if he wants me to call him by that silly name. I have told him that I want to be called Lady Muck; he had a giggle about that.'

Maud laughed. 'Oh Sally, you are a treasure. I knew I did the right thing to let you take care of the children. I think I can learn a lot from you.' Then her face turned thoughtful; Hugo never smiled at her, she had never heard his laugh, yet here was Sally able to have a joke with him.

'My Lady, you just have too big a heart.' They were disturbed by a sudden scream. Both ladies ran into the nursery where Louis was holding his head, and Hugo stood, defiantly holding a wooden soldier. Maud decided to follow Sally's lead. She stood with her arms folded and said in an icy tone: 'Hugo, go into your room. I will come and have a talk to you about this nasty conduct.'

'My name is not Hugo I am Peregrine, and I don't want... '

He did not get any further. Maud pointed at the door of his room. 'Out! Now!' she ordered. For a moment he hesitated; the lady who told him she was his mother had suddenly changed from a soppy woman into a virago, one to be feared and obeyed. He tried one more time, whinging: 'But he did not give it to me.'

'Hugo! Out! This moment!' Her tone said it all. He drooped to his room slamming the door.

She knelt next to Louis, petting him and telling him how brave he was to let Sally wash his forehead. 'Dear me, you are going to have a great lump on your head. Papa will say you have been in the wars. Where is your soldier?'

He pointed at the corner of the room where two soldiers lay, their muskets broken and their heads dented.

'What was this war all about Louis?'

'Hugo wants to kill all the English soldiers; he says they are bah-ters.'

'We do not use those words Louis, do not listen to him.'

'He wants me to say Peregrine to him, but Sally says "no".' This point was followed by a sob.

'You are right, Louis; his name is Hugo.' She hugged him and dried his tears with her handkerchief. 'I am very proud of you, my big boy.' The door had opened and Hugo watched this dialogue, his eyes narrow with jealousy.

Now he came out and yelled at the top of his voice: 'I hate you and I hate him! I hate you all!'

Maud got up and strode towards her son. 'I told you to go into your room, I did not ask you to come out.' He fled back and she closed the door after him.

The tone she had used was not her own. She was terrified of the thought that had struck her. She had almost uttered it. 'I hate you too!' Her own son - and that is what had been on the tip of her tongue. She walked out of the room, leaving Sally to deal with Hugo.

She sat in her bedroom, thinking over what had just happened. All the love she had felt for Hugo had turned into an empty feeling. When she looked at Louis there was a softening warmth; when she looked at Hugo, she felt nothing. In a matter of three days the longing to have her son back had vanished. She realised that she had wanted the baby back; the baby that was taken away from her. Not the boy who had been reared to be alien to her.

'My God, I am sorry that I am not a better mother, please help me love the boy, he has no one else.' Maud prayed in despair. For a moment she sat in silence, waiting for her heavenly Father to speak to her. Then a few truths struck her violently: Gerda was the only mother he had known and loved. In a far land she was in gaol and it was a miracle that she was not condemned to hang. Her father's intervention had at least bought her life, although death would have been friendlier to her.

Yet there it was: Gerda had been his mother.

They all had been very unprepared for the reunion. She had been too eager to see her son again, she had not given him the time to mourn the loss of the mother and the life he knew. She had expected him to be as happy with seeing her, as she was seeing him. She had forgotten that she was a stranger to him. They had warned her, but she had been too eager to heed the wise counsel. She had turned his life upside down and expected him to thank her and be happy. Suddenly a wave of pity for her eldest son engulfed her heart. He was barely six and they had not explained anything to him. A few remarks, that he was now with his real parents was not enough. Just saying that Louis was his brother did not mean anything to him. He was mourning Gerda, his life in Melbourne and everything he was familiar with.

She went back to the nursery and walked straight into his room. He lay on his bed, his face was smeared, where he had wiped away his tears. She took him by the hand and said: 'You are coming with me.' He looked up at her, fear in his eyes; the angry lady was taking him to have his punishment.

'Where are you taking me?' He asked, alarmed.

'You'll see,' she said in a non-comital tone.

In her bedroom she washed his face. 'You and I need to have a long talk, Hugo. I will be honest with you, and you must be honest with me.' she sat him down on the chaise in the window, and sat next to him.

'Hugo, do you miss Mutti?'

He nodded. This was something he had not expected. He looked warily at her.

'Do you know where she is?'

He shook his head.

'Hugo, Mutti is in gaol; she did a very bad thing and the police found out, so they arrested her.'

'But Philip Werner was a bad man,' he reasoned.

'What do you mean by that?' Maud asked wondering what he had been told about Gerda's husband.

'He was a bas…' he stopped remembering that he was not to use that word. He looked up to see if she would chide him. Maud smiled. 'You are a good boy to mind the words you are using. But tell me, why was Philip a bad man?' She probed further.

'I don't know. I think Mutti did not like him. She put a pillow on his head so he would not come with her to Melbourne, so it would be just the two of us.' Maud held her breath; Gerda had primed the poor boy to hate. She had taught him to be selfish, to the extent that it was right to kill someone.

'But that was not a nice thing to do, don't you think?' she asked the boy.

'But you only do it to people that you don't like.'

Maud was horrified at what she heard.

'Well, that is exactly the reason that Mutti is in gaol, Hugo. Gaol is not a nice place,' she told him. 'Mutti was wrong to put a pillow over Philips's head.'

'Mutti wanted to put a pillow on her father's head too, but he would not let her.'

'I am very relieved to hear that,' said Maud, wishing that John was with them. 'Hugo, did Mutti ever read from the Bible to you?'

He shook his head. 'What is that? A Bible?'

'It is the book that has God's words in it. It tells us what is good and things we should never do. It tells us also that God made us all, and because we are his creations, He loves us very much.' Maud waited for a response. None came.

'Do you want me to tell you the stories from the Bible, Hugo?'

'If you want to.' Hugo did not seem overly interested.

'From now on I will read a story to you every night.'

CHAPTER 35

hen Maud told John about the conversation she had with Hugo, he was visibly shocked: 'That means that Gerda killed Philip and not Kurt. And,' he raked his hand through his hair, 'that also means that we have to be very careful that he does not hurt Louis.'

'Do you think he would do that, John?' Now it was Maud's turn to be shaken. 'Surely not!' she said hopefully.

'Have a talk to Sally, Maud. Warn her not to leave the two alone. Ever! Until he knows right from wrong, we need to be one step ahead of him.'

'I will stay in the nursery more, especially, now I want to take it easy; I can play and talk with the boys. And when this little one is born,' she put her hand on the belly, 'I will stay even more often with them.'

And thus, the routines of the household were changed. Maud ate her breakfast and lunch in the nursery and only had the evening meal with John. Often Noah and Annabelle joined them, talking about their upcoming wedding. They had decided to get married in England, one month before going back to the Colony. While the couple spent most of their time with the Dowager, they were often quite exasperated by the interference in the planning of their important day. The Dowager wanted it to be the grand event of the year, the last great display of her family in society. Noah did not have the courage to tell her what he really wanted, so it was left to Annabelle to disappoint her mother.

'Mama, Noah and I want to get married in the church here, with the minimum of fuss. Just a wedding buffet after the ceremony and a family get-together in the evening. We might have a few friends, on the night, but nothing elaborate.'

'Darling!' Lady Eleanor had cried out in despair. 'Why don't you let me ask John if we can open the London house and then we may invite all the aunts and uncles and my old acquaintances from my younger years.' Noah looked in horror at his future wife. But Annabelle had answered quietly: 'Mama that would make it your party; my wedding will be done my way.' Noah had sighed with relief.

During their stay at the Dower House, they were subjected to heavy sighs and palpable silences. There was the occasional barbed remark about the common partners the House of Cheltenham had to receive as their own, but neither Noah, nor Annabelle reacted to these. For this reason, the atmosphere was not always pleasant and the young couple sought shelter with either John and Maud, or with Frederica and Richard.

As their wedding came closer, so did their departure to the Antipodes. As Hugo often came downstairs when Noah and Annabelle came to visit, he knew of their plans and always listened attentively when the grown-ups were talking.

Many a time he asked John if he could go back to the Colony with Noah and Annabelle, when they went. 'Because I do love to live in the Colony, Papa, and I would like to go back to my old house.'

'Hugo, your old house is sold. There is nobody in the Colony who can take care of you. Besides, Mama and I would miss you terribly if you went back again.'

Hugo would set his face in defiance. John saw that it did not make sense to the boy. Remembering his own urge to travel to the Colony, he said: 'When you are old enough, you can go back and I will buy you a farm or a business in the Colony. But you first need to learn your lessons, you will get nowhere without being able to read and write.'

Hugo threw himself on the lessons with his tutor, Mr George Stable. He was a perfect student and seemed to have no difficulty with anything that George put in front of him.

As promised Maud read Bible stories to both boys each day. Hugo was very interested in the story of Cain and Abel. And he had many questions: 'Did God send Cain away after he had killed his brother?', 'Where did he go?', 'When he was sent away, God still kept him safe, didn't he?', and 'A curse is not that bad is it?' Maud tried as good as was possible to answer his questions. It showed her that he was listening, and it showed that he was clever. Clever beyond his years.

When she told John how sharp his questions were, he was not as proud of his son as she had expected. He was worried.

'Maud, he has an unhealthy interest in this particular story. I am sorry you told him that part of the Bible.'

'So you don't think I should tell him the story about Joseph, then?' she asked sarcastically. 'These are good, wholesome stories, John. God is in the midst of all of them. And I do stress that when we talk about the stories.'

'Yes, but his heart will only hear what he wants to hear. At the moment you should be careful.'

Maud did not heed him; she was too delighted at how well her relationship with her eldest son was developing. Spending time with her boys brought her joy and her pregnancy advanced without difficulties. Maud felt she finally could be carefree and happy.

Four weeks before Annabelle's wedding a little girl was born to Maud and John. They were overjoyed. They called her Helena and she was a most beautiful baby. Maud showed her off to everyone in the house. The Dowager was euphoric over her granddaughter, and made all kinds of plans for when the girl had reached sixteen years of age, and could be launched into society.

Helena was the first child that Maud could fully enjoy. She took long times feeding her, she cossetted her and sang to her. Now, there was not always time to read the Bible or do the games with the boys. Time and time again, they were asked if they did not think Helena was the most beautiful present that God had given them. Louis would caress his sister, while Hugo looked on from a distance. Louis would sing a song to her, Maud joining in, humming the harmony. When this was how John found them; he thought it was the most enchanting scene.

'It seems Louis has inherited your voice, my love. You should sing more often together.' He put his arm around Hugo's shoulder, not noticing that the boy slowly stepped away from the loving gesture. He ruffled Louis' hair and told him he was a good big brother to soothe the baby.

The only thing marring the complete harmony in the family was the looming departure of Annabelle and Noah. As the day drew nearer, Hugo asked his mother, relentlessly, if he could go with them. At first, she answered him calmly that Papa had talked about his plan to buy him a farm when he had grown up, and that he just had to wait till that time. But as that reply was not satisfactory to the boy, he kept on and on, anticipating a different answer. In the end Maud became frustrated with him and said decisively: 'No! Now you can stop asking; you know the answer and it will not change.'

It had not helped that he had overheard Noah tell John that he would not mind taking Hugo with him so he could learn the farming ropes from a young age.

'I know his mind is set on it, John, and it will be good for him to get the hang of farming before he gets his own farm. You must remember how difficult it was for you to ask for help of neighbours, when you did not know what the best practice was. Farming in England is so much different from farming in the Colony.'

'Your offer is very generous, Noah, but already Maud and I have missed a lot of Hugo's life, and between you and me, I had hoped he would get used to life here and stay with us. As far as I can see he is settling in. I could not deprive Maud of the son she so longed for.'

Too soon the day came that boxes were loaded into a carriage and the tears of the Dowager flowed freely.

'Annabelle, my little Annabelle, I will never see you again. Why, oh why do you have to go so far away from me?'

'Mama, I will faithfully write to you; letters take less time, now that most ships have an engine to speed them up. Don't worry, Noah takes good care of me and don't forget, he makes me happy.' There were words of farewell, words of comfort, words of thanks and words of promise. Hands were shaken and hugs were exchanged. Then Noah and Annabelle Calder stepped into the carriage and it drove off.

Those who stood on the steps waved goodbye and lingered until the coach, hidden by the bend in the drive, was no longer visible. Then the sorry group dispersed: servants went on with their jobs, Maud with her arm around her mother-in-law, attempting to comfort her, John calling for his horse to ride out with his steward to inspect some of the fields. Sally took Louis' hand and looked around for Hugo. She called him a few times and asked a footman if he had seen Master Hugo. The answer was negative. She ran upstairs and found him sitting at his desk, leafing through a book about the Pacific Ocean.

'Oh, Master Hugo, I did not know you had already gone back to the nursery. Did you see Mr Stable?' she asked.

He shook his head and nonchalantly turned over a page.

She shrugged. George Stable was a good tutor and very well suited to his charge, even if he was a bit of a law unto himself. Sooner or later, he would join them to set work for Hugo, then she would take Helena and Louis out for a stroll in the grounds.

When Maud came in twenty minutes later, she found George Stable listening to Hugo reciting his tables and Sally dressing Louis into his outdoor clothes.

'Are you taking the little ones for a little sunshine?'

'Yes, My Lady, Mr Stable thinks it will rain this afternoon, so we will be back before lunch.'

'I will put Helena's bonnet on,' offered Maud. 'She has been sleeping well, hasn't she?'

'Yes, My Lady, she did not notice anything of the departure of Miss Annabelle… Mrs Calder, I mean.' Maud smiled at her. Sally had known Annabelle since she was ten years old… it was little wonder that she had to get used to the change of Annabelle's status.

Maud went into the baby's room and two seconds later there was a dreadful howl. She came running out and fell on Hugo.

'What have you done? You monster! You are nothing but the devil himself.' She yelled at him, clawing at him, pulling him off his chair and throwing him on the floor. Sally and George looked on in horror as Maud attacked her son. George leaped forward and plucked the raving woman off her son.

'My Lady, My Lady he is only a boy. What can be so terrible?'

Now Maud stood straight and pointed her finger at her son who got up and stood behind his tutor. 'He killed her, that beast killed my baby.' Now she sank to the floor and cried piteously. 'My little Helena, oh my baby, my beautiful baby.'

Sally took Louis out of the room and called out to one of the footmen to get my lord, as soon as he could. She hoped that he was still in the stables, or at least had not gone far yet. She called Faye and told her that my lady needed her in the nursery, and to bring her smelling salts. All the while George Stable was the only barrier standing between Hugo and his unhinged mother. A few times she got up from the floor to attack him, hit out at him and hurt him. Every time George held her back, speaking soothingly to her urging her to wait for my lord to come. Each time she sank to the ground, the cries of her weeping, a heartrending sound.

All through this Hugo stood motionless, with his arms folded, looking at the spectacle playing out before his eyes. George would later tell Sally that he was amazed that the boy showed no emotion at all. It was as if he was an outsider, not at all involved in the tragedy he had created.

CHAPTER 36

t did not take long for John to leap up the stairs to the nursery. They had caught him chatting with the steward before they had gone on their way.

'Maud, my love what is the matter?' he knelt next to her on the floor. 'Are you in pain?' Faye who had tried her best with the mistress, stood away from them.

'Helena', she cried, 'he killed my Helena.'

John looked questioning at George Stable. 'What does she mean?' he asked the tutor.

'We have not been in the baby's room yet, My Lord. My Lady came out, very upset. I have tried to keep her from hurting Hugo, that is all I could do. Sally took Louis outside.' For a moment John looked beaten, knowing deep in his heart that his greatest fear had come true.

He walked into Helena's room and it took some time before he came out. When he did, his face was ashen. He did not look at Hugo, but, in a mono-tone voice, said to Mr Stable: 'Take the boy to the library. Stay with him until I come and see you there.' Then he motioned Faye to leave them too.

When they had gone away and he was alone with Maud, he took her hand and led her to the chaise, where so often she had sat reading stories to the boys.

'Come my love.' She leant into him and together they cried for the loss of their two children. It was clear to John that Hugo could not stay with them, and he was sure that this time Maud did not want to have her son in her house anymore.

They went into the little room where their baby daughter lay, still and white. Perfect in every way, but now an angel on her way to her heavenly Father. A pillow lay on the floor next to the cradle.

'John, I did not want to believe it, but you were right. He put a pillow on her face, she suffocated. I knew it as soon as I saw the pillow in the cot. John, I don't think I want him to be my son. I don't think he ever was.' She lifted a pathetic face up to him. 'John, why is it that as soon as I think I am happy, something terrible happens?' She started crying again and John cried with her. Together they let their grief take over and they clung together in a vain attempt to make their heartbreak bearable.

It was a long time later that John found the courage to go into the library. He dismissed Mr Stable and turned to Hugo.

'Tell me what you have done.'

'I put a pillow on that little girl's face.' It was said without any form of sentiment.

'That little girl is your sister.' Hugo shrugged. John shivered; he had the feeling that, after all this time, the ghost of Gerda was right there in the room with him.

'Do you know that if the police find out you will be hanged?'

'What is that, what do you mean?'

'They will kill you too.' John thought he might shock him into feeling something, Anything at all.

'I did the same as Cain did, and God said that anyone who kills Cain will be punished seven times as much. It says so in the Bible.' Hugo looked John straight in his eyes, almost defiantly.

'Have you any idea how much grief you have caused your mother and me?' John tried another tactic.

Hugo shook his head.

That is when John realised that they could not possibly let the boy stay in England. 'Do you know how the Colony was started?' he asked.

'No'

'Eighty years ago, they put all the very bad people, thieves and murderers, and so on, on ships and sent them to Botany Bay or to Van Diemen's land. The Colony was one large gaol for bad people and that - that is the only reason that you are going back there. You have done something that is very bad and now, you are not allowed to stay in this country.'

Hugo's face shone. 'I am going back to Melbourne,' he said, excitement in his voice.

'No,' John said harshly. 'You are going back to work on the farm. You will sleep in the barn and you will work for your food. You are my eldest son. You could have been the master of this Manor and all its surrounding land, you could have had a lot of money. Now, I am giving everything to Louis.'

'I should have killed him first,' Hugo mumbled to himself.

John was horrified by this reaction. He asked George to come in again

'Mr Stable, I need to write a letter to Mr Calder. I would like you to accompany Hugo to Southampton. Can you sit with him while I write the letter, please?'

'My Lord, can I have a word, before you go?'

Outside the library door, George did not know how to bring more bad tidings to his employer. 'My Lord, while we were waiting for you, Master

Hugo mentioned his brother; it seems he wants to…' here George hesitated, but John nodded, and said: 'Never mind, Mr Stable, I know what he would like to do. The very reason he cannot stay with his family.'

'I am so sorry, My Lord.' George commiserated.

'Go in, and speak as little with him as you can. And Mr Stable… do not call him Master Hugo. He is just Hugo. And he can only have water, nothing else.'

John went upstairs again looking in on Maud who had gone to her bedchamber, being plied with laudanum by Faye.

'My darling, do you want to say goodbye to Hugo. I am sending him away within half an hour.'

'Yes, I will say goodbye to him. Faye help me up, I will need you to come with me.'

John's next stop was Sally, who had put a ring of flowers over the doorhandle of Helena's bedroom. She sat with Louis on the floor playing soldiers with him.

'Sally, I need you to pack a box with Hugo's belongings. He is going back to the Colony.'

'Certainly, My Lord.' Sally went about her task straight away. She felt regret, but most of all she felt relief.

John used the escritoire in the blue salon to write the most difficult letter in his life. He had to ask Noah to take the boy under his wings, as he had offered. Yet now, with the added warning for the safety of his own future offspring.

Dear Noah and Annabelle, he wrote,

> *It is with a leaden heart that I write this letter. Just after you left us, we lost out little darling daughter. What makes our*

grief beyond bearing, is the way we lost her. Hugo has, after the instructions of Gerda Werner, suffocated his sister with a pillow. We think he did this out of jealousy. As it is too dangerous for him to stay in England, I would like to accept your offer to take him back to the Colony. In view of the kind of actions he has shown himself capable of, I do fully understand if you do not feel comfortable doing so. Yet, I see no other way out, as staying here would see him hanged, and he is only six years old.

If you take him on, I beseech you not to spoil him. To make him work for his board, or send him out to work for some other farmer. Maybe the latter is preferable, because he would be with strangers, who would grant him no special favours. He needs to learn that his actions have consequences, yet as his father I wish for a certain amount of leniency for him. We are devastated; we have lost two children in one day. I do not know how Maud will carry on after this. Even for me it feels too heavy. But we must go on.

Mr Stable will bring this letter and Hugo to you. If you find the burden impossible for you, please send them both back and we will find another solution.

Farewell, you two have made the last year a very pleasant one and it is with great sadness we see you go. Your loving brother, John Beauchamp etc etc,

When the second carriage left that day, the steps were empty of well-wishers. John had told George that Mr and Mrs Calder would break their journey either in Swindon or, on the second day in Winchester. In either of those places, they might be able to catch up with them. He had also pressed on George's heart not to let Hugo out of his sight.

After they had gone, John and Maud spent a little time with the body of Helena, Maud put her prettiest dress on her and then they called the doctor and told him the full story. The doctor mumbled: 'Very unusual', and 'What a curious situation', and 'This is all very bizarre', all through the account of that day. But he knew John and did not doubt the veracity of their tale. He signed the death certificate and prescribed a draught for Maud so she would be able to sleep.

They finally called Sally to bring Louis to them. Telling him some of what had happened was the hardest thing John and Maud had to do. He did not understand the whole of the story, he just realised that his brother and his sister both had gone away, and that, again, he was the only child in the house. Maud stayed with him and slept in a bed next to him. He thought it was a treat; to Maud it was a small comfort to be with her boy, yet also a stark reminder that he was the one child she had left.

When all that was behind them, John rode to the Dower House to tell his mother the wretched news. If he had thought she would be sympathetic to his misery he was disappointed.

She blamed Maud for taking the boy in: 'After all, you did not know if he was even your son or just some urchin from Melbourne. She could not leave well enough alone, could she? She had to bring him over. I have always said that I did not believe the story of that tool shed. She probably lost the baby once you were gone.' John listened to her rant, hardly believing his ears. In the end he said in a bitter voice: 'Woman, do not blame my wife! She has suffered all these things because of your underhand conduct. If *you* would have left well enough alone,' he stabbed the air with an accusing finger, 'I would live happily and carefree on my farm in the Colony, with three healthy, happy children. Do not make the mistake of coming to the manor; you are not welcome!' He strode out of the house and made his horse gallop home.

He desperately needed to be with Maud and Louis.

Meanwhile the coach carrying Hugo and George Stable rumbled forth. They made good time and they planned to stop for a refreshment at Cirencester. The driver reckoned they would reach Swindon before dark: 'We are lucky the days are still long, else we would not be able to do it.'

Inside the carriage, there was mostly silence. Hugo did not want to talk much and George had orders not to make the trip a pleasant one. George read his book, every now and then he looked up at his charge, who was playing with a slingshot.

'Where did you get that?' George asked. 'I am sure that it is not yours. Isn't that the one that your Uncle Richard gave to Louis?'

'Yes, but Louis gave it to me as a farewell gift.' Hugo blustered. George was amazed at how easy the lie slid off the boy's tongue, and how little regret Hugo showed, not only at leaving his family behind but also for what he had done.

'Louis is a good brother. But you do not deserve a gift like that; give it to me. I will return it to your brother.' Reluctantly Hugo obeyed. George slipped the toy into his bag that was hanging on the door knob.

At Cirencester George left the carriage to get some refreshments, leaving the coachman to guard the carriage door, so Hugo could not come out. He was allowed to let the window down, enough to catch a little fresh air. As George was inside the inn, Hugo furtively put his hand into George's bag and slowly took out the slingshot, all the while looking out of the window as if he was interested in what went on in the yard. He felt around in the bag and found a shilling. There was a lot of activity in the yard:

other travellers were milling around, changing their horses and ordering some supper. As a lovely lady walked past and the coachman followed her with his eyes, Hugo leant out of the window, and aimed his shot at one of the horses' haunches. Then he let go. The shilling hit the horse hard on the rump. The animal panicked and tried to rear, whinnying loudly. This startled his mate and before anyone knew what was happening the two animals shot forward, rushing out of the yard, onto the road. Without the coach man to rein them in, they ran into a fence, where more panic got a hold of them. The coach was precariously rumbling behind them, as they shied away from the fence they ran to the other side of the road where there was a deep ditch. The coach overturned catching the horses unawares. The coachman came running as fast as his thick body would let him. He soon saw that the boy, who had still been hanging out of the window, cheering the animals on, had been crushed in the fall.

CHAPTER 37

After a restless night, John and Maud were having breakfast together. Later in the day they would go to the vicar, to arrange Helena's funeral; John had cancelled all his plans so he could stay with his wife. He had not spoken about his mother's reaction. He believed it would be too painful for Maud; his anger still burned fiercely in his heart and only with the greatest of difficulty was he able to hide it.

Maud had asked Sally to spend as much time outside in the park, so Louis would not catch fragments of conversations or gossip between servants.

'How are you coping, my love?' John asked, as he noticed Maud staring into nothing. It was obvious she had not slept well; she looked peaky and tired. In all his own grief, he felt for her.

'I feel guilty, John; I feel guilty that I am relieved that Hugo is gone. I must be a bad mother.' She sighed sadly. 'I keep telling myself that it is the best thing we could have done for him. He is going to be happy in the Colony, isn't he?'

'I am convinced he will be, Maud.' He held her hand and pressed it encouragingly. 'He will have no time to get into mischief there. I hope Noah will find him a good master. He has a good brain, so I do not doubt that he will learn fast and make a success of himself.'

As the breakfast room was at the back of the house, neither Maud not John had heard a carriage come up the drive. They looked up in astonishment when a footman, after profusely excusing himself, announced that he had taken the liberty to usher the vicar and Mr Stable into the library, as they said they urgently needed to speak with my lord.

Maud looked at John, anxious questions in her eyes. 'Why would Mr Stable bring the vicar?'

John did not answer but took her hand and drew it through his arm. 'Let's see what is so important, shall we?' he said it in a confident voice, though deep down he feared that it was an ominous sign.

On entering the library, they were met with the vicar's profuse excuses for the early hour of his visit, but in his estimation the circumstances justified his intrusion.

John impatiently waved away his apology, instead turning to George Stable: 'Well, Stable, did you get the boy delivered?'

'No, My Lord,' tears glistened in George's eyes. 'My Lord, there was an accident, Hugo did not survive the turn-over of the carriage.'

Maud sank on the closest chair and with her head in her hands could only utter: 'Oh no, oh no!' John looked grim. For a long while he could not trust himself to speak, his jaw working furiously in an attempt to control his emotions. Finally, he asked: 'Please, tell me the whole of it.' He motioned the vicar and George to take a seat, then he sat next to Maud.

There were very few questions left to ask, after George had told every detail of the events at the inn. George had just come out to the inn when he saw Hugo lean out of the window, slingshot in hand. He stressed that he should have taken the offensive weapon out of the carriage, but John corrected him, and said that he had made every logical provision for the boy's safety and that Hugo would have found some other way to do mischief.

George shook his head and started: 'If only I had…' But, to the vicar's astonishment, John would have nothing of it.

'You took all precautions necessary to safely deliver him to Mr Calder. The boy was a law unto himself, and no one could have prevented him from doing what he did.'

Neither John nor Maud shed a tear. The vicar gathered that their sorrow was beyond tears. When he said as much John cut him short too: 'Vicar we were planning to visit you today, to arrange the funeral of little Helena. It seems now we will have a double funeral. Will you be able to perform the service for us? I'd also would like to discuss where our children will be laid to rest?'

'My Lord, My Lady, please accept my sincerest condolences. Would you like the children to share a grave?' The vicar asked.

'No!' Maud had not meant to scream the answer as loud as she did. But her screech startled all in the room.

'I don't think that is a good idea,' John said in a much calmer manner. 'We will see you this afternoon, if that is convenient for you. We will come to the church to consider our options. I do not want to wait long before we bury the children, I want this to be over.'

Later, George could never convince himself that John's last word had not ended in a sob. He felt for these people; he had come to respect them. He loved the house and its relaxed atmosphere, and now he was sure he had to leave it, he was intensely sorry to say farewell to the family and his position.

'My Lord, if I may be so bold,' he said in a soft voice. 'I would like to stay to see Hugo buried. Do I have your permission?'

John looked at the forthright young man.

'Mr Stable, I would like you to stay on to teach Louis. Would you please consider remaining in your position?'

'Of course, My Lord, it will be my pleasure. Thank you.' He inclined his head, showing his esteem for the earl.

John never regretted his offer to George Stable. In the next few days, he was a wonderful support for him, arranging for Hugo's body to be brought straight to the church, and organising his coffin. Neither John nor Maud laid eyes on their son again; his head injuries so severe, that he was beyond recognition.

Even though the house was filled with guests, Maud mostly stayed away from the communal areas. One by one her relatives would come and sit with her. Anabelle and Noah, who had returned to Cheltenham Park when the notice of Helena's death reached them in Southampton, felt the loss of Hugo more than the other relatives. They heard the rest of the dismal story when they returned to the manor and had been appalled. Frederica and Richard, and Aunt Henry stayed with John and Maud. Marianna and Cornelis, and their two daughters, lodged with the Dowager, but visited every day. For a while, they all stayed on, after the heartbreaking burial of two children, an event that each one of the family found hard to forget.

With the uncles, aunts and cousins so close, Louis had ample attention. Yet he missed his mother, and every day he would ask: 'Where is Mama? She needs to read a story to me.'

George spent the most time with him and he told him that mama was not very happy at the moment, because she missed Hugo and Helena.

'But I am here,' Louis said with the wisdom of a child.

'Mama needs a lot of sleep; when she sleeps, she does not miss Helena so much.'

'Doesn't she miss me?' the boy would ask.

'She does, but she knows that you are here waiting for her, until she has rested enough. Just be patient, Louis, soon she'll remember that she need to read the stories to you.'

'I miss my Mama,' he repeated softly.

George felt the pangs of pity, not only for the boy but also for the parents.

When, via Faye, this conversation came to Maud's ears, she hurried out of her room, to the nursery. George was playing a game that taught French words to Louis. They were laughing about a silly sentence they had put together: 'La souris fume une pipe dans l'armoire'. George had made an illustration of a small mouse and an enormous pipe, next to a wardrobe that had clouds of smoke coming out of the doors. Louis was laughing out loud when Maud burst through the door. Totally ignoring George, Maud took her son in her arms and covered him with kisses.

'My Louis, I am sorry, I have missed you. I am going to read you a story every night, I promise.'

Louis beamed at his mother: 'I thought you had forgotten me,' he said.

'Never! My darling boy. How could I?

'Mr Stable said you were very tired.'

'Yes, I was, but then I remembered about our story-time and that woke me up.'

'That is what Mr Stable said,' said Louis.

Maud looked gratefully at George, and mouthed: 'Thank you,' to him. He inclined his head slightly.

From then on things seemed a little easier for Maud. Even if, after the last guest had left, the house seemed still and lifeless, her delight in Louis made her forget, for a little time. the pain of her loss. It was only during the nights that the full force of the tragic events hit her. John had taken to sleeping in his own room, so he would not wake her when she had finally gone to sleep. Yet, even as she slept, gruesome dreams would haunt her and often, she would wake up in tears. At the breakfast table she would eat little, stare into nothing and look like death warmed up. John would eat in silence or read his mail. Then they would go their own ways. Maud would jealously regard her husband's ways; he seemed to be unaffected by the death of their two children. He would go about his business, and at the dinner table he would talk at length about the tenants and their problems, the price of fodder for his horses, and other things that were meaningless to her. She would react appropriately, but did not understand how he could forget so soon; how he could pick up his usual life so easily.

One day, when she tried to talk about *Maere Green*, he cut her off, and saying they would soon get mail from Annabelle and Noah and then they could talk about the farm in the Colony. She felt wounded by his seeming disinterest in her memories of happier times. She knew from other conversations, that even the mention of Perk, made him set his face and shut down any further discussion. It was as if he had discarded the past; their happy, carefree past.

Thus, she concentrated her time and attention on Louis, who relished the time with his mother. While Louis did his work, she had long talks with George Stable. With him she was able to chat about Hugo without feeling hateful feelings. George had only known the boy as a diligent student, with an interest in learning. As an outsider he had liked him for his bright mind and ability think outside the box to find solutions, even if his last scheme had cost him his life. In the end she trusted him so much that she told him the events around Hugo's birth.

When Christmas approached, John proposed to go to London for the festive season.

'Last year we were anticipating the arrival of our son,' he said at dinner, one night. 'I think it would be an idea to celebrate Christmas in different surroundings this year. What would you say if we open the London house for a month or so. You could do some shopping. You could visit your own relatives, and I know Freddy and Richard and Mariane and her family will be there also.'

He looked expectantly at her. Immediately she had her suspicions.

'Is this a plan of your mother?' she asked, squinting at him.

'No.' he waited, saying no more. He had not thought she would react that way.

'I have never been to a large city like London; will I like it, do you think?'

All of a sudden, he saw her like he had done a long, long time ago: she was again that lovely young girl he had fallen in love with, uncertain, and depending on his opinion.

'My love, I'll take care that you will like it. We might take Louis to a pantomime, and we could go to the Museum, and the opera.' She smiled, and he thought sadly that he had not seen her smile for far too long.

'It sounds exciting.' She looked up at him. 'You will be there with me?'

'I will.'

'Your mother will be excited; she has wanted to go to London for such an age.'

'My mother will not be joining us.' Maud looked puzzled. 'I think that she is not the kind of company I would wish for us at the moment. It will be just our family, so we are free to enjoy our holiday our way,' he explained. He had not said anything about his mother's reaction to Helena's death and Maud had only seen the Dowager once, when she came to church for the funeral.

'I would like that, John. What a splendid idea!' There was a happy glow surging through Maud, and for the first time since the devastating events of the autumn, she felt a hint of happiness.

'I will organise it for the second week of December; that will give the servants time to air the house and get the kitchen organised.'

CHAPTER 38

Maud was in high spirits when she went into the nursery. As usual Louis had all kinds of news for her. His enthusiasm was contagious, and in an impulse, she kissed both his chubby cheeks.

'Why did you do that?' he asked surprised.

'Because I love your stories.' she said.

He smiled at her, and surprised her with his remark: 'You can kiss Mr Stable as well; he tells very good stories.'

'I cannot kiss Mr Stable, Louis. Ladies cannot just kiss any man.'

'Sally does,' he said with childlike logic. Mr Stable all of a sudden was very busy gathering some papers and Maud saw that he was in full blush.

'Then I think Sally is very special to Mr Stable, Louis. And I will tell you something else, something very important.' He looked up at her with a face so innocent, she just had to kiss him again. 'You should never tell on people who kiss, that is their business. And,' she added, more for George's benefit, 'kissing is something that grown-up people do in private, when there are no little kids watching.' Maud concluded that Ettienne had been too volatile for Sally and she had turned her sights onto George Stable, who would promise her a much more balanced future.

Just at that moment Sally came back into the nursery with a tray of hot chocolate and a pot of tea.

'Oh My Lady, I did not know you were here; are you having morning tea with us.'

'No, not today, Sally. I have a lot of organising to do. My Lord has decided to spend the Christmas holidays in London. I would like you to consider going with us.' Sally looked at George Stable and hesitated.

'Of course, I am asking you to come with us as well, Mr Stable.' There was distinct relief on both their faces and inwardly Maud was excited for the two young people.

When she related the situation to John during the evening meal, he looked faintly amused. 'And what do you think of that, my love?' he asked.

'They could do much worse. Good luck to them, they are nice people, both of them.' She spoke nonchalantly, but it had made her think of the times that she and John were in love, and of the time they had been so much closer than they were now. It brought her into a melancholy mood.

In the middle of that night Maud had one of her nightmares. She was back in the toolshed, bound and gagged. Hugo was standing over her. 'You are not my Mutti, I will put a pillow on your face. Then I will go back to Melbourne.' The evil laugh that followed was enough to make her want to scream. She woke up in a cold sweat, longing for John to be with her. She sat up in the dark trying to find peace, missing John and the safety of his arms. The chasm that had developed between them was hard to bear. Since the loss of Helena, they had drifted apart, each in their own grief. She remembered how she had felt when her love for him had first stirred her heart. How she had longed to have his strong arms around her, to feel safe in his embrace. In spite of the horrific dream, she smiled as she remembered the night she had lain at the foot of his pallet. A sudden thought struck her: He was only in the room next to her. What if she went to him again, just like that, just like she had done before?

She tiptoed out of bed and quietly opened the door that separated her room from his. She trod softly into the room. Instead of hearing the steady breathing of a sleeping man, there was a moan followed by something that sounded like a sob.

In two paces she was at his bed side.

'John, my love, are you unwell?' Like so many years before his strong arms reached out to her but instead of holding her at his breast, he leant against hers and she felt his sobs more than heard them. A wave of guilt swamped her. How could she have thought that the loss of his children would not affect him. How could she have been so selfish to think that hers was the only, or the greater grief? How could she have treated him in an aloof manner when he needed her. How could they live apart when they craved each other's comfort?

After a little while she said: 'John I am cold, let me in under the blankets.' Then he pulled her close and they lay entwined, silently being together.

'I am so sorry, my Maud.'

'What for? You must be mad to think that you did anything wrong. You showed strength and kept everything going. You are my strong man, my rock of a husband,' she caressed his face, still wet with tears.

'No, it is me, and my family's doing that you are here, that you lost the children, that you gave birth in a dark shed, that you...'

'Stop it John, where is your common sense? Do you really think I would have been happier in the bakery?' She almost had to laugh at that. 'You have given me all the love a woman can want. Others have spoilt what could have been, but never you, my love, never you. The only fear I have ever had is that I would lose your love. I could not live without that.' He kissed her and pressed her to him.

'Impossible!' he said 'I have always loved you and I always will.'

'Then I am content,' she whispered.

The Dowager was infuriated when she heard that the family would remove to London for the holidays. Without her! She wrote many angry letters to her daughters, accusing Maud of setting up her own son against her. But the letters they wrote back did not have the desired contents: Frederica bluntly told her mother that she was reaping the seeds she had sown, and even though Marianne was a little more tactful, the gist of her missive was the same.

Maud had wondered why her mother-in-law did not visit as she had before, neither were any invitations to have tea or lunch with the Dowager forthcoming. When she asked John about this, he told her that his mother had done all the damage to his family that he could bear and she was no favoured guest in his house anymore. Maud decided that in time she would go and visit the Dowager and offer a friendly hand, to try and mend the rift.

But not before Christmas.

Both Louis and Maud were in rapture over the city. London was very different from Sydney Town. There were stately homes, beautiful churches and wide roads. Maud loved London as much as she had loathed Sydney Town.

The London house was well lit and warm when they arrived late at night. The welcoming atmosphere caused Maud to love the house the instant she entered. She had written to her aunts and all three had promised to visit their unknown niece. It promised to be a wonderful holiday.

As she tucked Louis in bed on the first night in the city, he asked: 'Can we pray Mama? I fear that Helena and Hugo are missing out. This is such a wonderful adventure. I am so lucky. I want to pray that God gives them an exciting adventure in heaven as well.' With tears in her eyes, Maud prayed with her son. She wondered that Louis had such a big heart. He was John all over, she thought. It was the first time after all the misery, she was able to thank God for her family.

Town was exciting. Under the aegis of Freddy, Maud bought new dresses, hats and boots. For the first time in her life, she was interested in the latest fashions and every night John admired her for a new hairdo, a new dress, or another purchase. He met up with old friends, while she shopped. He showed her the family jewellery, yet she had to be talked into wearing the heirlooms that she thought were too valuable to come out of their locked boxes.

It was all too thrilling.

The night that her three aunts came to visit was the most stirring for Maud. She had invited them all for a dinner party, and all of them came to inspect the daughter that their eldest sister had borne in the Antipodes. For this occasion, Faye had woven her thick locks around a coronet of the Cheltenham sapphire collection, and knotted her hair in a chignon, at the back of her head. Her dress was of the latest fashion and John showed his pride in his wife by embracing her so fervently that he almost wrecked the effort that Faye had put into her mistress' appearance. As her dress was made of peacock blue material, he wanted her to wear the complete set of the Cheltenham sapphires. He kissed her slim neck after he fastened the heavy necklace. When he reviewed the effect, he was moved to exclaim: 'Perfect!'

The butler had been asked to make the guests comfortable in the oriental salon. Aunt Elizabeth arrived first with her husband Sir James McLodden, and their son Oliver, Aunt Lizzie was as chatty a lady as her husband was sour, without much to say for himself. Maud's cousin Oliver was a haughty young man, who showed his superiority by looking one up and down through his eye-glass. His self-importance was both ridiculous and rude.

Soon after, Aunt Gwendolyn entered, supported by her two sons, Gerald and Francis. There was a lot of moaning and groaning: 'Gerry, get my stick. Oh and don't forget my smelling salts. No not that chair, Francis, I will never get out of it, get me the seat over there, it is nice and high.' The young men obliged, without murmur.

'How are you, Lizzie?' she greeted her sister. With a nod to James, she said a short: 'McLodden,' Lord McLodden's response was the faintest inclination of his head. She turned to her nephew: 'Oliver, that tie looks absurd. Where did you get a piece of material like that?' and as she sank into the preferred chair she breathed a relieved: 'Ah yes, that is better.' Now she was comfortable, she waved away her sons as if they were her servants. They went to the window where they had a friendly chat with their cousin.

'Gwennie, will you ever learn some manners? We hardly see one another and when we do, you cannot say anything sweet.' said Lady McLodden.' I am quite appalled with you. Is it any wonder that I am loath to visit?'

'Never mind Lizzie, I am not as mobile as you are, although my sons are a great support to me.' she boasted.

'Yes, and you need it too,' was the snippy retort.

The door opened and two young daughters of Georgiana, Anna and Beatrice tripped in, arm in arm, each letting go to greet their aunts. Charles a handsome, young man of twenty years, followed with his parents, Georgiana and Walter Calhoun.

'My darlings,' exclaimed Georgiana happily, 'how lovely to see you. It's been an age!'

She went to her sisters and kissed them on their cheeks. Then she greeted Mr McLodden with a warm: 'James how are you? Busy as ever I wager. Those royals keep you on your toes?'

Again, Lord McLodden nodded slightly in the direction of his sister-in-law.

After a polite greeting, the young ones grouped together and it was left to the older generation to wonder where this daughter of Charlotte was hiding.

When John and Maud made their entrance, the three sisters stared agape at her. Georgiana clapped her hand over her mouth while the others could but stare. There was a strangled sound from Lizzie's mouth and Gwendolyn cried out: 'Lottie, Lottie is that you?'

Maud was quite overcome by their reaction to her. John saved the day by welcoming his wife's relatives:

'We are very glad you could all come today. Maybe we should get the introductions out of the way.' The younger crowd eagerly stepped forward to comply.

Maud started: 'I am Maud Beauchamp. This is my husband Sir John Cheltenham. I am the daughter of Charlotte Rochefort and Connor Stack from Sydney Town.'

Then the others followed suit. When all introductions were made, Maud said with a sweet giggle: 'I have invited you all here for dinner, at this early hour, so we would have time to chat; I would like you to tell me all about my family, especially about my mother.

'My dear you are the spitting image of her, and by the looks of it you have her sense of style and her spunk as well,' said Aunt Elizabeth. 'It seems that in you, we have our Charlotte back.'

CHAPTER 39

The younger generation seemed to be very impressed by the lady in blue. She was dressed a la mode and had done away with the crinoline that their mothers still wore. The bustle of Maud's dress had several over skirts and each layer had the most elaborate frills. From the blue calf-leather boots, with tassels at the end of the laces, to the golden coronet in her hair, Maud was a picture of elegance. Her ready smile and her friendly chatter, soon set the company at ease and no one was left out of the conversation. Even Lord McLodden felt he had something of value to add to the discussions that night.

Maud mostly divided her time between the sisters; each had new stories about her mother, and she hid all the information deep in her heart.

In her younger years, her mother had been the darling of society; a great hostess, when her sickly mother could not perform that duty. She had been determined to remain independent, after she married, not bending to a husband's whim. This put off many of her suitors. Except for Gervaise Beauchamp, Earl of Cheltenham. For two years, the two had a clandestine affair, waiting for Gervaise to become of age. After a disagreement with her sister, Lizzie accidently told her father of the couple's love for each other.

'Papa was livid,' Gwendolyn said, 'I have never seen him so angry. Mama expected him to drop dead of an apoplexy, but that did not happen. Lottie did not cry when she was found out, even though her heart broke.

She packed her bag and went away. A week later she came back, she had booked a cabin on a ship to the Colony, for herself and Esther. Poor Esther, she did not know what was going on, but Lottie was always her champion.'

'I can still remember how she rushed in, packed Essie's clothes in a large chest, ordering Pansy to help her. Promising Esther not to worry because they were going on a long holiday on a boat. She was so excited.'

'Oh, I can still see her walk into the library and tell Papa that she was taking Esther and that he would never see them again. She slammed the door, and he did not say one word to her.'

'Yes, all because he did not believe her. When he finally did, they were well and truly at sea. She only wrote to Mama, telling her how wonderful the sea voyage was and not to worry about them: she was taking good care of Esther.'

'He was a cruel man, our father, he blamed poor Mama that he only had daughters and that we were more worrisome than ten boys would have been.'

'Especially when Cheltenham was white-livered enough to obey his parents, and married the daughter of that silly baronet.' There was disdain in Aunt Lizzie's voice. 'He was held up to us as a shining example of obedience, even though he was not worthy enough to marry our sister.'

'No one liked her, his wife,' piped up Gwendolyn, looking accusingly at John. 'That must be your mother, Sir John, I am sorry to say this, but that was how it was.' John said nothing, but Maud felt she had to take her mother-in-law's side.

'I don't think the Dowager had an easy life. Being second choice is not very complimentary. But she bore it like a lady should.' That earned her a grateful smile from her husband.

'Your mother had a beautiful voice; like an angel.' Georgiana changed the subject.

'So does Maud,' John said, 'That is why I married her in the first instance.'

Now Anna joined in: 'I play the pianoforte; if I play, will you sing for us, cousin Maud?'

Maud gladly obliged; it would take the sting out of some of the stories that were told.

Together they looked at the music on top of the instrument, where they found a few pieces that they both liked and soon the room was filled with music. John's heart filled with pride when he saw that his wife was, again, beautiful and accomplished. Would she ever stop surprising him?

The rest of the company marvelled at how, in every aspect, like her mother Maud was. They discussed her modern dress and her audacity to wear blue. Who was brave enough to wear that colour, at a time that she would be still mourning her children. Beatrice was the one who spoke in her defence, saying that amongst so much melancholy, Cousin Maud needed to look for the bright things in life. After all she had to think of her little boy, and not make life for him a dreary affair. Mr Walter Calhoun agreed with his daughter; he said she was very right to champion their hostess.

Then dinner was announced and the family trooped to the dining room. The excellent dishes and the easy way Maud and John led the conversation away from the merest hint of discord, made the night a pleasant one. When the tea tray was brought in Maud told her aunts about life in the Colony. How Esther had found a husband and had a daughter. About the illness that had decimated the family and how John and she had met in the bakery. Maud was disappointed by how little interest there was for the niece who lived on a farm with her German husband and three children. There were no questions or remarks that showed even the faintest curiosity, the London relatives patiently listened, munching on the delicious macaroons that were served.

Soon after, the family members went home, one by one, feeling reconciled with life and their newly found relatives. They all promised invitations and more informal visits.

When John and Maud lingered in the empty salon, he voiced his admiration for the way she had handled her guests.

'You are a natural hostess, my love.' He pulled her close to him, 'and beautiful into the bargain,' he smiled at her. 'My Maud, I love you. I thank God, that he led me to you. Are you sad, hearing all the stories about your mother?'

She gave a gurgle of laughter at the thought that struck her: 'John we would have been brother and sister if your father had married my mother.' Then a little more serious she said: 'My mother was a wonderful person. She was a wonderful sister: She took Aunt Essie with her, because she knew that she would be unhappy in England. She made my father very happy, and she was the best mother one could wish for. I am very proud of her. The only regret I have is that she died far too young.'

'I would have loved to have known her.' John admitted. 'Do you think she would have approved of our marriage?'

'As it is now, I would say yes, but I think she would have wanted you to woo me properly.'

'And you? Is that what you would have wanted?'

'You did, but you did it while we were already married. John, I came to love and admire you in those first months at *Maere Green*. They were the happiest days of my life.'

'I would like you to be happy like that again, Maud. Do you think you can be that happy again?' He observed her anxiously, while she thought of the answer.

'In time I will be, John. It is just that those days were so innocent and simple. But I am content with you and Louis, my two men. You two give me joy.'

One of the most frequent visitors to the London house, was Aunt Henry. Maud was always glad to see her and found that the house seemed a little empty when she had gone.

Aunt Henry would tell her about the history of the Cheltenham family. In turn Maud would tell some of the stories to Louis, so he would know about his ancestry.

One afternoon Maud questioned Aunt Henry about the many portraits in Cheltenham House.

'Aunt Henry, this house is decorated so differently compared to Cheltenham Park. In the Park there are beautiful landscapes, but here, there is not one room without a multitude of portraits. I noticed, looking at the clothing that these are ancestors, but there are so many here, and none at the Park. Why is that?'

Aunt Henry nodded agreement. 'It's your mother-in-law's doing,' she said with a sigh. 'When they married, Eleanor counted on being a part of London Society; the great countess giving parties and soirees. Marrying my brother was an enormous triumph for any girl. But Gervaise was still mourning the loss of Charlotte. He decided to withdraw from London life, and closed the house. He made it clear that they would spend their life at the Park, and true to his word, he hardly ever set foot in the London house again. His man of business rented it out to diverse foreign ambassadors, and as such, it made him a lot of money.' Aunt Henry stopped, calling back the memories of yesteryear.

'In revenge she had all the paintings of his relatives brought to London and only had paintings that had no bearing on the Cheltenham heritage on the walls of the Park. It was her way of saying that his history, and even his heritage, was of no importance to her. Thus withholding it from his children.'

'Surely my father-in-law had some say over what happened in the house?' Maud suggested.

'He was like a crushed man, after Charlotte left. For a long time, he did not care what she did. They never had guests, they never visited anyone, in town or in the neighbourhood. That is why it was so important to her, that at least in the village, and among her servants she could display her rank of countess.'

'I have often wondered why rank is so important to some people.' Maud was pensively for a little while. 'If I look at my own relatives, the ones without a title are so much more amiable than those who have. Look at that conceited cousin, Oliver; I would be in disagreement as soon as I had a discussion with him.'

'Oho,' Aunt Henry laughed, 'Maud you forget that you have a title yourself, and you are higher in rank than cousin Oliver.'

'But I don't regard it,' said Maud in her defence.

'There are those who will say that it is easy for you to say that, because you are of a high rank.'

'Do you think I am haughty, Aunt Henry?' Maud asked perplexed.

'No, my dear, you have always been the same. And so has John.'

Maud was mollified.' I was so much happier when I did not have a title,' she said. 'What happened when they had children? You did say that your brother was happy with my mother-in-law.'

'Yes, but it was more because in the end he was resigned to his fate, and he was proud of his children. He loved them like a father should. And even there my sister-in-law put a damper on his happiness: by refusing to teach his children any of the Cheltenham history. What little they knew they found out from aunts and uncles. There is so much to tell about these relatives.' She indicated the paintings on the wall of the salon. 'For instance, I am certain that they have never heard of the curse of the second son. I certainly doubt if John ever heard of it.'

CHAPTER 40

Maud looked suspiciously at her aunt. 'Surely you are not superstitious? That sounds horrible! What is that all about?'

'We do not like to speak of it, but let me show you a few paintings and explain who they are. Then you can and tell me what you think.' She got up and went to the hall beckoning Maud to follow her. Pointing at the portrait of a man with a large moustache, and a helmet in the crook of his arm, she started to explain:

'This is the first Earl of Cheltenham, Martin Beauchamp. He was made an earl by King George, the first or the second, I forget which one. It was as a reward for saving one of his brood from drowning. He had three sons, the eldest was a wild one, daring his friends to do the impossible. Before he could inherit the title, he got shot during the hunt. He ran out in front of the hounds, boasting to his friends that his horse could outrun the dogs. So the second son became the next earl.'

Aunt Henry walked to another portrait. 'Meet The second Earl, Christian Beauchamp, He had two sons and three daughters. His eldest son was …'

'A wild one,' Maud filled in

'You are right.' Aunt Henry smiled. 'Arthur loved the drink too much. In a drunken stupor he jumped off a bridge into the Thames. He was only nineteen years then. So his brother Albert inherited the title.' They walked on to the next painting. 'This is him, the third Earl of Cheltenham. He had four sons. His eldest, Christian, drowned when his ship was lost in the Channel. Because he killed a man, he had to flee from England and was on his way to France. His brother Alexander became the fourth Earl of Cheltenham. Now Alexander had been living it up in France. He had stayed in Paris after the Bonaparte was done away with. I think that is why his elder brother tried to flee to him when he was in trouble. Anyway, Alexander married a French lady Francoise D'aureville, she was our mother, Gervaise's and mine.'

'Does that mean you didn't have a wild brother?' Maud asked.

'Of course, we did. Alphonse was going to inherit, but he had too many love interests, and died from wounds sustained during a duel with an irate husband of one of his conquests.' They had walked down the corridor to diverse rooms to follow the trail of portraits. The last portrait Aunt Henry had to look for, it was not in one of the salons or even the dining room.

'Let's have a look in the library.' Aunt Henry suggested. The painting they found was of a young Gervaise Beauchamp.

'Oh, look how much John looks like his father,' Maud cried out. 'How wonderful this is.' She walked closer to the portrait and tried to see the differences. These were hard to find. As she stood in the corner of the room, there, in a small alcove was another painting; it was small but it made Maud gasp with surprise. She thought at first it was a likeness of herself. But she realised that I could not be, the clothes were too old fashioned.

'Look! Here is a portrait of my mother!' she exclaimed.

Aunt Henry said: 'Ah, now I understand why Gervaise did not want Eleanor to ever come to the house. Heaven knows what she would have done if she would have found out that he had a painting of Charlotte. He would not be able bear it, if she destroyed it.'

Maud let her hand stray over the painting. Here was her mother, in the glory of her youth.

'Look how beautiful she is, and she looks so happy. Aunt Henry. I would like to take the painting back to the Park, and hang it there. What a gift, to have a portrait of my mother!'

'It will be a thorn in your mother-in-law's eye, Maud. Are you sure you want her to see it?' But Maud was quite adamant that she wanted the portrait of her mother with her, and the Park would always be their primary home.

'Mama, does not visit anymore,' Maud said. 'She and John have had an argument of some sort. I have thought that after we go back, I will visit her and try and make amends, Meanwhile I think I should take the painting with me; I have no other reminder of my mother, other than a few books.'

Later that day she related her conversation with Aunt Henry to John. She showed him the painting and asked him if it was right for her to take the likeness of her mother home. He thought it a splendid idea and suggested to hang it in the dining room where she could see it every day.

The curse of the second brother was another matter altogether. He had never heard of it before, and did not believe a word of it.

'That would mean that whatever happened, Hugo would turn out like he did. Utter nonsense Maud! All events around his birth and not growing up with us, *those* things are the cause of his death. He would have turned out better if we all would have stayed on the farm. By now he would be working at my side, learning everything there was to know about the land. We would have bought the Werner farm as well, and I would have built you the best farm house in the neighbourhood, even better than the Calder farm.

Maud looked at her husband, startled by the fierce declaration. She walked up to him and put her arm around his neck. 'John do you still pine for *Maere Green*?' she asked.

'Every single day. Maud. Every single day.'

'Oh, my love,' she said, emotion shaking her voice. 'Do you want to go back? I don't mind giving all this up.' Her hand indicated the luxury around her.

'No, I cannot. William would make a muddle of the estate, and this is Louis' inheritance,' he answered wearily.

'Let's go back to the Park, then. We do not have to stay here all of January. Let's go home, John.'

POST SCRIPT

From then on, life in Cheltenham Park became their shared future. John was often seen working on the land with his tenants, and Maud tended a flock of fowl and a large vegetable garden. These produced more than the household needed. As a result, there was no hunger or poverty in their neighbourhood; every bounty was shared. Thus, the people around them, villagers, tenants and servants alike, adored and respected their master and mistress.

Not so the gentry, who thought that the title was wasted on the Earl and Countess of Cheltenham. Invitations seldom came and even their relatives dropped them from their acquaintance. The blue dress, together with the other luxuries that Maud had bought in London, were all folded away in a trunk, never to be worn again. Her granddaughters found the chest and its treasures at the start of World War I and deduced that their grandmother must have been a grand dame in her youth.

Fortunately, the Dowager did not witness any of these developments; that same winter, she died of a severe cold that would not settle, or maybe her demise was the result of loneliness. The dower house was once more shut up.

The Beauchamps were blessed with two more children: Maria and Laurent. They were mostly taken care of and educated by Sally and George

Stable, who married shortly after Maria's birth. Their two sons grew up together with the Beauchamp children.

Louis loved his siblings and was a wonderful eldest brother. When he grew up, he joined the army. He married a girl from the village and had three beautiful daughters.

If a curse of the second son ever existed at all, it was broken by the birth of the three girls.

Louis came back from the Boer war with many decorations. Yet these meant nothing to him, as the atrocities of war had rendered him a disillusioned man. His daughters grew up to be courageous girls, whose work for the women's suffrage was substantial; their great- grandmother Charlotte, would have been proud to call them her own.

Clara never came to England and the aunts did not try to connect with the daughter of their younger sister. They could not believe that a simpleton like Esther could have produced a capable woman like Clara. Maud and she wrote each other often, and they exchanged photographs of their families. They explained to their children who their cousins were and told them the history of their life in the Colony and their friendship.

Gunter was the only one to travel to England, he became the truest friend Louis ever had.

Maud and John were happy – as happy as they would have been in the Colony. When, at a ripe old age, they died within a week of one another, they were buried in adjoining graves, sharing one headstone. Engraved on it, besides their names and dates, there was the inscription: 'God has been good to us'.